E-MAIL

A LOVE STORY

E-MAIL

A LOVE STORY

by Stephanie D. Fletcher

DONALD I. FINE BOOKS

New York

for Snikky Snak

DONALD I. FINE BOOKS
Published by the Penguin Group
Penguin Books USA Inc., 375 Hudson Street,
New York, New York 10014, U.S.A.
Penguin Books Ltd. 27 Wrights Lane,
London W8 5TZ, England
Penguin Books Australia Ltd, Ringwood,
Victoria, Australia
Penguin Books Canada Ltd, 10 Alcorn Avenue,
Toronto, Ontario, Canada M4V 3B2
Penguin Books (N.Z.) Ltd, 182-190 Wairau Road
Auckland 10, New Zealand

Penguin Books Ltd, Registered Offices:
Harmondsworth, Middlesex, England

Published in 1996 by DONALD I. FINE BOOKS
an imprint of Penguin Books USA Inc.

1   3   5   7   9   10   8   6   4   2

PUBLISHER'S NOTE
This is a work of fiction. Names, characters, places, and incidents either are the
product of the author's imagination or are used fictitiously, and any resemblance to
actual persons, living or dead, events, or locales is entirely coincidental.

ISBN 1-55611-477-X
CIP data available

This book is printed on acid-free paper.

Printed in the United States of America

WELCOME TO THE
LUXNET INFORMATION SERVICE
COMMUNICATIONS HELP CENTER

LuxNet offers two ways for its members to communicate with each other: public bulletin boards and private electronic mail.

BULLETIN BOARDS

LuxNet provides over 50 different bulletin boards to appeal to the varied interests of its three million subscribers. Bulletin boards are the places where public discussions are conducted. If your interest is in connecting with a large number of members about specific topics, this is the communication method you want. To learn more about bulletin boards, simply click your mouse over the BB icon on the screen.

ELECTRONIC MAIL

Every LuxNet subscriber has a personal mailbox for receiving private e-mail communication. If you are interested in communicating privately and one-on-one with another LuxNet member, this is the method you want. To learn more about electronic mail, simply click your mouse over the MAIL icon on the screen.

WELCOME TO THE
LUXNET INFORMATION
SERVICE
BULLETIN BOARD HELP CENTER

To see a list of the 50 bulletin boards topics offered by the LuxNet Information Service, click the mouse twice over the LIST icon. When the list appears, use the arrow key to locate the topic in which you are interested. Click the mouse twice over the topic title and you gain entrance to the top of the bulletin board.

WELCOME TO THE
LUXNET INFORMATION SERVICE
ADULT TOPICS BULLETIN BOARD
INFORMATION & GUIDELINES

The Adult Topics Bulletin Board is a special service offered by LuxNet. In this forum, topics of a mature nature are open for discussion. These topics include Sexuality, Relationships, Women and Men.

This board is not appropriate for children and is therefore open only to members who are sixteen years of age or older. Participation is offered only to the "A" ID of each family or to members of a family who are sixteen years of age or over and are designated by the "A" ID.

Entry into the Bulletin Board requires the use of a password. To register as a user of the Adult Topics Bulletin Board community and to designate a password, click the mouse twice over the REGISTRATION icon.

Due to the sensitive nature of many of the topics under discussion on the Adult Topics Bulletin Board, we ask members to cooperate in adhering to its guidelines, which follow:

Each individual is responsible for any note he or she posts on the board. This is a public forum and is open to millions of diverse individuals. Make sure personal conduct is in line with that which would be deemed appropriate at any other large public gathering.

Courtesy and respect for others are expected.

Profanity and use of obscene or grossly repugnant language is prohibited. For example, racism and "hate" comments are not allowed.

No advertising of any kind is allowed.

No illegal behavior will be tolerated. For example, threatening language and harassment are prohibited.

Any notes which violate the LuxNet guidelines should be reported immediately to the Adult Topics Representative (ATR) by clicking the mouse twice over the ATR icon on the screen.

Infractions of the rules listed above will result in a return of the offending note and may result in barring from use of the board or in suspension of membership.

To gain entry into the Adult Topics Bulletin Board, click the mouse twice over the ADULT icon.

IN BED WITH A COLD

************* ADULT TOPICS BULLETIN BOARD *************

TO: ALL   10:00AM EST
FROM: KATHERINE SIMMONS S102248A   01-05-93
SUBJECT: IN BED WITH A COLD

Hi!
   I am a 44-year-old woman who is suffering from a miserable cold. My bedside table is laden with an assortment of remedies and a box of Kleenex. Sigh! It looks like I may be cooped up here for a week.
   The words "bored" and "antsy" describe me at the moment. The stack of magazines by the bed and the TV have no appeal. I crave distraction in the worst way.
   I am new to the Adult Topics Bulletin Board. This is the first public post I have ever made and I really don't know how this works. But, if you are willing, I would enjoy some correspondence. Is there someone out there in computerland who might have mercy on this poor suffering woman?

Katherine

************* ADULT TOPICS BULLETIN BOARD ************

TO: KATHERINE SIMMONS S102248A   10:07AM EST
FROM: PAUL HO R114738B   01-05-93
SUBJECT: IN BED WITH A COLD

Hi Katherine!
I'm a 27-year-old handsome guy who lives in Eugene, Oregon. I'm 5'9", and I have black hair and brown eyes. I weigh 161 pounds.
I like older women. Please tell me about you, either here or by e-mail.

Love, Paul

************ ADULT TOPICS BULLETIN BOARD *************

TO: PAUL HO R114738B   10:30AM EST
FROM: KATHERINE SIMMONS S102248A   01-05-93
SUBJECT: IN BED WITH A COLD

Dear Paul . . .
Like I said, I am 44 years old. I am 5'6", and let's just say I have an average build. My hair is a coppery color and I wear it shoulder length. My eyes are large and hazel. On more than one occasion I have been told that I am attractive.
I was born and have lived in the South all my life. It goes without saying that I have a Southern accent.
I am well educated, but I do not work for money. Perhaps I am what one would call a "domestic goddess." That works.

Now what?
Katherine

************ ADULT TOPICS BULLETIN BOARD ************

TO: KATHERINE SIMMONS S102248A   10:36AM EST
FROM: TIMOTHY FLETCHER P333978A   01-05-93
SUBJECT: IN BED WITH A COLD

Dear Katherine,
    Sorry to hear you have a cold today. I'll be delighted to keep you company, since I don't go into work until 2:30. My wife has already gone to work. While the cat's away the mouse can play ;-}
    If you'll check your mailbox, you'll see that I've left you some medicine. If it makes you feel better, perhaps you'll send a little my way. I'm sure you must have an excellent bedside manner.

                              Regards,
                              Tim

************ ADULT TOPICS BULLETIN BOARD ************

TO: TIMOTHY FLETCHER P333978A   10:46AM EST
FROM: KATHERINE SIMMONS S102248A   01-05-93
SUBJECT: IN BED WITH A COLD

Dear Tim . . .
    I hate to sound obtuse and impolite, but just exactly what kind of games did you have in mind playing while your "cat's away"? Remember, I am a rank novice at all this.
    It took me most of yesterday just to figure out how to get around. By accident, I stumbled upon the Adult Topics Bulletin Board which required a password and was closed to children under sixteen. Rather like forbidden fruit, isn't it?
    The only e-mail I have gotten so far has been junk mail from Lux-Net . . . you know, welcoming me aboard or peddling something. It will please me to find some real e-mail in my mailbox. I'll look for yours in a minute.

                              Learning the ropes . . .
                              Katherine

************ ADULT TOPICS BULLETIN BOARD ************

TO: KATHERINE SIMMONS S102248A   10:50AM EST
FROM: BUCK BRAZEMORE X455045A   01-05-93
SUBJECT: IN BED WITH A COLD

Dear Katherine,

I've stayed home this morning to catch up on some paperwork and am taking a little breather, entertaining myself for fifteen minutes or so by watching the exploits on the board. It's unusual for me to show up on a weekday. I usually log on for an hour or two in the evenings after work and I do a little "board surfing" on the weekends, too. It beats TV. Over the past three months this has become a hobby.

You're a new face around here and will probably be swamped by replies from the horny inhabitants of this place. But, if you need information or advice, let me know. You can always find me in the subject, BUCK'S BASEMENT.

> At your service,
> Buck

************ ADULT TOPICS BULLETIN BOARD ************

TO: BUCK BRAZEMORE X455045A   11:01AM EST
FROM: KATHERINE SIMMONS S102248A   01-05-93
SUBJECT: IN BED WITH A COLD

Dear Buck . . .

You are just the person I need! Thank you for your generous offer of help and advice. I will take you up on it. I have several questions already. I don't like to read instruction manuals, they are too mathy for me. I need someone to teach me. And, the first things you can teach me are what your "basement" is and how to get there!

I would appreciate any information you care to offer at this point. There seems to be so much to learn!

> Your eager student . . .
> Katherine

************* ADULT TOPICS BULLETIN BOARD *************

TO: KATHERINE SIMMONS S102248A   11:16AM EST
FROM: MAHMOUD OUALIAH F690423D   01-05-93
SUBJECT: IN BED WITH A COLD

I would like to meet you. Do you wish it? I am exchange student of Morocco. I like to talk to a woman.

Mo

************* ADULT TOPICS BULLETIN BOARD *************

TO: MAHMOUD OUALIAH F690423D   11:42AM EST
FROM: KATHERINE SIMMONS S102248A   01-05-93
SUBJECT: IN BED WITH A COLD

Dear Mo . . .

No, I am afraid I don't wish to meet you today. You see, I have this horrible cold and it is almost impossible to look attractive with a runny nose. Have you ever noticed that?

Hey, I hope you realize that I am kidding. I am sure that you are an extremely interesting person. It would be delightful to learn about your country, since it is one to which I have never traveled. But you must realize that the likelihood of our living within a short drive of each other is highly unlikely. There are over three million subscribers to LuxNet, and we live all over this country.

Anyway, good luck with your studies!

Katherine

************* ADULT TOPICS BULLETIN BOARD *************

TO: KATHERINE SIMMONS S102248A   11:54AM EST
FROM: DONALD HAYNE N019272B   01-05-93
SUBJECT: IN BED WITH A COLD

Dear Katherine,
    Please look in your mailbox. I've sent you some e-mail. It's very long and I hope you'll like it and write back to me. I've sent many women long e-mail notes and they hardly ever write back. It's a bummer. Please write back. Please!

                    Lonely Don

************* ADULT TOPICS BULLETIN BOARD *************

TO: DONALD HAYNE N019272B   12:05PM EST
FROM: KATHERINE SIMMONS S102248A   01-05-93
SUBJECT: IN BED WITH A COLD

Dear Don . . .
    I can't wait to read your e-mail to me and I promise I will write back to you! However, first I must go and learn about e-mail and my mailbox.

                    Learning . . .
                    Katherine

WELCOME TO THE
LUXNET INFORMATION SERVICE
ELECTRONIC MAIL HELP CENTER

Each member of the LuxNet community has a personal mailbox in which to receive and send private electronic mail (e-mail) to other LuxNet members. The address of a member's mailbox is his member number. Each family has an option to sign up as many as four members from the "A" ID through the "D" ID. Each ID has its own private mailbox.

If there is unread mail in a mailbox, the member will be alerted by a flashing NEW MAIL bar in the upper right-hand corner of the screen. The mailbox may be accessed by clicking the mouse twice over the NEW MAIL bar.

When the mailbox screen comes into view, the unread mail is shown as entries on a grid in the order in which it was received. Each entry is identified by the name of the sender and the title of the message. Individual entries may be accessed by clicking the mouse twice over the identifying number.

To move to your mailbox at any time, click the mouse twice over the MAIL icon. A red flag will appear if there is no new mail.

----------------------------------- MAILBOX -----------------------------------

FROM: THOMAS FRANKEN D454572A   10:30AM EST
SUBJECT: IN BED WITH A COLD   01-05-93

Dear Katherine,

I'm a handsome 37-year-old man. I'm 6'2", and I have straight blond hair and pale blue eyes. I work out every day at the gym and have the body of an 18-year-old guy.

Women think I'm sexy. I've never had any complaints, if you know what I mean. That is probably because I'm well endowed. My penis is six inches long when it's soft and a whopping 8 inches when fully erect. I've had lots of practice, so I really know how to use my tool.

Well, what do you think? Would you like me to show you how I can ring your chimes?

E-mail me and tell me about you, your measurements, what you like to do in bed, and stuff like that. Then we'll take it from there, okay? I promise you, you won't be sorry.

                    Tom-Tom

----------------------------------- MAILBOX -----------------------------------

TO: THOMAS FRANKEN D454572A   12:29PM EST
SUBJECT: IN BED WITH A COLD   01-05-93

Dear Tom-Tom . . .

My Goodness! I do not think I have ever had such a comprehensive introduction to anyone in my life!

I hope you will forgive me if I am not forthcoming with the information you have requested. I am in shock at the moment and do not feel up to the task. Perhaps there is another woman wandering around computerland who has fewer inhibitions.

How lovely for you that you are so confident in your sexual prowess. I am sure your partners are very fortunate indeed. Good luck.

                    Stunned . . .
                    Katherine

-------------------------------- MAILBOX --------------------------------

FROM: SEAN MCGREGOR W776432C   10:32AM EST
SUBJECT: IN BED WITH A COLD   01-05-93

  Do you suck cocks?

-------------------------------- MAILBOX --------------------------------

TO: SEAN MCGREGOR W776432C   12:45PM EST
SUBJECT: IN BED WITH A COLD   01-05-93

Sean . . .
  Allow me to answer your question with a question. Why do you ask?
It would seem to me to be totally irrelevant for you to have such information at your disposal. Can you convince me this is something you
need to know?

                        Bewildered . . .
                        Katherine

-------------------------------- MAILBOX --------------------------------

FROM: TIMOTHY FLETCHER P333978A   10:37AM EST
SUBJECT: IN BED WITH A COLD   01-05-93

Dear Katherine,
  Just lie down and let me massage away those aches and pains from
being in bed so long. That's right. Just slip right out of those nighties
and stretch out on the bed on your stomach. Let me drizzle a little
of this eucalyptus oil over your back, bottom and legs. I have very
strong, experienced hands and I'm sure that I can make you feel better.
  I'll start at the nape of your neck, gently rubbing circles down the
length of it. MMMmmmm, you have a pretty neck. Then I'll move to
your shoulders, kneading out the soreness in your muscles and joints.
Next, your back will benefit from my expert hands. You'll groan as I
massage deeply.
  As my hands move over the swell of your bottom, I feel you tremble
a little. I give your glutes my special attention, stroking and squeezing,
allowing a hand to slide down to the pliant flesh of your inner thighs
occasionally. Then, your legs, from the tops of your thighs, behind your

knees, over your calves and to the soles of your feet are treated to the delights that my strong masculine hands have to offer.

Would you like to turn over?

A physical therapist . . .
Tim

---------------------------------- MAILBOX ----------------------------------

TO: TIMOTHY FLETCHER P333978A   12:58PM EST
SUBJECT: IN BED WITH A COLD   01-05-93

Dear Tim . . .

Now there's a first . . . computer massage! Although I must admit it was entertaining and I actually do feel a little better, I think I will pass on the offer for a display of your manual dexterity on my flip side.

Thank you anyway.

Appreciatively . . .
Katherine

---------------------------------- MAILBOX ----------------------------------

FROM: CHARLES LESLIE G654390B   10:40AM EST
SUBJECT: IN BED WITH A COLD   01-05-93

Dear Katherine,

I'll tell you right off the bat, I'm a married man. At 50, I'm finding my predictable married sex to have something lacking, but I'm not willing to risk having a real-life affair for several reasons.

This medium offers the possibility of connecting with persons of the opposite sex and engaging in sexually arousing conversations that benefit both parties without risking AIDS or the emotional and marital problems which might result from adultery.

I've been gratified by two sexually explicit e-mail relationships with women on this board. Those affairs have run their course and I'm looking for another woman who might share my desire for a roll in the computer hay. Would you be interested?

I'm 5'9" and weigh 189 pounds. I have brown eyes and gray hair, what's left of it <G>. I own a freelance accounting service which I run out of my home office. I enjoy golf and most spectator sports.

I generally like a full-figured woman and I especially like very large breasts (I mean really big ones I can bury my face in). I like to give head and I like to get it. And I like a variety of positions, but my favorite is probably with the woman on top.

Well? What do you say?

Love,
Charlie

---------------------------------- MAILBOX ----------------------------------

TO: CHARLES LESLIE G654390B   01:01PM EST
SUBJECT: IN BED WITH A COLD   01-05-93

Dear Charlie . . .

I say, "Holy Mackerel, let me out of here!" But, before I leave, I will tell you that I would not be your ideal woman. You would probably find me lacking in the bosom department.

Feeling like a resident of the
Twilight Zone . . .
Katherine

---------------------------------- MAILBOX ----------------------------------

FROM: DONALD HAYNE N019272B   11:30AM EST
SUBJECT: IN BED WITH A COLD   01-05-93

Dear Katherine,

I'm a 24-year-old guy. I'm 5'10" and weigh 152 pounds. My hair is brown and I have gray eyes. Some people told me that I'm nice-looking. I'm disabled and use a wheelchair. I live in a group home with five other guys. We have a computer we share in the common room.

I'd like to meet a woman who will write to me about romance and sex. It's been hard to find anyone who's interested. I don't get it. You can't see over the computer. What difference does it make if I'm in a wheelchair? I can come up with some interesting and sexy writing just like anybody else.

Here is something I have written. I've sent it to about twenty women and most of them didn't even write back to me, maybe one or two. Will you write back to me?

It was dark and we stood on the balcony looking at the ocean and the moon. It was beautiful. I put my arm around you and we kissed. Then we stood there for about another hour just looking at the beauty.

I went inside and put some music in the tape player. It was nice slow music. I asked you if you wanted to dance and you said yes. We danced for about an hour. You were a good dancer and so was I. While we danced we kissed some more. It felt great!

After we danced we went inside and sat on the couch and we kissed some more. We were alone. I put my hand on your breast and you sighed and let me feel it. It felt good to me to have my hand on your breast. You enjoyed it too. Then I put both of my hands on your breasts and rubbed them slow. They were big and soft. You sighed again. You took your blouse off and let me feel your breasts as much as I wanted because you liked the way it felt. It made you want to have sex with me.

You put your hands in my sweat pants and held my penis. You squeezed it a little and I really liked it. It got hard as a rock.

You were hot so you laid on the couch and pulled off your pants and underpants. You were naked. You let me look at you for about fifteen or twenty minutes. Then I felt all of your body even your vagina. You sighed and really liked it!

We kissed some more and then I laid on you after I pulled my pants off. We had sex for about an hour and a half. It felt real good until we stopped. Then we got dressed and talked for a long time.

Will you please write to me?!

Lonely Don

---------------------------------- MAILBOX ----------------------------------

TO: DONALD HAYNE N019272B   01:30PM EST
SUBJECT: IN BED WITH A COLD   01-05-93

Dear Don . . .

You really did send me a long letter! Although I hate to add to your disappointment in being unable to find a woman who is interested in writing to you about romance and sex, I must also decline your offer. However, you need to know it has nothing to do with the fact that you are disabled.

You see, I have a cold and am just bored. I decided to visit this bulletin board on a whim, as a way to entertain myself. I was curious and had no idea what people do here.

I am married and am really not interested in talking to strangers about sex. The way people communicate here has really shocked me.

Anyway, thank you for responding to my note. I hope you find a pen pal.

Regards . . .
Katherine

---------------------------------- MAILBOX ----------------------------------

FROM: JOHN DAVIS P674501A   12:35PM EST
SUBJECT: IN BED WITH A COLD   01-05-93

Dear Katherine,

I'm a 47-year-old DWM who lives in Indianapolis. I'm six feet tall, have brown hair and eyes, and a slim athletic build. I'm a runner. I manage a string of hosiery stores.

I'm looking for a slim attractive divorced or single woman between the ages of 25 and 40 who might be interested in establishing an e-mail relationship with the goal of meeting in person at some point. If you fit the description and feel this is something you might consider, please send me your particulars via e-mail.

If you're fat, married or a smoker, don't bother replying.

John

---------------------------------- MAILBOX ----------------------------------

FROM: HARVEY SONDHEIM H094683A   12:42PM EST
SUBJECT: IN BED WITH A COLD   01-05-93

Kathy,

How about some hot phone sex? I'll call you or you can call me collect. E-me back and give me your number or let me know if you're interested and I'll send you mine. I have a hot rod in my hand that needs some attention and I know how to make you wet, believe me.

Hard and horny,
Harvey

------------------------------------- MAILBOX -------------------------------------

TO: HARVEY SONDHEIM H094683A   01:40PM EST
SUBJECT: IN BED WITH A COLD   01-05-93

Dear Harvey . . .

Well, I'm afraid you will have to stay in that condition. There is no way in the world I would give a complete stranger my phone number, much less engage in phone sex with him. I am amazed that you would offer to give me your number. Aren't you afraid you might hook into someone who isn't playing with a full deck? Luckily, I am.

Dumbfounded . . .
Katherine

------------------------------------- MAILBOX -------------------------------------

FROM: CHRISTINE COMPTON Z474215B   12:45PM EST
SUBJECT: IN BED WITH A COLD   01-05-93

Dear Katherine,

I'm a 30-year-old woman who lives in Florida. I'm pretty and out-going. Recently I've been feeling that I must be bi, since I'm finding myself being very sexually attracted to women. My husband has actually been encouraging me to follow up on my urges because he's always had a fantasy about a menage a trois.

It's occurred to me that it might be possible for me to begin exploring female relationships by connecting with a woman on this board; either one who is experienced in bisexuality or who shares my desire to explore the possibilities. I hope it does not offend you that I'm approaching you.

Sincerely,
Chris

---------------------------------- MAILBOX ----------------------------------

TO: CHRISTINE COMPTON Z474215B   01:45PM EST
SUBJECT: IN BED WITH A COLD   01-05-93

Dear Chris . . .

After some of the e-mail I have received today, your polite request for intimacy has been a breath of fresh air. Unfortunately, I must tell you that I am not drawn to women sexually and the prospect of engaging in a sexually charged relationship of any kind with another female does not appeal to me.

You are fortunate to have a husband who is willing to encourage you in your search for fulfillment.

Bye now . . .
Katherine

---------------------------------- MAILBOX ----------------------------------

FROM: JASON KEMPER G101721D   12:52PM EST
SUBJECT: IN BED WITH A COLD   01-05-93

KATHERINE
CAN I EAT YOUR PUSSY?

JAY

---------------------------------- MAILBOX ----------------------------------

TO: JASON KEMPER G101721D   01:53PM EST
SUBJECT: IN BED WITH A COLD   01-05-93

Jason . . .

And just how, may I ask, do you plan to accomplish that feat? You must know something about modems I do not.

Annoyed . . .
Katherine

---------------------------------- MAILBOX ----------------------------------

FROM: BUCK BRAZEMORE X455045A   01:00PM EST
SUBJECT: IN BED WITH A COLD   01-05-93

Dear Katie,

I'm fixing to go out into the field and thought I'd check in on you before I take off. Well, are you in shock? I know what happens to a new woman when she shows her pretty face on this board. I talked my wife, Linda, into giving it a try a month ago and I got to see first hand. Men don't get the same reaction.

I'm guessing men outnumber women about twenty to one here, so you can count on being swamped with replies on the board and e-mail in your mailbox whenever you make a public post on the BB. You'll get a ton more late this afternoon after people get off work, and tonight. Most people who work get on the board at night or really early in the morning. But, there's a three-hour time difference between the East Coast and the West Coast, so the communication is kind of staggered. During the day, you see a bunch of college kids, but you'll see people who work out of their homes or who do shift work and stuff like that, too.

In answer to your questions: My basement is just a subject on the bulletin board called "BUCK'S BASEMENT." I started it for fun about six weeks ago. As long as a subject gets replies, it stays up. If a subject gets no replies in 48 hours, it drops off. My subject stays up because several of my computer buddies routinely post there. We just kid around, it's lots of fun. To get there, you just log back onto the BB and pull up the alphabetized list of subjects. Go down the list until you see my basement, then click twice. That's it! But, watch that first step, it's loose! <G>

Another tip—lots of people see what you write on the board, so don't put anything on there you want to keep confidential. For example, never put your address or phone number up there. I wouldn't even tell the city where you live. You don't know who might get hold of it. I saw a woman post her phone number one time and I wondered how many obscene phone calls she got, she probably had to have her number changed. You'll see lots of people on the board saying, "check your mailbox" or "e-me" or something like that. This is just the way people tell each other they have something private to talk about. E-mail is private.

I'd like to get to know a little bit about you if you're willing. I promise to be the perfect gentleman.

Gotta get going. If you have any questions, just let me know.

> Still at your service,
> Buck

---------------------------------- MAILBOX ----------------------------------

TO: BUCK BRAZEMORE X455045A   02:02PM EST
SUBJECT: IN BED WITH A COLD   01-05-93

Dear Buck . . .

To be sure, my morning was not dull! I never dreamed people communicate like this over computers . . . what a revelation! I am amazed, incredulous, insulted and yet utterly fascinated and oddly attracted. Perhaps I am delirious with fever or am suffering from a NyQuil-induced hallucination.

Yes, I will tell you a little bit more about me, if you will return the favor. You seem like a normal person in a sea of bozos. I have become very curious about you. Why are you here? Are there others like you?

You say you have a wife named Linda. Well, I have a husband named Tom and twin teenage boys, Greg and Stephen. I have a good deal of education, but I don't work for money and my time is pretty much my own, now that the twins can drive. My life is good, but lately I have been feeling, oh I don't know . . . maybe restless.

At the moment, I am feeling tired. I think I'll go and take a nap. I will come back after dinner and see if there is NEW MAIL from you.

> Until later . . .
> Katie

P.S. I like the new nickname, it makes me feel young.

---------------------------------- MAILBOX ----------------------------------

FROM: BUCK BRAZEMORE X455045A   07:30PM EST
SUBJECT: IN BED WITH A COLD   01-05-93

Dear Katie,

I like finding you in my mailbox. Are you feeling better? Have you gotten over your shock at what goes on around here?

I guess I'm pretty normal, if anyone who wanders around in this strange place can be accused of that. I'm almost 40, my birthday is the day before Valentine's Day. I've been married for eighteen years and am the father of two rowdy boys, Cody and Jeremy, ages 13 and 11. I have a degree in geology from Texas A & M.

I live in the Hill Country of Texas near the little town of Kerrville and own a small but prosperous oil-drilling operation. Most of my business is outside this country. For example, I'm negotiating a contract at the moment with some people in Israel. I sank three successful wells for them two years ago. I also have a consulting contract with Parks and Sparks, the well-fire and blowout specialists. They are the guys who got so much publicity during the Kuwait conflagration. Sparky McCallum (the "Sparks") has been my friend since kindergarten.

You might be interested in the way I look. I'm 6 feet tall and wiry. I haven't weighed in lately, but I suspect I might weigh 175 or thereabouts. My hair is a nondescript brown and I have blue eyes. I don't look like Mel Gibson, but no woman has ever thrown rocks at me either.

I'm outside a lot in my work and I like that. I'm especially interested in paleontology and have a humdinger of a fossil collection. Texas is a great place to live if you like fossils. It was at the bottom of a big shallow ocean at one time and, during another period, a lot of the large dinosaurs, the big carnivores and stegosauri and the like, roamed here.

Well, I have some stuff to do in the equipment shed tonight, so I need to vamoose. Please, send me a note and tell me some more about you and let me know if you have more questions. I'll look for you in the morning.

A new friend,
Buck

---------------------------------- MAILBOX ----------------------------------

TO: BUCK BRAZEMORE X455045A   08:30PM EST
SUBJECT: IN BED WITH A COLD   01-05-93

Dear Buck . . .

Yes, I am a little better; the worst is over, but I'm still congested and have aways to go before I will feel human again. You know what I mean, everyone has to slug it out with a bad cold every now and then.

I am alone tonight (this is not unusual and is probably just as well since I am sick). Tom travels a lot in his business and he is a workaholic, I guess. He is the manufacturer's agent representing Ishii copiers. The whole Southeast is his territory. He is at one of his district offices in Charleston, Birmingham or Columbia. I forgot which one this time. He rents condos in all three cities for convenience. He will call before ten and remind me where he is. The kids have gone out for hamburgers and then to the library with their girlfriends, Allison and Jill. They ought to be home about 10:30 since it is a school night.

Thanks to your advance warning, when I logged back onto LuxNet after my long nap and dinner, I was not surprised to find eighteen new replies on the BB and twelve new e-mail messages in my mailbox. It took me almost two hours to reply to everyone. I don't think I can keep this up, but you are right when you say, "it beats TV."

Perhaps you are interested in MY appearance. I am 5'6" and my weight fluctuates between 135 and 150 during the course of a year. I peak after the Christmas holiday and ebb in the summer. I am not a thin woman, but I am certainly not fat.

I think I must still be attractive. I still get compliments and appreciative looks, although they are becoming fewer and farther between. When I was in college, at UNC-Chapel Hill, my sorority sponsored me in the Maid of Cotton contest. I was beautiful then. Now, in my forties, I have my good days and my bad days. Sometimes I look at my face in the mirror and like it better than when it was younger (it looks more interesting and complicated), other days I look like the mother of teenagers (and it scares the daylights out of me).

I hate to confess this, but I am still vain. My beauty was always a source of power for me; I took it for granted, and although I'm still attractive, "attractive" is not the same as "beautiful." What comes after attractive? It makes me cringe to think.

I am amazed that I'm revealing this insecurity to you. It seems easy to let barriers fall down in this place! Maybe it is the anonymity or something. Anyway, perhaps this is what draws some people. You can use it like confession.

I will check out your basement. It will have to be tomorrow, though. I just had a belt of NyQuil before I began this note and I can feel it kicking in.

See you later . . .
Katie

BUCK'S BASEMENT

TO: CLIFF NOTES L896112C   07:30AM EST
FROM: BUCK BRAZEMORE X455045A   01-20-93
SUBJECT: BUCK'S BASEMENT

Cliff, Ole Buddy,

I see that you and Sue have been making out on the couch down here again. What a mess! Now, you two get busy and clean it up. We're gonna need it when we set up the card table for the poker game.

Will you be around tonight?

> Rallying the troops,
> Buck

TO: BUCK BRAZEMORE X455045A   07:57AM EST
FROM: CLIFF NOTES L896112C   01-20-93
SUBJECT: BUCK'S BASEMENT

Buck, My Man!

Hey, sorry about the mess, but that's what's so great about this basement, right? It's the perfect make-out pad. Maybe we should drag a couple of those old mattresses down from the attic and put them over there in the corner. You know, with a lava lamp and a beaded curtain, we could have it looking really great. Let's do it! As a matter of fact, consider it done. It'll be my contribution to the atmosphere for tonight's soiree.

I'll have to ask Sue to get after those stains with the saddle soap and a little elbow grease. I have a morning meeting and am out the door. See you tonight.

> Hasta la vista,
> Cliff

************* ADULT TOPICS BULLETIN BOARD *************

TO: CLIFF NOTES L896112C   08:15AM EST
FROM: SUSAN VENEER G740094D   01-20-93
SUBJECT: BUCK'S BASEMENT

Cliff!
    What's the big deal making me clean up the couch! :-(It's mostly YOUR mess! No fair! So what if you have to go to work, I've got to go to school.
    I'm gonna get you for this. :-)

> @-->->----Sue Veneer----<-<--@

************* ADULT TOPICS BULLETIN BOARD *************

TO: KATHERINE SIMMONS S102248A   08:16AM EST
FROM: BUCK BRAZEMORE X455045A   01-20-93
SUBJECT: BUCK'S BASEMENT

Hey, New Girl in Town,
    Wanna be the hostess tonight at the poker game? You can be my date and take care of the refreshments—don't forget the beer. Why don't you decorate the place, too? Just use your imagination—cost is no object. <G> That's what's so great about this virtual reality.
    We will crank up about 7:00 EST and have a fine old time. Whaddaya say?

> Asking sweetly,
> Buck

************* ADULT TOPICS BULLETIN BOARD *************

TO: BUCK BRAZEMORE X455045A   08:30AM EST
FROM: KATHERINE SIMMONS S102248A   01-20-93
SUBJECT: BUCK'S BASEMENT

My Dear Buck . . .

Why, of course, I will be delighted to be both the hostess and your date! What fun! You are allowing me carte blanche with the decorations and refreshments? How about if we have a 70s theme, since Cliff is dragging the mattresses down from the attic and has already set up the lava lamp and beaded curtain?

I'll see if I can find someone to bring a black light, a strobe light and some incense, then I will look into scrounging up some Jimi Hendrix, Vanilla Fudge, Cream, Santana and Quicksilver Messenger Service albums (Oh, yes, and I will bring some James Taylor just for me). Everyone will need to come in costume, as well. I better make a run to the Goodwill shop to see if I can find something especially good.

> The Hostess with the Mostest . . .
> Katie

************* ADULT TOPICS BULLETIN BOARD *************

TO: KATHERINE SIMMONS S102248A   08:42AM EST
FROM: CAROL BEATTY N771200C   01-20-93
SUBJECT: BUCK'S BASEMENT

Dear Katie,

May I please help? I'll bring the tofu burgers, sprout salad and Alice B. Toklas brownies for dessert. Oh yes, and how about a couple of bottles of some Boone's Farm wine? <LOL>

I love JT, too!

> Still a hippie at heart,
> Carol

************* ADULT TOPICS BULLETIN BOARD *************

TO: CAROL BEATTY N771200C   08:56AM EST
FROM: KATHERINE SIMMONS S102248A   01-20-93
SUBJECT: BUCK'S BASEMENT

Dear Carol . . .

By all means, pitch right in! Let's make it pot luck, then everybody will be content.

I am always happy to find someone who also loves James Taylor. When I was a student at UNC-Chapel Hill (many moons ago), his father was the dean of the medical school. Occasionally, I would see one of the Taylors walking nonchalantly down the main drag, Franklin Street. Once in a while it would be James, but more frequently it would be one of his siblings, Kate or Livingston. I had such a massive crush on JT back then. It was one of those "small-town boy makes good" things. His music can still reduce me to a love-sick adolescent.

Let's drink some Boone's Farm and listen to JT tonight!

> Humming "Fire and Rain" . . .
> Katie

************* ADULT TOPICS BULLETIN BOARD *************

TO: KATHERINE SIMMONS S102248A   09:07AM EST
FROM: CAROL BEATTY N771200C   01-20-93
SUBJECT: BUCK'S BASEMENT

Dear Katie,

I'm pretty new here and have been watching BUCK'S BASEMENT this week. It looks like so much fun. I'll be home tonight, so I'd love to jump right in. What are the rules?

I'm 39 and live in Florida. My son is school-age and I have a six-month-old at home. I'm taking this year off from my job in middle management at a largish bank. What do you do?

> Having another cup of coffee,
> Carol

************* ADULT TOPICS BULLETIN BOARD *************

TO: CAROL BEATTY N771200C   09:20AM EST
FROM: KATHERINE SIMMONS S102248A   01-20-93
SUBJECT: BUCK'S BASEMENT

Dear Carol . . .

Believe it or not, I have only been around here two weeks myself. I wandered into this place while recovering from a cold. The cold is almost over, but I have become hooked on the Adult Topics Bulletin Board. I have never experienced anything like it!

There really don't seem to be any rules here except for the LuxNet guidelines. You can read them by hitting the "guidelines" button when you first log on.

As for tonight: What I have learned is one shows up at about 7:00 EST and just jumps into the fray. I don't have a clue how many people are involved, but it is rather like an interactive free-for-all. Buck Brazemore is the emcee of sorts. He has asked me to be his "date" and the hostess for tonight and I am at a loss as to what that means exactly. I suppose I will get on-the-job-training.

I am 44 years old and I live in the South, too. We are almost neighbors. Like you, I am at home. However, my babies are seventeen years old. I have twin boys, Greg and Stephen, who are seniors in high school. They can drive now, so they don't need me much anymore (except to wash their clothes, clean their rooms and provide them with huge quantities of food).

I wish I could stay and talk for awhile, but I need to go take a shower and get dressed. I am meeting two friends for a shopping/lunch thing at 10:30. See you tonight.

                                        Your new bosom buddy . . .
                                        Katie

************* ADULT TOPICS BULLETIN BOARD *************

TO: ALL   06:58PM EST
FROM: BUCK BRAZEMORE X455045A   01-20-93
SUBJECT: BUCK'S BASEMENT

Hi, Guys and Gals!

It is I, your host for the evening. Don't I look sharp in my Nehru jacket, bell-bottoms and sandals; and how about my John Lennon glasses, headband and Fu Manchu mustache? My date for tonight, the Lady Katie, has set the theme for tonight's poker game and party. Isn't it a dandy?

Now, let's see who will show up and what will happen!

Your host,
Buck

************* ADULT TOPICS BULLETIN BOARD *************

TO: BUCK BRAZEMORE X455045A   07:09PM EST
FROM: KATHERINE SIMMONS S102248A   01-20-93
SUBJECT: BUCK'S BASEMENT

Buck!

My Goodness, you do look divine! And how do you like my outfit? You will notice I am wearing a lime green and electric pink psychedelic-print halter top with my patched, hip-hugger bell-bottoms. Do you like my puka-shell necklace and matching headband? Don't my clogs and white lipstick just grab you? My blonde wig is reminiscent of Alice in Wonderland, n'est-ce pas? And I am wearing patchouli oil just for you.

Now, come with me into the party room and tell me how you like the atmosphere. Ravi Shankar's sitar music is on the player, there is a haze of sandalwood incense wafting around and the black lighting makes my lips and bell-bottoms glow an unearthly violet-white. The food is displayed on an Indian print cloth on the floor. And there are mattresses illuminated with lava lamps in the corner behind the beaded curtain.

Sue Veneer and Cliff Notes dragged the couch into the adjoining room and we set the card table up in there. Well, what do you think?

The Hostess with the Mostest . . .
Katie

************* ADULT TOPICS BULLETIN BOARD *************

TO: KATHERINE SIMMONS S102248A   07:17PM EST
FROM: BUCK BRAZEMORE X455045A   01-20-93
SUBJECT: BUCK'S BASEMENT

Lady!

OOOOOoooeeeee! Get over here and kiss me with those white lips
and let's see what the black light does to those lip prints. If they look
real good, we'll have to experiment with them later on, if you get my
drift. <wink, wink>

You've done a great job fixing the place up. It needed a woman's
touch. Now, let's go greet our guests.

                                        The Host with The Most,
                                        Buck

************* ADULT TOPICS BULLETIN BOARD *************

TO: ALL
FROM: CLIFF NOTES L896112C   07:18PM EST
SUBJECT: BUCK'S BASEMENT   01-20-93

Greetings!

Check it out! Here I am, making my entrance wearing a tie-dyed T-
shirt and Earth shoes. I decided not to wear any pants. Excuse me while
I make a beeline over to the mattresses to stake out my turf. And speaking of my turf, where is my main squeeze, Sue Veneer?

Babe, get yourself over here and bring a couple beers with you.

                                        A party animal,
                                        Cliff

************ ADULT TOPICS BULLETIN BOARD ************

TO: CLIFF NOTES L896112C   07:28PM EST
FROM: SUSAN VENEER G740094D   01-20-93
SUBJECT: BUCK'S BASEMENT

Hi, Honey! <kissing you passionately on the lips>
   Here's your beer. How do you like my black leather miniskirt and
see-through blouse? Did you notice I am going braless tonight? :-)
Wanna go in the other room and mess up the couch again?

                    @-->->----Sue Veneer----<-<--@

************ ADULT TOPICS BULLETIN BOARD ************

TO: SUSAN VENEER G740094D   07:31PM EST
FROM: CLIFF NOTES L896112C   01-20-93
SUBJECT: BUCK'S BASEMENT

Squeeze o' mine,
   I have a better idea than messing up the couch again. Are you available?

                    No pants,
                    Cliff

************ ADULT TOPICS BULLETIN BOARD ************

TO: CLIFF NOTES L896112C   07:39PM EST
FROM: SUSAN VENEER G740094D   01-20-93
SUBJECT: BUCK'S BASEMENT

Dear Cliff,
   Just give me about ten minutes to get rid of my roommate. I'll E you
when the coast is clear.

                    @-->->----Sue Veneer----<-<--@

*************ADULT TOPICS BULLETIN BOARD *************

TO: BUCK BRAZEMORE X455045A   07:41PM EST
FROM: WILLIAM RAMSEY Y082176A   01-20-93
SUBJECT: BUCK'S BASEMENT

Hi Buck,

   Thanks for the invitation. I'm making the scene wearing a fantastic
dashiki and looking like Sly (the lead singer in the group Sly And The
Family Stone). Do you remember his song, "I Want To Take You
Higher"? It seems I heard that every day I was in Vietnam.

                              Picking out my Afro,
                              Will

*************ADULT TOPICS BULLETIN BOARD *************

TO: WILLIAM RAMSEY Y082176A   07:46PM EST
FROM: BUCK BRAZEMORE X455045A   01-20-93
SUBJECT: BUCK'S BASEMENT

Buenos Noches, Padre, <giving you five>

   Whoa, I'm shocked! Since you are a man of the cloth, I expected you
to show up in your chaplain's get-up. By the way, what did chaplains
wear in Vietnam?

                              A civilian,
                              Buck

************* ADULT TOPICS BULLETIN BOARD *************

TO: BUCK BRAZEMORE X455045A   07:50PM EST
FROM: WILLIAM RAMSEY Y082176A   01-20-93
SUBJECT: BUCK'S BASEMENT

Buck,
   Since I was in the field, I wore fatigues like everybody else, except I
also wore a little cross on my lapel. Although I thought about wearing
my Air Force threads tonight, I was afraid it might prompt someone into
staging a demonstration. <G> Besides, I look infinitely more cool in
my dashiki.

                         Shooting you a peace sign,
                         Will

************* ADULT TOPICS BULLETIN BOARD *************

TO: ALL   07:51PM EST
FROM: KENNETH LONG T017643A   01-20-93
SUBJECT: BUCK'S BASEMENT

Hello Everyone,
   I'm wearing a body-hugging polyester shirt with a fringed leather vest
and matching leather pants. I'm looking for a date. Is there anyone
around for me?

                         Arriving stag,
                         Ken

*************ADULT TOPICS BULLETIN BOARD *************

TO: KENNETH LONG T017643A   08:00PM EST
FROM: CAROL BEATTY N771200C   01-20-93
SUBJECT: BUCK'S BASEMENT

Hi Ken,
I'll be your date. What's your sign? I'm a Virgo—not!
I'm wearing a baby-blue gingham granny dress with matching plat-
form shoes and eye shadow. Be sure to catch the false eyelashes, too.
How do you like my peace medallion?
Wanna dance?

> Frugging up a storm to the Mamas
> and the Papas,
> Carol

*************ADULT TOPICS BULLETIN BOARD *************

TO: ALL   08:02PM EST
FROM: PAULA LEVY U345109A   01-20-93
SUBJECT: BUCK'S BASEMENT

Hi Guys,
Don't I look amazing in these outrageous hot pants and thigh-high
boots? And take a gander at this string bikini top. They don't call me
"Peaches" for nothing. Anybody out there want to do the hot e-mail
thing? I need it.

> On the prowl,
> Peaches

*************ADULT TOPICS BULLETIN BOARD *************

TO: PAULA LEVY U345109A   08:06PM EST
FROM: PETER CHO L884653   01-20-93
SUBJECT: BUCK'S BASEMENT

Peaches!
I do! I do! E-mail me right now and tell me what you want!

> The big,
> Peter

************* ADULT TOPICS BULLETIN BOARD *************

TO: PAULA LEVY U345109A   08:16PM EST
FROM: JOHN HINSON D772553A   01-20-93
SUBJECT: BUCK'S BASEMENT

Dear Peaches,
   PLEASE, check your mailbox! Is something wrong? Why won't you
answer my letters?

                          John

************* ADULT TOPICS BULLETIN BOARD *************

TO: ALL   08:30PM EST
FROM: RICHARD FLEMING K129543A   01-20-93
SUBJECT: BUCK'S BASEMENT

A WARNING TO ALL GUYS!!!!
WATCH OUT FOR PAULA LEVY, AKA "PEACHES"! SHE'S A
C**CK TEASER AND A B**CH!

                    ONE WHO KNOWS!
                    RICH

************* ADULT TOPICS BULLETIN BOARD *************

TO: RICHARD FLEMING K129543A   08:40PM EST
FROM: PAULA LEVY U345109A   01-20-93
SUBJECT: BUCK'S BASEMENT

Dick,
   That does it! I've warned you five times to stop hounding me. I'm
gonna sic the Lux police on you, turkey! Now, STAY AWAY FROM
ME!

                          P.

************ ADULT TOPICS BULLETIN BOARD ************

TO: ALL   08:47PM EST
FROM: JOHN W. KELLY JR. A041178A   01-20-93
SUBJECT: BUCK'S BASEMENT

<<<<<<<<<<<< I'M NAKED!!!>>>>>>>>>>>>>>>>

Streaking,
Johnny Kelly

---------------------------------- MAILBOX ----------------------------------

FROM: BUCK BRAZEMORE   07:52 EST
SUBJECT: BUCK'S BASEMENT   01-20-93

Dear Katie,

I'm afraid I'm going to have to leave you in the lurch tonight. You'll have to handle BUCK'S BASEMENT without me. You can do it, the Wednesday night crew is usually pretty tame.

I have a small herd of longhorns, one bull, eight cows, two calves and a steer. They're my pets really. Senorita, one of my cows, is acting like she might calf tonight. She's young and has been having some trouble. Anyway, I have her in the barn and I'm fixing to go down there in a minute. I may need to hang around for awhile.

Here are the answers to your questions from yesterday:

<G> = Grin

<VBG> = Very Big Grin

<SEG> = Shit-Eating Grin

<LOL> = Laughing Out Loud

<LMAO> = Laughing My Ass Off

<LMAOAROTF> = Laughing My Ass Off And Rolling On The Floor

:-) :-(;-} 8-[etc. = Little face things that show emotion (I think they're goofy!)

---<---<---@ = A little flower thing Sue does all the time

The Lux Police = A term for the censors who work for Lux—they're the ones who decide whether a post is offensive and they deal out punishments if necessary.

Well, I better get going. I'll E you tomorrow.

Adios,
Buck

---------------------------------- MAILBOX ------------------------------------

TO: BUCK BRAZEMORE X455045A   08:15PM EST
SUBJECT: BUCK'S BASEMENT   01-20-93

My Dear Buck . . .

Gee, thanks! Just what I need . . . trying to manage that unruly bunch, and me a raw recruit! But, of course, I understand your predicament and I admire the way you care for your animals.

Over the past week, I have found a lot to admire about you. You have certainly been kind and helpful to me and have kept your promise about being a gentleman. What a rarity in this place! I enjoy watching you relate to others, too—you always seem so upbeat and positive. When I try to imagine my Buck, I see a cowboy in a white hat . . . a good guy. Are you really like that?

Will you tell me some more about the real you? For instance, what were you like growing up? Why did you choose to study geology? How did you meet Linda? Why are you here? If I am getting too personal, please forgive me. It's just that I'm getting very curious about this man who stood me up for a heifer tonight.

All ears . . .
Katie

---------------------------------- MAILBOX ------------------------------------

FROM: BUCK BRAZEMORE X455045A   12:58AM EST
SUBJECT: BUCK'S BASEMENT   01-20-93

Dear Katie,

Well, it's almost midnight CST, so you're probably in your bed asleep and won't get this 'til morning. Senorita finally had a bull calf and it wasn't easy, but it's over now. We always call bull calves "Dinner."

We don't give them real names or we get attached to them. And that won't do since we either have to sell or butcher them.

I dropped in on the board for a minute just now. Wow, there were eighty-something replies in five hours! It got kind of wild and woolly after 9:00 with all that streaking and going-on. But you did a good job. You had those guys eating out of your hand.

I'll be happy to tell you some more about me, but it'll have to wait until tomorrow. I'm plumb worn out!

> Your Cowboy,
> Buck

---------------------------------- MAILBOX ----------------------------------

TO: BUCK BRAZEMORE X455045A   07:49AM EST
SUBJECT: BUCK'S BASEMENT   01-21-93

Dear Cowboy . . .

"Dinner"?! How funny! <laughing> Please tell me about longhorns. I am a city slicker and cattle ranching sounds so exotic. I don't know a thing about it.

I must tell you that I am really enjoying this! Every morning, the minute the boys are out the door, I run into the loft (where I keep my computer) and log on. Each day the NEW MAIL sign is flashing. Most of the stuff is dreadful, but you are usually there, too. After I read the mail, I go downstairs, fix a cup of coffee and then come back up here to compose my replies. Then I go and play on the board. It has become my routine. But, one day last week, I looked down at myself at three o'clock in the afternoon to discover I still had on my nightclothes. This is addictive, isn't it?

I am looking forward to learning more about you. Also, do you know anything about the other people who play on the board? For example, who is that guy you called "Padre," what is the story with Cliff Notes and Sue Veneer and what's with the nom de plumes?

> Curious . . .
> Katie

------------------------------------ MAILBOX ------------------------------------

FROM: BUCK BRAZEMORE X455045A   07:30AM EST
SUBJECT: BUCK'S BASEMENT   01-21-93

Dear Katie,

    I'd like nothing more than to wile away the day with you. Unfortunately, I'm late getting up this morning and need to go out and make a living. Damn! <LOL> I'll write to you this evening after I get home.

Saddling up,
Buck

MOTHER'S
MORNING OUT

FROM: CAROL BEATTY N771200C   07:57AM EST
SUBJECT: MOTHER'S MORNING OUT   01-21-93

Hi Girl!

My son has just boarded the school bus. Tiffy has been nursed and is
playing contentedly nearby with her Busy Box. I only breast feed her
twice a day now and she should be totally switched over to the bottle
by early next month, so we'll both be ready for me to go back to work.
I have a few minutes to myself, so I thought I'd write. This is a nice
distraction and it's convenient—an instant conversation partner.

My maternity leave will be over in six months. I have mixed feelings
about that. Part of me would like to just stay home, but most of me is
claustrophobic and bored stiff.

I've been having some e-mail fun with that Ken Long guy who
showed up in BUCK'S BASEMENT last night looking for a date. He
seems like a nice normal person. Some of those men give me the creeps.

Do you happen to have a really good easy cookie recipe? One of my
girlfriends from work is having a bridal shower for a mutual friend and
she's asked me to bring four dozen cookies. I hate to cook. Any ideas?

Uh-oh! I smell something suspicious. Tiffany probably needs a
change. Write me if you get a chance.

> Your friend,
> Carol

---------------------------------- MAILBOX ----------------------------------

TO: CAROL BEATTY N771200C   08:39AM EST
SUBJECT: MOTHER'S MORNING OUT   01-21-93

Dear Carol . . .

I would like to have a female computer buddy since I have been feeling lonely lately. Let's chat regularly.

I have been having some "e-mail fun" with Buck Brazemore for a little over two weeks. He is a really nice guy, not at all like some of these gross weirdoes. Buck is sweet and helpful and I am really enjoying getting to know him.

Being at home with a baby really is complicated, isn't it? The first three years after my twins were born are kind of a blur. I was too exhausted to be bored. I breast fed them for twelve months and it seems my entire life centered around feeding infants. Many days, I would walk around my house dressed only in my nursing bra (with the flaps open) and sweat pants. I remember just barely escaping flashing a UPS guy when I absent-mindedly headed for the door in that outfit. I just happened to catch my reflection in the hall mirror. I wonder what kind of reaction I would have gotten if I had opened the door like that? <laughing>

I never developed a romantic feeling about nursing . . . it was simply a job to me. Once, I remember looking at the cover of a La Leche League booklet, with its picture of this blissful-looking Madonna gazing down at her nursing baby, and feeling a pang of jealousy.

One of my friends who had delivered her daughter three months before Greg and Stephen were born confessed she had sexual feelings when she breast fed. I looked at her in disbelief. Who had energy for sexual feelings? I felt like a dairy cow.

Three afternoons a week, I paid my neighbor's sixteen-year-old daughter to come over after school and just play with the boys for two hours. I remember watching the clock impatiently and praying for 3 o'clock to hurry up and get there. When the girl arrived, I would hand the babies over and go immediately to my bedroom and crash. Having two infants at one time is incredibly tiring.

At the same time I was dealing with the demands of new motherhood, Tom got the Ishii account and began building his business. Most of the time he was gone, preoccupied or fatigued, too. So, I did not have much help with the twins from him. As I think back on that time, it seems the boys and I became a unit and we kind of disengaged from Tom. The boys have managed to hook back up with their father, but I have had some trouble.

Recently, when Tom turns his cool blue eyes in my direction they give me the shivers. Either he studies me with a sad curiosity, like he is searching for something he lost and has no hope of recovering, or he looks strangely guilty. I'm afraid to question him. What I don't know won't hurt me . . . that's become my philosophy.

Wow, this note took a strange turn! Again, I marvel at how quickly walls come down in computerland. Thanks for listening.

Here is a good easy recipe for Happy House Cookie Bars:

2¼ c. unsifted flour	1 tsp. vanilla
1 tsp. baking soda	2 eggs
1 c. softened butter	1 12-oz. pkg. chocolate chips
½ c. sugar	1 c. chopped nuts
1 c. brown sugar	

Preheat oven to 375. In a small bowl combine flour, baking soda and salt; set aside. In a large bowl, combine butter, sugars and vanilla, beat until creamy. Beat in eggs. Gradually add flour mixture. Mix well. Stir in chocolate chips and nuts. Spread into a greased 11"×13"× 2" pan. Bake for 25–30 minutes. Cut into bars when cool.

Your friend . . .
Katie

---------------------------------- MAILBOX ----------------------------------

FROM: CAROL BEATTY N771200C   10:24AM EST
SUBJECT: MOTHER'S MORNING OUT   01-21-93

Hi!

Tiffy is in her crib taking her morning nap and I have some more time on my hands. Thanks for the cookie recipe! It sounds perfect—just my speed.

I can only try to imagine what it must have been like to have twins without help. Ed doesn't help me with our kids either. He has never changed a diaper or fed either of the children. He actually got mad when I became pregnant with Tiffany because this year he wanted to buy a boat.

He had been complaining for three years about the weight I had gained after Eddie was born and I suggested maybe if I went off the pill, I could lose 10 pounds. He won't wear condoms and I guess my diaphragm didn't work. Anyway, I got pregnant and he got pissed off.

Ed is impatient, controlling and selfish and our marriage isn't doing well at the moment. That's one reason I'm enjoying Ken so much. It's nice to talk to a man who's supportive and encouraging for a change. What a breath of fresh air.

The Orkin man is at the door. I'll catch you later.

> Your friend,
> Carol

------------------------------------ MAILBOX ------------------------------------

TO: CAROL BEATTY N771200C   11:01AM EST
SUBJECT: MOTHER'S MORNING OUT   01-21-93

Dear Carol . . .

Tom was in the delivery room when Greg and Stephen were born. After the nurse put them on my chest, he put his arms around us and cried. I think he wanted to help with the twins (when he was home, he did change diapers and feed them when they could eat solid food), but I think he felt pretty useless and thought the best way he could help would be in being a good provider. He certainly threw himself into his career.

I thought about working after the children started school. When they started first grade and I was suddenly free every day until 3:00, I suggested to Tom that I might like to find an enjoyable part-time job. He looked stunned and hurt, asking me sincerely if I didn't think he provided well enough for us.

Anyway, I gave up the idea of working, since the idea seemed to bother Tom so much and we didn't need the money. I became a "professional volunteer," like so many of the wives in our circle of acquaintances. I got involved in the PTA at school (I was president by the time the children were in the 8th grade), Boy Scouts and the art museum. I have spent my whole adult life in the service of others in some capacity, it seems.

I envy your career and wonder how my life might have been different if I had worked somewhere other than here at home and as a volunteer. Actually, I did work for a bank in San Francisco for a very brief time during the early 70s. That year I learned so much. For example, I learned how to get around using mass transit. I had never set foot on a bus before then. It was in the days before BART, so I had to take three modes of transportation from Oakland to my job on the very top of Nob Hill. I would catch a bus near my apartment and take it over the bridge, then transfer to a streetcar which went down Market Street and (after stopping to buy a cruller and some coffee on the corner) I would take a cable car up the hill. That was my favorite leg of the commute. Weather permitting, I liked to sit in the open front of the car and watch the city during my ascent. That was when I was young and anything seemed possible. Now, I am middle aged and nothing seems possible.

Well, time to go to the grocery store, the cleaners and the library. I am so glad you dropped by to visit. Let's do this again.

Your friend . . .
Katie

SHOW N' TELL

FROM: BUCK BRAZEMORE X455045A   7:30PM EST
SUBJECT: SHOW N' TELL   01-21-93

Dear Katie,

First, let me answer some of your questions about the people around here. Over the past two months, I've learned that Will Ramsey, the guy I call "Padre," is a counselor of some kind and a retired Methodist minister who lives in Chicago. He was a chaplain in Vietnam. He is the Professional Contributor on the ADULT TOPICS BB and has a subject on the board he calls, THE CHAPLAIN'S ROOM. Peaches is one of the resident heartbreakers and likes to drive the guys crazy with her famous hot e-mail. She loves 'em and leaves 'em. Johnny Kelly, the streaker, is a cardiologist from California. He kind of appears and disappears. I don't know much about him. Cliff Notes is a married guy in his thirties who lives in Cincinnati. He owns a small insurance agency. I think he told me he has two people working for him. Sue Veneer is a college kid and must be about twenty. She writes me short e-mail notes a couple times a week. Sue is really stuck on Cliff and their relationship has graduated from the e-mail stage to the phone stage. She told me in a note this week that he is going to drive out to see her. They make an odd couple, don't they?

As for the nom de plumes, you'll see a lot of them, some funnier than others. I think people take on these other identities in an attempt for more anonymity. If you'll notice, all the pseudonyms have a B, C, or D at the end of their member number. That means the primary member (the A) has used one of the other ID numbers available to him as a LuxNet subscriber. Usually, those numbers go to children or relatives. The fake names are funny, but most of the time I don't trust people who use them. It makes me think they have something to hide.

Now, about me (and this is true stuff):

I was born and raised just outside the little town of Kerrville, Texas. My daddy owned a 640-acre ranch which I inherited five years ago. I grew up around horses and cattle and in the beautiful landscape of the Texas Hill Country. I liked to learn and loved school, which was pretty unusual for a young guy who grew up in these parts. My Mamma was probably responsible for that. She'd been a high school English teacher before she married Daddy and, as her only child, I guess I absorbed her zeal for reading books of all kinds.

I met Linda in the eighth grade. She was the prettiest girl in the county and I mooned over her all through high school. She was the best barrel rider you ever saw and she was the Rodeo Queen, an irresistible combination for this ranch boy. Sparky and I were rivals for her attention, some months she'd be my girlfriend and others she'd be his.

I went to college because I wanted to get married. Linda's family was dirt poor and she's ambitious. She told Sparky and me she was going to marry the one who could provide for her best. She made no bones about it. Neither Linda nor Sparky made very good grades and ended up dropping out after high school. I was accepted at Texas A&M for the honors program in geology. I chose paleontology and petroleum engineering as my allied sciences. Like I hinted earlier, I've always loved the land. And I wanted to learn more about the creatures that lived here all those millions of years ago. I started collecting fossils when I was six. Anyway, Linda and I got married my senior year. I was accepted into the graduate program and attended the first semester, but it just got too blamed hard working, adjusting to marriage and going to school. Our marriage has never been what you'd call smooth. Linda and I aren't much alike and don't like to do many of the same things.

It's kind of funny the way things turned out. I've done okay, my business is steady and I have this ranch, but Sparky is the one who really made it big. He's been making money hand over fist all along. He and Randy Parks started Parks and Sparks when they were both in their early twenties. They made millions off the Kuwait disaster. He has a huge spread over near the YO Ranch. He even keeps 1500 acres just for exotics like ibex, kudu, Thompson's gazelles and other African game.

Well, I've really been rambling and am about to run out of space. Now, it's your turn to show n' tell.

Your cowboy,
Buck

--------------------------------- MAILBOX ----------------------------------

TO: BUCK BRAZEMORE X455045A   07:50PM EST
SUBJECT: SHOW N' TELL   01-21-93

Dear Cowboy . . .

I enjoyed your last e-mail.

I guess it should not surprise me people would want to hide themselves under some form of cover around here. The pen names make sense. And it must be a temptation, and quite easy, to lie about other things and get away with it. Actually, having a computer is a little like having Aladdin's lamp, isn't it? I mean, in computerland, you can become the man or woman of your dreams.

I have noticed many men begin their notes to me with something like, "I'm a tall good-looking guy . . .," and then follow it with a description that sounds like some movie star or professional athlete. Women do the same thing. Jeez, if you took at face value all the claims, you would think computerland is populated by a race of supermen and starlets. I'll bet underneath these personas created for public consumption are a bunch of pretty average people; the folks who wouldn't get a second look at a PTA meeting, on campus or in the company cafeteria. How strange. But, no harm done, I guess. Why not be the person you have always wanted to be?

I believe you, though. You seem so real, I can almost touch you. Thank you for opening yourself up to my scrutiny. Now I guess it is my turn.

My father was a successful entrepreneur. He designed, developed, produced and successfully marketed a high-quality line of textile machinery. His corporation, ProTex, was the leader in its field for twenty years.

As a result of my father's financial success, my family had lots of advantages. We lived in a big pretty house in the best part of town. I went to a private boarding school during high school and became a debutante when I was a sophomore at Grace (the Southern "girls' school" I attended). My two sisters and I were spoiled.

I transferred to the University of North Carolina at Chapel Hill from Grace. At the time, it was a custom for a young woman in my circle of friends to attend an all-female two-year college and then transfer into the university for the sole purpose of locating an appropriate future provider . . . to earn the coveted "MRS" degree. <G>

An integral part of the plan was to become a member of an acceptable sorority (a rich source for dates and, eventually, bridesmaids). Like everyone else I knew, I moved cattlelike through the events of rush week, visiting all the sororities on the row, watching skits, smiling and trying to impress the sisters with my charm, wit and really great clothes. <laughing> I was a shoo-in because I was a legacy (with many of the women in my family having been sorority girls in the past, including my mother).

My boyfriend that year lived in the fraternity house next door. I met Jeff up in the limbs of a big oak tree because I had been invited to be an ornament (quite a coup) for the occasion of the induction of new members into "The Order of the Tree Toads." The popular members of the order, dressed in white lab coats with their nicknames emblazoned on the back, climbed up into the tree about midmorning. They took cases of beer and pretty young women with them. In the late afternoon, from their lofty heights, the young princes were entertained as they watched the drunk chosen ones attempting to make it into the elite group by climbing without assistance up the twenty feet to join them. The whole thing seems barbaric to me now. It is amazing no one was seriously hurt or killed.

I was lavaliered right away and shared my joy at a special candlelight ceremony at the sorority house. It wouldn't be long until I was pinned, then engaged and finally married after graduation. Or, at least, that was the plan.

However, the Vietnam War got in the way. It changed everything. Jeff's lottery number was seven. He became desperate and despondent. Like all the other young men, he was forced to face the terrible choices: joining the military, finding some way to get out of serving in the military, running away or rebelling. The young women saw their embryonic husbands and lovers being shipped off to the Asian war or being transformed into strangers.

Jeff was a senior with lackluster grades. My boyfriend was not a candidate for graduate school, so his student deferment would expire at graduation. I imagine he felt like a trapped animal. He broke up with me, moved to an apartment complex off campus and became lost in a haze of alcohol and drugs. He stopped going to classes, frequently becoming drunk or stoned by 1 o'clock in the afternoon. In two months he had flunked out of school. He eventually returned to his hometown where he enlisted in the Marines.

Buck, it is embarrassing for me to admit it, but this little personal crisis is actually what led this one-time cosseted, superficial Southern Belle to eventually become a human being. It was necessary for me to be personally affected before I paid attention to what was happening in Southeast Asia. I was shaken and stunned. My paradigm shift was sudden and complete. I would never be the same.

When my world view changed, everything about me changed. My former friends didn't recognize the new me. *I* didn't recognize the new me. Within weeks I became a war protester. I went from wearing sorority-girl clothes to wearing overalls and a headband. I marched in demonstrations and studied the geography of Vietnam. By spring my transition was complete.

That May after my junior year, against my parent's wishes, I packed my convertible and took off for California, by myself. I was not exactly "Easy Rider," but I was looking for America just the same.

Three years later I learned Jeff was blown to bits by a mine planted in a rice paddy. What a waste! If women ruled the world there would be no war.

I need to go now. The boys have a basketball game tonight and I will go and catch the last part of it. Tom is out of town, so what else is new?

Fondly . . .
Katie

---------------------------------- MAILBOX ----------------------------------

FROM: BUCK BRAZEMORE X455045A   08:52PM EST
SUBJECT: SHOW N' TELL   01-21-93

Dear Katie,

I was a senior at A & M in 1975, the year the war in Vietnam officially ended. I was spared, but I knew lots of boys who got killed or totally screwed up from being in the fighting. I knew guys who flipped out like your old boyfriend, too.

Vietnam didn't hurt my friend Sparky, though. He enlisted in the Air Force when he was 18 and saw plenty of action during his three years in Nam. That hellhole is where he learned how to contain big fires. He became a fire-fighting specialist in the service and parlayed those skills into a business when he got back home.

There used to be an old ramshackle deer blind in the field behind the

McCallums' house. When Sparky was about 14 his parents let him fix it up and the shed became his place. In Sparky's blind I tried my first cigarette, had my first drink of liquor and shot my first wad over the Playmate of the Month.

When the weather was warm he liked to sleep out there. One spring night he woke suddenly. He looked out the window and saw the big house going up in flames. He burned his hands and arms trying to get in to save his parents and little brother, but it was no use. Since then fire has been Sparky's big enemy and it's natural he would make his job fighting it.

Oil well fires are real dangerous and expensive problems for the petroleum industry. It takes somebody who has no fear to tackle them. That sure describes Sparky. He came back from overseas a war hero with all kinds of decorations, including a Purple Heart. There were big write-ups about his heroic deeds in the Houston, Dallas and Austin papers. In one of those articles it mentioned that Sparky would like to start his own well-fire business. A retired Air Force colonel in San Antonio read the story and later bankrolled Sparky and Randy. The rest is history.

I wonder what would've happened if I had served in Vietnam. If I hadn't gone to college and married Linda, things might have turned out different.

I've never been one to just sit and watch TV. Every night after supper, Linda, Cody and Jeremy watch three or four particularly stupid sitcoms. I was looking for something to occupy my time while my family tubes out and I found the ADULT TOPICS BB. Yes, I sit in front of a screen for hours just like they do, but at least this requires some interaction with another human being. I find it interesting. I find you interesting.

When I'm at the ranch, I have the habit of being on the computer from about 6:30 until 8:30 (that's Central Time) almost every night. On Thursdays, I usually stay on 'til 10:00 or so. Every Thursday, Linda spends the night in town with her girlfriend, Becky. They take some craft class early on Friday mornings. This time she said it's tole painting, whatever that is. The kids are old enough to get themselves in bed, so Thursday has become my Lux Night.

When I'm out of the country in a backwater somewhere, I'm off the computer for a month or more. I spent last April and May in Hassi, Algeria, and next October or November, I'll probably be in Negba, Israel. That is, if these negotiations work out, and it is looking pretty good. If everything clicks, I'll fly out and meet their representative in Tel Aviv sometime next month to sign the contract.

At the moment, I'm nursing my second beer and imagining you must be sitting on some bleachers somewhere. I hope it's one of those crystal clear winter nights—and I wish I could be with you, Katie.

Lonesome,
Buck

---------------------------------- MAILBOX ----------------------------------

TO: BUCK BRAZEMORE X455045A   10:13PM EST
SUBJECT: SHOW N' TELL   01-21-93

Dear Cowboy . . .

Well, I'm back. The boys' team won and they are out celebrating. I told them they had to be home by 11:00. It is cold (almost freezing) and not "crystal clear," but cloudy and spitting rain, but it still would have been nice to have had your company. Your e-mail notes are becoming the bright spots of my days and I am enjoying our time together more and more.

My husband is in Charleston tonight, so I have decided to join you in a glass of wine since a little alcohol makes a nice lubricant when one is showing and telling. And, doesn't it make this rather like a date? <laughing> I mean, here we sit, having a drink, revealing to each other the little corners of our lives and delighting in each other's company. I love this!

Although I promised myself I would never let anyone on the computer know exactly where I live, how can I not tell you? You have pinpointed where you live. Since you are trusting me, I will trust you. <Taking a deep breath> I live in Charlotte, North Carolina. It is a nice medium-size city and, at the moment, it seems a little like a boomtown.

Charlotte is in the middle of the rolling hills of the Piedmont of the Carolinas. It does not have a river, ocean or mountains, but it does have trees. Giant oaks, maples and other hardwood trees provide a lush green canopy in the spring and summer and a splendid show of color in the fall.

I have lived here all my life, except for the rebellious year I lived in California after my junior year at UNC. My parents thought I would only last a week or two in San Francisco, since I didn't take much money with me (they wouldn't give me any, so I cleaned out my little Christmas Club account which had about $300 in it) and I had never shown much independence. However, I confounded them (and myself) by getting a job as a teller in the California National Bank in the Fairmont Hotel and renting a little studio apartment in Oakland.

Now, as I think back on those months when I lived simply and took care of myself, it seems it was the happiest time in my life. It was the only time I ever worked for a salary and supported myself. I felt free, unattached and capable. But the next year I caught pneumonia in the late spring and my mother flew out to take care of me. During those three weeks she managed to shame me into returning home to finish my education. I frequently wonder how my life might have been different if I had not come back with her. Maybe I would have finished college in California and found a career there. Was it a lost opportunity? Like you, I will never know if my life would be better or worse if I had chosen a another path when I was young. I guess middle-aged people always wonder about missed chances.

Is this boring you, Buck?

> Your date . . .
> Katie

---------------------------------- MAILBOX ----------------------------------

FROM: BUCK BRAZEMORE X455045A   10:30PM EST
SUBJECT: SHOW N' TELL   01-21-93

Dear Katie,

No ma'am, I don't find you boring at all! I'd like to know all about you if you'll let me. I've been looking for someone like you. Please don't ask me why, because as I just typed the last sentence, it came as a complete surprise to me. All I know is you're special. I'm getting sweet on you, to tell you the truth.

This IS a date. We're spending an evening getting to know each other just like a couple in the real world. It's kinda odd that we're both married, can't see each other and are separated by more than a thousand miles, though. <G>

I like the idea of your tree-rich place. I love trees, but they have a hard time out here in this rough land. We have lots of post oaks and live oaks on this ranch. They don't grow very tall and the trunks are usually all gnarled up from the effort of surviving in harsh conditions. But I like the twisted shapes of the trunks. They have character and a story of suffering to tell. Unfortunately, there's a terrible disease that has been attacking the live oaks and lots have died. No one can find out how to save them. The other day, I heard someone on the radio say that in twenty years there won't be any more live oaks in the Hill Country of Texas. They'll just slowly disappear like the American chestnuts and the Dutch elms.

I like to visit cities, but I couldn't live in one of any size, there just isn't enough space in them. I need to be able to look out and see the land every day. I need to put my hands on it. It would make me feel trapped to be surrounded by walls of houses and buildings and to have the land covered up with roads and concrete parking lots. I imagine I'd feel like a bug in a bottle if I had to live in San Antonio, Austin or Charlotte.

In one of your earlier notes, you asked me if I was a cowboy. To tell you the truth, for the past three or four years I have been thinking of myself as one of the vanishing breed of cowboy/poets. I love to be out on the land and to think about the mysteries and the beauty it offers up. Up 'til now the rock shells and bones have had my attention, but lately I have been thinking about men and women—the mysteries and the beauty.

Probably it's the beer speaking, or maybe it's the fact that I'm a month shy of 40, but it seems at this point in my life I want to be a cowboy/poet in earnest. Oh, I don't mean quit my work, abandon my family and roam around driving cattle and singing mushy songs. I'm just missing some-thing and I want to connect with the richness in life again and maybe let my emotions lead for awhile. Do you understand what I'm trying to say? If you do, will you please tell me? <LOL>

                              Your Cowboy,
                              Buck

---------------------------------- MAILBOX ------------------------------------

TO: BUCK BRAZEMORE X455045A   10:43PM EST
SUBJECT: SHOW N' TELL   01-21-93

My Dear Buck . . .

Actually, I think I do know what you mean about craving to be a cowboy for real at this point in your life. And I suspect the "cow" is not as important as the "boy" in the word.

You know how much I love James Taylor. One of my all-time favorite songs of his is one titled, "Sweet Baby James." Maybe you know it; it was on a top-10 album back in 1970. Anyway, the beginning is about a young cowboy and it paints a warm, idealized picture of his solitary existence. It is a pretty song, a lullaby. It used to give me goose bumps and it also gave me the romantic image of cowboys I carry around with me to this day (rather like the ones I still harbor for knights, Robin Hood and astronauts).

In addition to wanting to recapture a youthful image of yourself, I think you must be a romantic, or at least a wannabe. Me too! It is especially hard to be halfway through my life and to think what I have experienced of passion and romance is all I am likely to get. It strikes me as sad that romance has so little place in the modern world. The freshness of it is always greeted by arched eyebrows and sneers of the cynical and world-weary. It seems to be gone from my marriage and I miss it so much. It would be a reprieve to find romance again.

Musing . . .
Katie

---------------------------------- MAILBOX ------------------------------------

FROM: BUCK BRAZEMORE X455045A   10:58PM EST
SUBJECT: SHOW N' TELL   01-21-93

My Sweet Katie,

I vaguely remember that James Taylor tune, but I've always liked Country/Western music best. It sounds like you've pretty much hit the nail on the head, except the "cow" in "cowboy" is pretty important to me, too.

This morning, you asked me to tell you about longhorns. Well, I don't have many and have only been raising them for three years. They have something to do with my strange middle-age desire to be a real cowboy. You just can't be a cowboy without longhorns. Linda doesn't appreciate the symbolism—maybe you will. Here's their story in a nutshell:

The longhorns came from the Andalusian cattle the Spaniards brought to Mexico while they were colonizing and proselytizing. Some animals were abandoned and some strayed and these creatures became wild. The ones with the longest legs, resistance to diseases and ease in calving were the ones that survived and reproduced. So the original longhorns were simply a product of natural selection. They could travel long distances in search of forage and water, had incredible endurance and prospered on the hot Mexican range.

After the Civil War, returning Texan soldiers found no work and bleak economic conditions. Like magic, the longhorns solved their problems. The cattle could be bought for $5 a head in Mexico, or they could be rounded up or rustled for free, then be driven to the railhead at Abilene or Kansas City, where they could be sold for $20 a head. The animals actually fattened on the journey.

Some people made a pile of money. This was the time of the cattle barons and the huge ranches known as "RIs," or "Rhode Islands," because they contained at least as many square miles as the smallest state. The King Ranch was one of them.

This short span of thirty-something years from the late 1860s to about 1900 was also the time of the REAL cowboys. It's hard to believe that colorful part of American history was so short.

When the pioneers poured in and settled the West, they built fences as they went and the range became blocked. And more railroads were built, so long drives weren't necessary anymore. After the big drives petered out, most of the longhorns were bred with other strains of cattle. But, the government established the Wildlife Refuge for the protection of a small herd of the original longhorns and certain famous Texas families (like the Peelers, Marks, Yates, Phillips, Wrights, Schreiners and Butlers) saved other small herds of pure-blood longhorns. Now, only animals that can be traced back to one of these small herds can claim to be true longhorns. It's kinda like having a pedigree among dogs.

Longhorns are pretty critters. They are known for their spectacular and gigantic horns, especially the steers, but they are also known for their colors and patterns. For example, I have two of the cutest heifers. "Scoot" is a tricolor. She has a white hide and it looks like someone spattered her all over with paint brushes full of red and black paint.

"Fancy" has a pure white background with a black ring around her nose, black ears and black stockings.

Linda thought I was crazy when I bought my Bull, "Macho," a pure-blood descendant from the Wildlife Refuge herd, and my first three cows, also pure "WRs." Like I said, I figure I need real longhorns if I want to be a real cowboy. It's the principle of the thing.

A cowpoke,
Buck

---------------------------------- MAILBOX ----------------------------------

TO: BUCK BRAZEMORE X455045A   11:03PM EST
SUBJECT: SHOW N' TELL   01-21-93

Dear Cowboy . . .

What an interesting story! I hope you will forgive me, but it made me chuckle a little. I mean, I have heard of men buying sports cars, sailboats, motorcycles and even airplanes in response to middle age, but you are the first man I have ever met who bought a herd of cattle. <laughing> I like your midlife hobby. It shows spirit and originality. Buck, you are one of a kind and I am becoming very fond of you.

Unlike you, everything my husband does is somehow related to his work. When we go out to dinner or to a performance or sporting event we take a client or two along. Tom packs a briefcase of paperwork and a portable fax machine when we go on vacation. He doesn't enjoy any hobbies or outside activities except snow skiing and I suspect the only reason he likes to ski is it gives him an opportunity to compete with his brother, Ben (who always goes with us). After all these years, their sibling rivalry is still fierce.

I don't understand how Tom can keep from burning out. He is on the road almost constantly. The word "recreation" is not in his vocabulary. One day he might just explode.

The boys just came in. I need to go.

Yours . . .
Katie

---------------------------------- MAILBOX ----------------------------------

FROM: BUCK BRAZEMORE X455045A   11:46PM EST
SUBJECT: SHOW N' TELL   01-21-93

Dear Katie,

   You won't get this 'til in the morning, but I want to send it off before I lose my nerve. I'm beginning to think of you as my sweetheart. Is that okay?

Love,
Buck

SHE-MAIL

TO: CAROL BEATTY N771200C   10:17AM EST
SUBJECT: SHE-MAIL   01-25-93

Dear Carol . . .

Good morning! I am dyeing my hair at the moment and have 45 minutes to kill while the developer is doing its thing. This is dead time (meaning I would simply die if anyone saw me at the moment). <laughing> Even Tom and the boys are not allowed to see me in this condition. I hope you know what I mean. Few things are more unattractive on this woman than a head (and lately eyebrows) slathered in the rusty-looking goo which ensures my medium auburn hair color. Man, the indignities we women suffer in the pursuit of youthfulness! Oh well, at least this provides me with the perfect opportunity for sending an e-mail in your direction.

Something really strange is beginning to happen. Over the weekend, Buck's e-mail has taken on an unmistakable romantic tone and I have found myself not only encouraging him, but responding in kind. The thing is, I am really enjoying this make-believe romance. I don't know what has gotten into me! We are both married, yet we are acting like we are in love. Have you ever heard of anything so bizarre? Do you think I need a shrink? <laughing>

> Your friend . . .
> Katie

------------------------------------- MAILBOX -------------------------------------

FROM: CAROL BEATTY N771200C   10:54AM EST
SUBJECT: SHE-MAIL   01-25-93

Girl!

Where have you been? Do you mean to tell me you haven't heard what has been going on over the computer between men and women all over this country and the world? You're not alone by a long shot. Cyber romances are flaring up all over the place. Everywhere you look there are articles in the media about computer love and there are exposes on all the talk shows. I've been reading or hearing about the phenomenon for at least the past year. That's why I even bought and installed the LuxNet software. I'm really curious about this thing.

Several people at the bank are into the BB scene and they've told me all about it. You can find bulletin boards EVERYWHERE. There are the big networks like LuxNet that connect millions in this country and other countries, and then there are the small local BBs which just serve a specific city or area code and involve maybe a couple hundred people. Anyone with a computer, a telephone line, a modem and communication software can tie into a net.

On ALL the BBs, men and women are meeting and hooking up. It doesn't matter if they're already married or not. There was a couple on a talk show last week who said they were going to get married ON the computer. Apparently it will be quite an event on the CompuCon net in June. Hundreds of people are expected to be on hand, on their 'puters, for the happening. It seems they met on the network's GOLF BB, of all places. Anyway, at the end of the interview, you found out that both of these people had been married to others when they met through their modems last year. They got divorced from their spouses, met in person (not necessarily in that order) and now they're engaged.

At work, just before I left on my maternity leave, there was this married guy in the commercial loan department who got caught and then fired for using the computer at work to connect with his computer honey in Oregon. He didn't get fired for having a girlfriend, he got fired for using the bank computer for HOURS to communicate with her. I have been wondering how they caught him. Anyway, everybody was stunned. John was the nicest guy in the world and the one you would least suspect of having a girlfriend on the side, even a computer girlfriend. You know the type, he had pictures of his wife and kids all over his office. He was my son's T-ball coach last summer.

I think the incident with John is what REALLY piqued my interest about this thing. The woman in the office next to John's is one of my best friends. She is the one who gave me all the details and she told me John had been using LuxNet. That is why I decided to try it instead of one of the other big nets. I'm afraid to hook up to a local BB because I might run into someone I know.

Ken is divorced with no kids and lives in Des Moines. He is 32 and our 7-year age difference doesn't seem to bother him. We started being romantic with each other almost right away. Why not? Like you said, this is make-believe and it has instantly gotten rid of my boredom. <G>

About hair: I have mine frosted. They put one of those plastic bags over my head and then pull strands out with a crochet hook thing and then put that lavender stuff on it. There I sit, looking like an alien with these purplish tentacles sticking out all over my head. Talk about unattractive! Not only that, but it costs a fortune. Why don't men do stuff to their hair as they get older? No fair!

Actually, now that I think about it, a few men DO do stuff to their hair. For example, they wear toupees. Last week, I went to Sears to exchange the electric screwdriver I got for my grandfather for Christmas and the guy who waited on me OBVIOUSLY had on a hairpiece. Man, it stuck out like a sore thumb. They all do. I can spot a rug at fifty paces. And then there are those seventy-year-old fellas who look like they dye their hair with Mercurochrome. Who do they think they're kidding? Wait a minute! Who do we think WE'RE kidding? <LOL> Hey, but we aren't as bad as the grandpas with the orange hair, are we?

Your pal,
Carol

---------------------------------- MAILBOX ----------------------------------

TO: CAROL BEATTY N771200C   11:34AM EST
SUBJECT: SHE-MAIL   01-25-93

Dear Carol . . .

What??!! I am totally caught off guard by your revelations about computer romance. I admit to not watching the talk shows (they just embarrass me too much, or something) and my ears do not prick up when I hear the word, "computer"; quite the opposite. As a matter of fact, I am pretty much a computer illiterate and used to avoid any contact with one if possible, and that includes reading anything about them. It stuns me to learn this universe exists under my nose and I have been oblivious to it.

Writing and receiving these love letters over the past two days is making me feel a little sneaky (there is no way I would let my family know about my little secret), but our make-believe romances with Buck and Ken are harmless as long as we don't let them get out of hand, right?

Since Tom is gone so much, it helps me not be so lonely. The exchanges are entertaining. It is like being a character in an interactive novel or an actor in a play. Those people on the talk show and the guy at your office must have lost control.

It is really fun and exciting to find Buck's letters in my mailbox. Although it seems incongruous, this high-tech venue actually offers a wonderful opportunity for romantics! In many ways, with its dependence upon language and writing, it harkens back to an earlier time when people communicated through letters. Then, lovers sent their tender or smoldering sentiments to each other by messenger or in sweet-scented letters in the overland mail. I feel like Juliet or the heroine in some Victorian novel. <laughing> And the most important thing is I feel young and desirable again.

Maybe this is the antidote I need for my midlife crisis (or whatever it is). I hate to be so unoriginal, but I seem to have all the symptoms. I have been feeling so old and looking back on my life and asking the old question, "Is that all there is?" I am going through "the change" and it took me by surprise. Menopause is something my mother or great aunt went through. There must be some mistake. I am terrified by my fading beauty and every time I look at my naked body in the mirror it astounds me it can be so disloyal. How can it just give in to the law of gravity without even putting up a fight? <laughing> I am self-absorbed, restless and feeling trapped.

Tom is spending more and more time out of town. Sometimes he is gone four nights a week. Even when he's home he seems distant and troubled.

I feel alone and wonder if I might be slightly depressed. Some harmless computer-generated love with Buck may be all I need. How could it hurt?

Your friend . . .
Katie

---------------------------------- MAILBOX ----------------------------------

FROM: CAROL BEATTY N771200C   12:24PM EST
SUBJECT: SHE-MAIL   01-25-93

Dear Katie,

Don't feel alone. There are probably lots of people who don't know what happens in computerland. I think people who are comfortable using computers in their jobs or at school are the ones who are most likely to venture into the realm of the nets during their free time.

For example, I used a computer every day in my job at the bank. I work in the personnel department and am the Employee Benefits Specialist. The tool holds no mystery for me. I bought this laptop last year when I was pregnant, so I could work at home some days if I didn't feel like going into the office. Being pregnant in my late thirties was no picnic. I was always exhausted, especially during the last two months.

Hey, I agree 100% about computer love giving us a new lease on life. It's easy to forget misery and pain when one is caught up in a whirlwind romance. Who cares if it's computer-generated? I think it's the best thing since control-top pantyhose.

Gotta run. I'll e you again tomorrow.

                              Your pal,
                              Carol

BANQUET

TO: ALL   05:25PM EST
FROM: KATHERINE SIMMONS S102248A   01-28-93
SUBJECT: BANQUET

My Dear Friends . . .
   In the spectrum of human relationships, romance is the opulent banquet. How appealing to all the senses is a glistening, heavy-laden and fragrant table! Can you see the flickering candles with the light scintillating off the surfaces of china, crystal and silver? Can you smell the rich and provocative aromas which trigger autonomic responses of hunger within the body? Textures invite exploration and flavors invite discovery. The temptation is always to eat too much . . . Isn't that the case with romance?

Katie

************* ADULT TOPICS BULLETIN BOARD *************

TO: KATHERINE SIMMONS S102248A   05:32PM EST
FROM: BUCK BRAZEMORE X455045A   01-28-93
SUBJECT: BANQUET

My Darling Katie,
   Will you forgive me for this? I'm hard-pressed to resist.
   Taking two chocolate-frosted donuts off one of these spiffy silver

trays, I plaster them against your sweet, pink and perky bosoms. Yummy, what a sight!

> Yelling, "FOOD FIGHT!" and
> heading for the hills,
> Buck

************* ADULT TOPICS BULLETIN BOARD *************

TO: BUCK BRAZEMORE X455045A   05:40PM EST
FROM: KATHERINE SIMMONS S102248A   01-28-93
SUBJECT: BANQUET

Cowboy!
  Oh yeah? Well, creeping up behind you and quickly pulling out your waistbands, I deftly dump a steaming platter of Fettucini Alfredo down the back of your pants and then proceed to execute a perfect major wedgie.

> Giggling hysterically and getting
> the heck out of Dodge . . .
> Katie

************* ADULT TOPICS BULLETIN BOARD *************

TO: KATHERINE SIMMONS S102248A   05:43PM EST
FROM: NORMAN CONQUEST B767792B   01-28-93
SUBJECT: BANQUET

HEY KATIE!
  As you turn around to see who is yelling at you, I smack you right up the side of the head with a huge handful of mashed potatoes and gravy, which proceeds to slide down your neck and into your donuts.

> Taking off like a bat out of Hell,
> Norman

************ ADULT TOPICS BULLETIN BOARD *************

TO: NORMAN CONQUEST B767792B   05:46PM EST
FROM: KATHERINE SIMMONS S102248A   01-28-93
SUBJECT: BANQUET

But Norm, unfortunately you are not fast enough!

I catapult a huge lemon meringue pie which smashes right into the back of your head. It plasters into your hair and makes it stand up like a cresting wave.

> Rolling on the floor . . .
> Katie

************ ADULT TOPICS BULLETIN BOARD *************

TO: NORMAN CONQUEST B767792B   05:50PM EST
FROM: SPRING FORTH X329054B   01-28-93
SUBJECT: BANQUET

Hey, you big Stud Muffin,

Watch this! I stick the nozzle of a whipped cream can down the front of your pants and fill 'em up. Then I goosh it around a little. This won't be the first time you've had cream in your jeans, will it? <SEG>

> Hee-Hee!
> Le Printemps

************* ADULT TOPICS BULLETIN BOARD *************

TO: SPRING FORTH X329054B   05:56PM EST
FROM: NORMAN CONQUEST B767792B   01-28-93
SUBJECT: BANQUET

OOOooooo, Honey!

I like it when you do that! And speaking of honey, watch as I fill your unprotected cleavage with this squeeze bottle. And speaking of "squeeze bottles" . . .

Is your old man around? Can I call? Check your mailbox.

> Creamy and looking to be
> creamier, <VBSEG>
> Norman

************* ADULT TOPICS BULLETIN BOARD *************

TO: SPRING FORTH X329054B   05:56PM EST
FROM: KENNETH LONG T017643A   01-28-93
SUBJECT: BANQUET

Spring!

Bombs away! I lob three raw eggs in your direction and chortle with glee as I hear the SMACK! SMACK! SMACK! indicating direct hits on your noggin.

> Heading for cover!
> Ken

************* ADULT TOPICS BULLETIN BOARD ************

TO: BUCK BRAZEMORE X455045A   05:57PM EST
FROM: CLIFF NOTES L896112C   01-28-93
SUBJECT: BANQUET

Bucky!
   Think fast! Using the form of an Olympic discus thrower, I send an extra large Sicilian pizza, with anchovies and extra cheese, spinning through the air. SPLAT! Boy, is your face red!

                         Laughing like a hyena,
                         Cliff

************* ADULT TOPICS BULLETIN BOARD ************

TO: CLIFF NOTES L896112C   06:00PM EST
FROM: SUSAN VENEER G740094D   01-28-93
SUBJECT: BANQUET

Heads up, Baby!
   A pint container of Ben and Jerry's Chunky Monkey just went down the front of your Fruit of the Looms.
   Hand me a spoon and I'll help you clean up the mess. Or, do you want me to use my excellent ice cream cone licking technique instead?

                         Eyeing your sugar cone,
                         @-->->----Sue Veneer----<-<--@

************* ADULT TOPICS BULLETIN BOARD ************

TO: KENNETH LONG T017643A   06:03PM EST
FROM: CAROL BEATTY N771200C   01-28-93
SUBJECT: BANQUET

Hi Ken!
   I am amusing myself by firing peas through a straw at you, then pelting you with other small missiles, including marshmallows and olives. I need some grapes.

                         Looking for a slingshot,
                         Carol

************ ADULT TOPICS BULLETIN BOARD ************

TO: CAROL BEATTY N771200C   06:08PM EST
FROM: KENNETH LONG T017643A   01-28-93
SUBJECT: BANQUET

Carol!

Although I am ecstatic to see you, it doesn't keep me from dumping a 16-oz. container of Breyer's strawberry yogurt down the back of your pantyhose. Take that!

Give me a minute and then look for me in your mailbox. Have you got time for a little e-mail "chat"?

Yours,
Ken

************ ADULT TOPICS BULLETIN BOARD ************

TO: KATHERINE SIMMONS S102248A   6:23PM EST
FROM: CAROL BEATTY N771200C   01-28-93
SUBJECT: BANQUET

Girl Friend!

I'm having fun flinging Happy House Cookie Bars at you and watching them bonk you on the head. And, here, try washing them down with this quart of breast milk—KASPLOOSH!

You're so prissy. I just LOVE messing you up!

Yukking it up,
Carol

************** ADULT TOPICS BULLETIN BOARD *************

TO: CAROL BEATTY N771200C   06:48PM EST
FROM: KATHERINE SIMMONS S102248A   01-28-93
SUBJECT: BANQUET

Carol!
  Some friend you are! <wiping the milk out of my eyes and dusting
the crumbs off my turtleneck> Ugh!
  Two can play at this game! Your eyes pop out as I launch two huge
spoonfuls of baby food at you. Yessss! The strained peas spatter against
the side of your face and into your carefully coifed frosted hair.

                        Squealing with glee . . .
                        Katie

--------------------------------- MAILBOX ----------------------------------

FROM: WAYNE ROONEY F362238A   08:10PM EST
SUBJECT: BANQUET   01-28-93

HARLOT!!!
    THE WAGES OF SIN IS DEATH!!!!!

--------------------------------- MAILBOX ----------------------------------

TO: WAYNE ROONEY F362238A   10:10PM EST
SUBJECT: BANQUET   01-28-93

Wayne . . .
  Gee whiz, will you please lighten up?! You have a right to your opinions and beliefs, but what is so sinful about a little food fight? I usually
just ignore your notes, but this one is rather scary. Please don't bother
me any more. If you continue to pester me, I will alert the Lux Police.

                        Katherine

---------------------------------- MAILBOX ----------------------------------

FROM: BUCK BRAZEMORE X455045A   10:23PM EST
SUBJECT: BANQUET   01-28-93

My Darling Katie,

What a hoot! I just checked the BB and BANQUET already has close to a hundred replies! People are coming out of the woodwork. I've never seen anything like it in all my born days. There were some pretty risque posts, but I don't imagine they'll stay up long, the Lux police have probably already been alerted. There have been a bunch of guideline infractions.

I hope you'll forgive me for trashing your subject. I know you made it for me. I had no idea my donuts would cause such a ruckus. It seems we have rustled up a little audience or fan club on the BB over the past week. Have you noticed? They must be the same kind of people who like soap operas. Anyway, that might explain the huge number of people who jumped in when I plastered you with the donuts.

Katie, I really would love to see your face. Would you send me a picture? Please! My address is, PO Box 45A, Kerrville, Texas, 78029. If you e-mail me your address, I'll send you a picture, too.

The past three weeks have been great! I feel happier than I have in years. It's you, Katie.

> Glad to be alive,
> Buck

---------------------------------- MAILBOX ----------------------------------

TO: BUCK BRAZEMORE X455045A   10:40PM EST
SUBJECT: BANQUET   01-28-93

Cowboy . . .

Jeez, you should see my mailbox; it is packed! I must have fifty messages. I am so glad you convinced me it is not necessary to respond to all these jokers. Now, I just hit the "delete" key if a note offends me. There go my hard-won finishing-school manners right down the drain. <laughing>

Some of these guys are trying to have a private food fight with me. You are right, the whole thing is hilarious. And how bizarre to have a food fight on a computer. God, we are acting like a bunch of adolescents! Isn't it fun?

There is this one guy, Wayne Rooney, who makes me a little nervous, though. He is always sending me these notes with religious overtones, commanding me to repent. I wonder what his problem is?

I guess Katie and the Cowboy are celebrities now. We will have to start wearing sunglasses and raincoats when we make our appearances on the board. <laughing>

I am enjoying this so much! My days are beginning to revolve around the computer. I plan everything around it and I am finding I feel irritable and unhappy if I must leave the house, even to go to the grocery store. I have been late paying my bills and yesterday I forgot to feed the dog. Really. I am a little frightened at what this means, but I am loving it too much to look carefully.

Yes, I will mail a photo to you. I will throw caution to the wind and give you my address, too. It's 3650 Old Church Road, Charlotte, NC, 28207.

> Hooked . . .
> Katie

---------------------------------- MAILBOX ----------------------------------

FROM: BUCK BRAZEMORE X455045A   11:13PM EST
SUBJECT: BANQUET   01-28-93

Dear Katie,

You have made me one happy man! I can't wait to see what you look like. Please mail your picture early tomorrow at the post office and maybe I'll get it on Saturday. I promise I'll mail mine to you first thing. Man, this is really exciting, isn't it?

I think Wayne is a bubble off plumb, if you get my drift. He raves at everybody. I get notes from him from time to time and he posts about 10 random Bible verses a day on the board. It must cost him a fortune. He's kinda heavy on the !!!!!!s, ain't he? <G> I think he's harmless, though.

I forgot to tell you this before.

Last night, Linda, the boys and I had dinner with Sparky. He doesn't have any family in Texas except a great uncle who lives in Fredricksburg. My parents took him in after the fire and he lived at our ranch for about three years until he enlisted in the Air Force. He's like a part of my family—a combination friend/brother/cousin. Sparky's a bachelor, but he has an overseer, six ranch hands and three women (one who cooks) working for him, and they all live on his ranch.

At least once a week, Sparky goes with us to eat at a Mexican restaurant in Kerrville called the Three Amigos. The woman who owns the place makes the best fresh tortillas any of us have ever eaten—and we've eaten a few.

While I was sitting there last night, I had the strangest desire. I wanted you to be sitting at the table with us. For some reason, it felt like it would have made the scene perfect. We could be the FOUR amigos.

> Good night,
> Buck

THE CHAPLAIN'S ROOM

*************ADULT TOPICS BULLETIN BOARD *************

TO: ALL   09:08AM EST
FROM: WILLIAM RAMSEY Y082176A   01-29-93
SUBJECT: THE CHAPLAIN'S ROOM

Thought for the week:

In Book II of Plato's *The Republic* there's a story of a Lydian shepherd named Gyges who comes to possess a magic ring. The ring allows its wearer to become visible or invisible at will.

In many ways, the computer can be like the Ring of Gyges. It enables us to be faceless in our involvements with others. What happens when we use this magic our modems offer us? Is the power of invisibility good or bad?

> Offering food for thought,
> Will Ramsey
> Professional Contributor,
> Adult Topics Bulletin Board

************* ADULT TOPICS BULLETIN BOARD *************

TO: WILLIAM RAMSEY Y082176A   10:47AM EST
FROM: CATHERINE VAN ALLEN Z101011A   01-29-93
SUBJECT: THE CHAPLAIN'S ROOM

Dear Will,

I've recently had a bad experience with the "Ring of Gyges." I'm a 37-year-old single woman looking for a single man with whom to develop a relationship. I met "John" on the SINGLES BB. He seemed to be just the man for whom I was looking. He said he was close to my age, single and looking for a serious relationship.

After four months of sending passionate e-mail to each other, I thought we had fallen in love and we made plans to meet to see if we would be compatible in real life. About this time, I saw a post from another woman to him on the ALTERNATIVE LIFESTYLES BB. She was accusing him of lying to her. I sent a private e-mail message to her and asked about her accusations. For the past week, this woman and I have been comparing notes. It seems "John" is none of the things he has been telling me. He's 30 years old, married and apparently he has lied to several women.

I feel betrayed, angry and very sad that my "John" does not really exist. What should I do?

> Desperately unhappy,
> Cathy

P.S. What does "Professional Contributor" mean?

************* ADULT TOPICS BULLETIN BOARD *************

TO: CATHERINE VAN ALLEN Z101011A   12:30PM EST
FROM: WILLIAM RAMSEY Y082176A   01-29-93
SUBJECT: THE CHAPLAIN'S ROOM

My Dear Cathy,

You aren't alone in being abused by a person pretending to be someone he or she is not. Like Gyges, many people find the temptation to use this power of invisibility for selfish ends too great to resist.

You must feel sad and alone. Unfortunately, not many in the real world will be able to understand your emotional pain. If you'd care to write to me on a personal level, please feel free to e-mail me. I may be able to plug you into some supportive resources in your community.

In answer to your question, Professional Contributor is a status LuxNet gives to a group of people who provide services to the subscribers of the network. In return for free subscriptions and usage of all additional-fee services offered by LuxNet, a Professional Contributor makes himself or herself available (when convenient) to members. There is one Professional Contributor for each bulletin board. I'm the PC for adult topics. I'm a retired Methodist minister and Air Force chaplain. For the past ten years, I've been a relationship counselor in private practice and I write a bimonthly syndicated newspaper column which is published in six Midwestern dailies. Once a week, I introduce a topic on this BB and I reply to private e-mail which is directed to me.

Yours truly,
Will Ramsey

************* ADULT TOPICS BULLETIN BOARD *************

TO: WILLIAM RAMSEY Y082176A   02:17PM EST
FROM: ANDREW PRINGLE O546836B   01-29-93
SUBJECT: THE CHAPLAIN'S ROOM

Dear Will,

I have a happy outcome to report. I met my fiancee, Helen, on the MUSIC BB under the MARY CHAPIN CARPENTER subject. Although it was a great temptation, since I'm a paraplegic and my fiancee is 12 years older than I, neither of us lied about ourselves. We corresponded for six months before we finally met in person in a group of Mary Chapin Carpenter fans from the board who gathered at a concert in Memphis.

We never would have met without the "Ring of Gyges". We like the idea that it's the inner people who meet first here. Where else could something like this happen?

Just adding my two cents,
Andy

************* ADULT TOPICS BULLETIN BOARD *************

TO: ANDREW PRINGLE O546836B   03:20PM EST
FROM: WILLIAM RAMSEY Y082176A   01-29-93
SUBJECT: THE CHAPLAIN'S ROOM

Dear Andy,
   Yours is the kind of story which makes me happy and gives me hope.
You express an excellent point. This new technology allows people to
become connected before they see each other. Age, race, gender and
physical appearance do not enter into the equation here. This is the way
it should be in the real world, isn't it?
   Thank you for sharing your happy ending with me.

                                    Regards,
                                    Will Ramsey

************* ADULT TOPICS BULLETIN BOARD *************

TO: WILLIAM RAMSEY Y082176A   04:32PM EST
FROM: KATHERINE SIMMONS S102248A   01-29-93
SUBJECT: THE CHAPLAIN'S ROOM

Dear Will . . .
   I am new around here and have enjoyed reading your "Thought for
the week" on the past two Fridays. You always introduce a concept
worth thinking about. It also pleases me to read the advice, comfort and
encouragement you offer to those who seek you.
   You are evidence that not all people succumb to the temptation of
using this "Ring of Gyges" toward selfish ends. While you admit to
receiving remuneration for the services you render, the assistance and
referrals you provide are much more valuable than a subscription to
LuxNet and use of its extra fee services. Must the power of invisibility
always corrupt (like in the stories of the "Ring of Gyges" and *The
Hobbit*)?

                                    One of your admirers . . .
                                    Katie

************* ADULT TOPICS BULLETIN BOARD *************
TO: KATHERINE SIMMONS S102248A   06:00PM EST
FROM: WILLIAM RAMSEY Y082176A   01-29-93
SUBJECT: THE CHAPLAIN'S ROOM

Dear Katie,
   No, I don't think the power of anonymity always corrupts. However, it takes will-power and character to resist the pull of using it for ill.
   I've been counseling on-line for more than a year now and based upon the reports of people who have shared their experiences with me, the unhappy stories seem to outweigh the happy ones by about three to one. Now, granted, I'm sought out more by people who have had bad experiences, but I still suspect there's a lopsided ratio. It does seem married people have more problems with it than single people, though.

                         Sincerely,
                         Will Ramsey

THE FOUNTAIN
OF YOUTH

TO: BUCK BRAZEMORE X455045A   04:01PM EST
SUBJECT: THE FOUNTAIN OF YOUTH   02-01-93

My Dear Cowboy . . .

It just thrills me to log on and find the NEW MAIL blinking! The response is reminiscent of the way I reacted when I was a teenager and would hear the phone ring . . . especially if I were expecting a call from someone really special.

Anyway, you can imagine the thrill when I found two unread letters from you this morning! It was like having the phone ring and it be the captain of the Deerfield football team, inviting me up for the Deerfield/Choate Weekend. My adolescent idea of Heaven! <laughing>

It is really amazing we both have birthdays during the same week, isn't it? Hardly anyone seems to be born in February. This must be some kind of sign. <laughing> Next Sunday is my 45th and your 40th is the following Saturday. Wanna trade? Pul-eeeeeease! Yuck! As you can tell, I am having a hard time adjusting to middle age and I think I know why.

When the twins were three years old and I took them to the pediatrician for their routine check-up, I expressed some concern that the boys had not gone through a ''terrible two'' stage. I asked Dr. Whedon, with some trepidation, if it meant I was in for a double whammy during their adolescence. He was reassuring, telling me that people come into this world with their dispositions pretty much intact. If an individual does not have problems with the developmental steps of toddlerhood, it is likely he will adjust easily to the other transitions in life. His observations recently resurfaced when I realized *I* had been a ''terrible two'' and a "teenager from Hell." Why should I expect my midlife passage to be easy?

You are the best birthday present imaginable. In the face of this rather depressing marker in time, you revive me. Though this may sound goofy, our connections have become like tiny sips of some magical elixir of youth . . . sweet, bracing, slightly intoxicating. It is hard to believe there is no cost. Many would sell their souls to drink from the Fountain of Youth.

Thirsty . . .
Katie

---------------------------------- MAILBOX ----------------------------------

FROM: BUCK BRAZEMORE X455045A   11:57PM EST
SUBJECT: THE FOUNTAIN OF YOUTH   02-01-93

Sweetheart,

Don't feel alone. I'm beginning to feel like one of Pavlov's dogs myself. When I see the NEW MAIL flashing I have an automatic physical response. My heart thumps in my chest, a lump forms in the back of my throat and another thickening has recently started developing in a different portion of my anatomy. Can you guess where? It could get embarrassing.

I don't mean to be coy. I don't really know how to ask you this except straight out. Will you describe your body to me, Katie? I need to put more form to you. I think about you all the time and it's getting real frustrating not being able to "see" you.

Yours,
Buck

---------------------------------- MAILBOX ----------------------------------

TO: BUCK BRAZEMORE X455045A   07:10AM EST
SUBJECT: THE FOUNTAIN OF YOUTH   02-02-93

My Cowboy . . .

You have asked me to tell you about my body. There is nothing I would like more than to undress for you. But, how does one accomplish this intimate act over the computer? <Sigh!> I will try.

I am not a thin woman, but I am certainly not fat. Probably, "womanly" is the word which describes me best. My breasts are small and have very sensitive, pinkish, quarter-size nipples which sometimes become slightly tinged with lavender. My waist is trim and my hips are full. I have a slightly curved belly and a neat triangle of fine, straight pubic hair. Unfortunately, I was standing behind the door when they gave out legs.

I do not possess the voluptuousness of a Renoir bather, nor the undulating curves of Rubens's women. Titian is the artist who worshipped my body's form. His "Venus of Urbino" could be my twin, in body and attitude—In an art historian's language, I possess the same soft gentle "landscape" and the same "unselfconscious sexuality."

Are you familiar with "The Venus of Urbino"? The Venus lounges nude and languorous on a chaise. In one hand she loosely holds full-blown blossoms while her other hand curls into the warm place between her legs. She has no shame of her nakedness and she looks with a steady eye at those who would appraise her.

When I was younger, several people told me I look like her. It bothered me at first. The Venus was a little too ripe for my taste. But I grew to like the resemblance. I even bought a print of the painting at the gift shop at the Metropolitan Museum of Art in New York. When I was in my mid and late twenties and a warrior in the sexual revolution, it pleased me to play the role.

Somewhere over the years, I have lost touch with the Venus. However, she is there still . . . just under the surface. I don't know when my lush sexiness was replaced by this image of the conventional society matron. It must have happened very slowly. Suddenly I miss this aspect of my personality. I am perfectly ready for her to take over my life for a while! I love being naked for you.

> Can you see me?
> Katie

---------------------------------- MAILBOX ----------------------------------

FROM: BUCK BRAZEMORE X455045A   08:00AM EST
SUBJECT: THE FOUNTAIN OF YOUTH   02-02-93

Sweetheart,

Your description has made me horny! Your body sounds so sexy and sweet. I haven't seen Titian's painting, but I can imagine it. And I'll go out sometime this week and find a book with the picture in it. I need to see it.

Your disclosure has made me want to tell you about my body. I wonder if you'll find it as exciting as I find yours. This morning after I got out of the shower, I scrutinized myself in the mirror so I would be able to describe it to you.

My body is hard, because both maintaining a ranch and my work are physically demanding. My muscles are almost knotty in places, especially the ones in my forearms. The skin of my face, neck, hands and arms is brown as a nut and the rest of my body is fishbelly white. My shoulders are broad and one of them is slightly lower than the other because I broke it the first time I rode a bull when I was 17 years old. My torso is tight and I have narrow hips. My pubic hair is a dark, thick tangle and it makes an inverted triangle from my navel, widening down to my penis. I guess my penis is of average dimensions. It's a dusky pink color and lists slightly to the left. My legs are long and sinewy and have six or seven good-sized scars as a result of my youthful local rodeo days.

I just laughed, thinking how I might look draped over some piece of cushy furniture. Our bodies must be complete opposites. I like to think of the contrast between your smooth softness and my scarred hardness.

It embarrasses me a little to tell you this, but I want you to know. Imagining your body and telling you about mine has made me hard. And letting you "see" this boner has given me the guts to ask you something that has been in the back, and sometimes the front, of my mind for the past two weeks. Would you like to try some computer sex with me?

I confess, I'm not exactly a computer sex virgin—but almost. Before you showed up I tried it a few times with some of the regulars on the board. For example, Peaches was willing to oblige on two occasions. Every Sunday afternoon, she sends her stuff out to a mailing list she limits to 25 guys.

I kinda picture Peaches to be like one of those prostitutes who followed various armies throughout history. I reckon soldiers would line up twelve deep outside the tents of those camp followers. Talk about sloppy seconds. Ugh! I wonder what she gets out of playing this role.

Needless to say, masturbating while reading one of Peaches's generic gang bangs was not satisfying. But it was mildly stimulating.

I can imagine that reading sexual fantasies written by you especially for me would be highly stimulating AND totally satisfying. It would give me pleasure trying to excite you, too.

Let's take the next step. Be sexy with me, Katie. Let's be naughty on the board and passionate in our mailboxes. Let's make love.

Proposing,
Buck

---------------------------------- MAILBOX ----------------------------------

TO: BUCK BRAZEMORE X455045A   08:12AM EST
SUBJECT: THE FOUNTAIN OF YOUTH   02-02-93

My Cowboy . . .

I am ready and eager to learn how to make love with you and will follow your lead. Please teach me right now. I can't wait!

Feverish and virginal . . .
Katie

---------------------------------- MAILBOX ----------------------------------

FROM: BUCK BRAZEMORE X455045A   08:25AM EST
SUBJECT: THE FOUNTAIN OF YOUTH   02-02-93

Honey,

Yesssss! I'm so excited at the thought of having sex with you I'm afraid I might trigger the smoke alarm. It's a good thing Linda went into town at the crack of dawn today.

It'll take me a while to write something good enough for your first time. It won't take too long, though. All I have to do is unzip my jeans, let my imagination go wild and then take "dick"tation. I called the field office and told them to do the first tests without me. I'd like to take the morning off and just make love to you until after lunch. Are you up for that? I sure am! See? <G>

Why don't you relax and change into something more comfortable? Or better yet, get naked. I like the thought of you sitting at your computer and reading my hot e-mail in the nude. In about an hour you'll find me in your mailbox all hot and bothered.

Your lover,
Buck

************* ADULT TOPICS BULLETIN BOARD *************

TO: ALL   07:00PM EST
FROM: BUCK BRAZEMORE X455045A   02-02-93
SUBJECT: THE FOUNTAIN OF YOUTH

Howdy folks!

My basement got real torn up after our little shindig the other night, so I've called in a cleaning crew. The supervisor said it may take a week before it's fit for human habitation again. In the meantime, I thought it might be nice to open up a friendly neighborhood bar. I'm thinking of calling it "The Fountain of Youth." How does that sound?

Anyhow, I've set up a little operation here. The specialty of the house is the elixir of youth on the rocks. It's mighty tasty and good for what ails you, especially if what ails you is being over the hill. <G> Here's my price list:

Small———Free
Medium———First-born child
Large———Your Soul

I also have Lone Star beer in tall brown bottles and on tap and I make a pretty mean Margarita. Of course, you can have a jigger of tequila if you want, the salt and limes are on the counter. Your credit's good with me. Now, what's your pleasure?

Your grinning bartender,
Buck

************* ADULT TOPICS BULLETIN BOARD *************

TO: BUCK BRAZEMORE X455045A   07:12PM EST
FROM: CLIFF NOTES L896112C   02-02-93
SUBJECT: THE FOUNTAIN OF YOUTH

Buckaroo,

I have a youthful fountain myself. Unfortunately, it's only able to dispense two or maybe three beverages a night. I wouldn't be able to open a successful bar. What's your secret?

Puzzled,
Cliff

************* ADULT TOPICS BULLETIN BOARD *************

TO: CLIFF NOTES L896112C   8:00PM EST
FROM: BUCK BRAZEMORE X455045A   02-02-93
SUBJECT: THE FOUNTAIN OF YOUTH

Pardner,

My secret? I've got THE Fountain of Youth. You know, the one people have been looking for all these years.

It's been spewing up a storm today. Even I'm amazed and impressed by the display. Don't you think it's fitting to name this bar after such an incredible geyser?

Cocky,
Buck

************* ADULT TOPICS BULLETIN BOARD *************

TO: BUCK BRAZEMORE X455045A   08:08PM EST
FROM: KATHERINE SIMMONS S102248A   02-02-93
SUBJECT: THE FOUNTAIN OF YOUTH

My Darling Bartender . . .
    Oh goody, my favorite drink! However, I do not like my elixir of
youth on the rocks. I prefer it warmed, like a brandy which has been
heated gently over a flame.
    May I have it the way I want it?

                        Still thirsty . . .
                        Your Best Customer

************* ADULT TOPICS BULLETIN BOARD *************

TO: KATHERINE SIMMONS S102248A   08:17PM EST
FROM: BUCK BRAZEMORE X455045A   02-02-93
SUBJECT: THE FOUNTAIN OF YOUTH

My Darling Customer,
    Yes Ma'am! You may have it any way you want it. It's Lady's Night
here at the Fountain of Youth and YOU are the lady. As you know, I
aim to please. Where should I aim next time? <G>

                        Frisky,
                        Buck

************* ADULT TOPICS BULLETIN BOARD *************

TO: CLIFF NOTES L896112C   8:20PM EST
FROM: SUSAN VENEER G740094D   02-02-93
SUBJECT: THE FOUNTAIN OF YOUTH

Cliff Babe,
    Is it "Happy Hour" yet? Actually, I'm in the mood for a "Happy Hour
And A Half" or even a "Happy Two Hours"! What do you say?:-)

                @-->->----Sue Veneer----<-<--@

************* ADULT TOPICS BULLETIN BOARD ************

TO: SUSAN VENEER G740094D   08:28PM EST
FROM: CLIFF NOTES L896112C   02-02-93
SUBJECT: THE FOUNTAIN OF YOUTH

Sweet Sue,
   Hold the phone! Two hours? Ma Bell already loves me this month,
but how can I resist "Happy Hour And A Half" with you?

                              Stand By—
                              Cliff

************* ADULT TOPICS BULLETIN BOARD ************

TO: BUCK BRAZEMORE X455045A   08:36PM EST
FROM: WILLIAM RAMSEY Y082176A   02-02-93
SUBJECT: THE FOUNTAIN OF YOUTH

Hello Buck,
   I suppose I'll have one of those specials. Make it a small one, though.
According to your price list, it's all I can afford, the larger sizes seem
a bit steep. <G> However, at 62, a little jolt from the Fountain of Youth
sounds mighty tempting.
   Did you finish repairing your fences last weekend? How are the negotiations going with the Israelis? Seems we haven't touched base for a
week or so.

                              Your friend,
                              Will

************* ADULT TOPICS BULLETIN BOARD *************

TO: WILLIAM RAMSEY Y082176A   08:49PM EST
FROM: BUCK BRAZEMORE X455045A   02-02-93
SUBJECT: THE FOUNTAIN OF YOUTH

Glad to oblige, Padre, <handing you a shot glass>
    Luckily, my herd is small, so I only have two-thirds of my property
fenced. However, no rancher ever finishes repairing fences. It's an ongoing chore. I did get a bunch done this weekend, though. And I'll hear
from the Israelis tomorrow or the next day. I'm pretty sure I'll be flying
out to Tel Aviv at the end of the month. It's almost a done deal.

                         Chewing the fat with a regular and
                         wiping the bar,
                         Buck

************* ADULT TOPICS BULLETIN BOARD *************

TO: BUCK BRAZEMORE X455045A   09:05PM EST
FROM: JOHN W. KELLY JR. A041178A   02-02-93
SUBJECT: THE FOUNTAIN OF YOUTH

Hi Buck,
    Nice looking place you've got here. Does the elixir of youth have
alcohol in it? If not, give me a shot. Otherwise, I'll just take a Shirley
Temple. I'm on the wagon.
    Where are the babes?

                         Pulling up a stool,
                         Johnny

************* ADULT TOPICS BULLETIN BOARD *************

TO: JOHN W. KELLY JR. A041178A   09:19PM EST
FROM: BUCK BRAZEMORE X455045A   02-02-93
SUBJECT: THE FOUNTAIN OF YOUTH

Hi Johnny,
    Long time no see. How's it going? You'll be happy to know that I
have both nonalcoholic elixir of youth and the kind that'll give you a
buzz.

The only babe in the bar at the moment is my babe, Katie. Sue Veneer just took off with Cliff Notes. You know how they are. But, I reckon a few more women will wander in before the night's over. Maybe you'll get lucky.

> Handing you a glass with a parasol
> and a cherry,
> Buck

A PROPOSAL

FROM: JOHN W. KELLY JR. A041178A   10:09AM EST

SUBJECT: A PROPOSAL   2-03-93

Dear Katie,

I think the term for a person like me is "lurker," meaning I watch what happens on the board, but rarely participate myself. In my lurker status, I've been admiring your witty and articulate writing. For the past week, I've been following you, pulling up your number and reading all your public posts. It was no accident that I showed up at THE FOUNTAIN OF YOUTH last night. I saw you there.

I can tell you and Buck have a computer romance going, but I'm wondering if you have room on your dance card for another admirer. I don't see any reasons why a woman shouldn't entertain as many suitors as she chooses in this place. Do you? Might as well look at the menu, right? No one else needs to know. I can keep a secret and promise to be the picture of discretion on the board.

I live in California, in Marin County. Over the past two years, I've been gradually withdrawing from my practice as a cardiologist, with the goal of retiring completely next year. At present, I only schedule procedures two mornings a week, so I have lots of time, a big chunk of which I would enjoy filling with you.

I've been divorced for five years, but have a long-standing relationship with an independent woman named Janet. She has her own home about twenty miles south of San Francisco, but she keeps an outpost in one of my guest rooms. I also have a terrific 15-year-old daughter named Megan who lives with her mother at the moment. She spends one week night and every other weekend with me.

Katie, it's tempting to create a character for you and to present myself

87

as someone I'm not. For instance, it would be easy to tell you I'm young, incredibly handsome and sexy. Although I like to believe I can be sexy on occasion, the other stuff would not be true and I'd like to be honest with you. I'm a recovering alcoholic and my recovery is dependent upon my being honest with myself and others. I've been in recovery for six years now. AA saved my life.

I'm 54, not quite 5'11" and weigh about 190 pounds. My hair is gray and my eyes are brown. I'm an energetic person.

I own fifteen acres of land and relish tackling big landscaping projects on my property. My favorite toys are an old Caterpillar bulldozer I bought at an auction four years ago, and any one of my several chain saws. I like to cook and eat and I have appetites for things other than food which I enjoy indulging. I'm a little kinky where sex is concerned.

I want to know you. Do you crave adventure as much as I?

> An explorer,
> Johnny

---------------------------------- MAILBOX ----------------------------------

TO: JOHN W. KELLY JR. A041178A   10:32AM EST
SUBJECT: A PROPOSAL   02-03-93

Dear Johnny . . .

I must tell you, I had a good laugh when I found your e-mail in my mailbox just now. I have also noticed you when you have appeared on the board (especially the time you started the streaking frenzy in BUCK'S BASEMENT). You have a namesake who is a fire-and-brimstone televangalist, but since you are not from the South, perhaps you have not heard of him.

The Johnny Kelly with whom I am familiar is a caricature really; a buffoon. He looks to be about sixty years old and about five feet tall. He is known far and wide for his uniform, a powder blue suit, white tie and white platform shoes. He is also immediately recognized by his amazing jet-black pompadour hairstyle. If he wore a cape and sunglasses he would look like a miniature Elvis impersonator. He hosts a locally produced TV show called the "Hallelujah Hour," which airs at 7:00 on Sunday mornings, and a syndicated radio show of the same name which is heard on Wednesday mornings and Thursday evenings. Most Southerners immediately recognize his distinctive, high-pitched plaintive voice. One of the popular local morning

DJs has made his career by lampooning "Dr. Johnny" and his equally diminutive wife, "Sister Sally."

Johnny and Sally were arrested last year for throwing eggs at the owner of an adult bookstore. The store owner was minding his own business and mowing his lawn when the two munchkinlike Kellys began pelting him. It was in all the papers. Dr. Johnny claimed God had given him instructions "to egg the Devil." What a riot! Just after the incident, somebody made a fortune selling T-shirts with what looked like raw eggs splattered all over them. I bought one and like to wear it when I am feeling particularly devilish. Perhaps I should put it on now because I think I WOULD like to "look at the menu" a little, as you suggest.

However, will you do a favor for me . . . will you change your name? May I call you Jack? It is my favorite nickname for a man whose given name is John. I love the name for many reasons, not the least of which is the fact that it carries with it a certain kind of straightforward masculinity. So are you willing?

I hate to say this, but I am still an attractive woman. I say, "I hate to say this" because it sounds so typical. It seems everyone in computerland is at least attractive, if not gorgeous. Nevertheless, it is true.

I am 5'6" and have an average build. My best features are my large and expressive olive green eyes. My hair is reddish and a medium length. My teeth are pretty and I have a nice smile. I smile a lot and love to laugh.

Although I have lived in other places (including California), I was born and raised in North Carolina, so I have a Southern accent. People who are not from the South don't seem to understand there are huge differences among Southern accents and they tend to lump them all together. Nothing irritates a Southerner more than hearing a bad Southern accent in a movie or on TV. For example, it would really grate on my nerves to hear an East Texas accent coming out of the mouth of someone who is supposed to be from Tidewater, Virginia. My accent has the slight nasal quality and twang to it which one normally associates with the Tennessee/Carolina regions. It is not quite as pretty as the classic Georgia/Alabama/Mississippi version, but it is nice.

I am married to a handsome and successful man named Tom. He owns his own business which represents the Ishii Corporation in the Southeast. Japanese copiers have a solid reputation and he has built a prosperous and thriving company. He is very focused on his career like so many men in the Power Years, and he travels a lot. Lately he has been spending quite a bit of time in Charleston, SC, and I don't see him for days at a time. Last week he was only home on Monday night. He got home about

7:30 and left for Charleston early Tuesday morning before I got up, so I saw him for a total of about 2 hours last week.

Tom and I have fraternal twin boys who will be eighteen soon. Next year, they will be in college and I guess I will be retired from my job as their nurturer. I don't think I'm ready to retire.

Becoming obsolete . . .
Katie

---------------------------------- MAILBOX ----------------------------------

FROM: JOHN W. KELLY JR. A041178A   10:58AM EST
SUBJECT: A PROPOSAL   02-03-93

Dear Katie,

I have no qualms about changing my name to Jack for you. No one calls me Johnny anyway; it just sounded cool to me. However, after hearing your story, the name has lost its sex appeal. <LOL> Please, by all means, call me Jack.

I like it that you're Southern and have an accent. It makes you seem exotic. I hate to admit this, but I've rarely met anyone who lives below the Mason-Dixon line and I've never set foot in the South, unless you count airport layovers.

Like so many Californians, I came here from somewhere else. I was born and raised in Ohio, but went to undergraduate school and medical school at Stanford. I liked California so much I decided to stay here. I lived for a short while in San Diego, right after I completed my internship and residency, but moved back here after two years. I love the San Francisco Bay area; it suits me.

Janet Gordon, my "significant other," is 50 and chief marketing executive for Phototech Corporation, the company which manufactures the portrait packages promoted by discount stores all over the country. She is well paid and self-reliant. She was married once before, but has been single for 19 years. Her daughter and grandson live in Phoenix.

Jan and I have a good relationship. We both value our privacy and give each other plenty of space. However, she spends lots of weekends and one or two nights a week over here. Once in a while I spend a night at her place, too.

Janet is handsome, intelligent and funny. In addition to being a good sex partner, she's my friend. She enjoys the same kind of erotic experimentation I do. We've managed to maintain a monogamous relationship for three years and I feel very fortunate to have such a compatible woman in my life.

Lately, I have been feeling a little obsolete myself, so I know how you feel. It seems like only yesterday I was on the cutting edge and now my techniques are considered rather conservative—kind of hard to swallow. I'm not exactly eager to retire, but I don't mind too much, since I'm financially secure and I have other interests in my life.

I love nothing more than being outside, changing the landscape. It pleases me to make something chaotic and overgrown into something beautiful. Maybe I'm a sculptor at heart.

I prefer the challenge of big jobs. For example, three years ago, I created a half-acre pond behind my house. I dug it out using my bulldozer. It's really nice now that it's finally filled with water. It's fringed with pampas grass on two sides and I planted a weeping willow on the bank nearest the house. It's become the home for a family of Canada geese. I'm proud I created this place.

Two years ago, I built a dirt road to the back side of my property where it drops off into a deep canyon. At the end, overlooking the abyss, I built a deck, so I can watch the sun set over the ridge between my property and the Pacific Ocean. It's become my favorite spot.

Probably my most gratifying pastime is pruning trees. My bulldozer has become very handy for accomplishing this chore. I simply drive it up to the tree in need of pruning and raise the bucket up as far as it will go. I climb up into the bucket and it becomes the perfect, stable platform for bracing myself as I use my chain saws to lop off limbs. I've amassed a huge brush pile at the bottom of the canyon as a result of all my hard work and the large trees closest to the house have become elegant and sculptural.

The other day, I was wondering about why I love to landscape so much. It's a rather unusual hobby. However, it strikes me that it mirrors what I'm doing inside myself. I'm moving and changing my interior, bringing order to the clutter.

When I was drinking, my life was a mess, a giant tangled, impenetrable jungle. My sobriety has become a bulldozer for me. It's torn down some of the ugliest tangles and let the light in. I'm building ponds and roads, now. I'm adding things of beauty. You could be one of the ornaments, Katie.

A landscaper,
Jack

--------------------------------- MAILBOX ----------------------------------

TO: JOHN W. KELLY JR. A041178   11:15PM EST
SUBJECT: A PROPOSAL   02-03-93

Dearest Jack . . .

I am glad you find me exotic. Since you have never set foot below the Mason-Dixon line, perhaps I may unburden you of two stereotypes about Southerners which continue to be promoted in books and movies and on TV.

First, not all Southerners are ignorant. However, I think there is a rule of thumb for writers and directors which goes something like this: If you want someone to seem REALLY dumb, the character in question should be given a Southern accent.

Second, the use of "you all," or of the contraction "y'all," is not a sign of brain damage. The terms are simply the plural form of you. I doubt very seriously that Europeans (who also use the second person plural) snicker or look incredulously at someone who uses that form. What's the big deal? End of sermon. <laughing>

I'm glad to find a kindred spirit! I love that you write to me using analogy and metaphor. I think in pictures. It's the way I learn best and make sense of the world.

I have always been a visual person. I forget which side of the brain it means I use, but I use that side exclusively. I am not mathy at all. The fact I am so visual might explain why I majored in art history and why I am a collector. Art speaks to me.

I really like the way you compare landscaping to your self-altering processes. I understand exactly what you mean. And I wonder if I am not engaging in a big landscaping project of my own. I feel big hunks of terrain being pushed around. I wonder what I am using for a bulldozer? I also wonder if you will "make the earth move" for me. <laughing>

                              Off to bed . . .
                              Katie

COFFEE BREAK

FROM: CAROL BEATTY N771200C   08:01AM EST
SUBJECT: COFFEE BREAK   02-04-93

Dear Katie,

I've really been enjoying our morning chats! After I put Tiffy in the playpen, I get a cup of coffee and then come in here to talk to you. This time has become my coffee break. Only a computer friend could understand or appreciate what I've been experiencing lately. My other friends would undoubtedly think I've gone off the deep end. Sometimes I wonder myself. <G>

Like you, I'm wallowing in my love letters. Every day this week, I've found at least three in my mailbox. Ken is a nice mix of romantic, sweet, and HOT. We've even started treating each other to some computer sex twice a day. Wow! You need to try it. You won't believe it.

It dawned on me this morning, after I read Ken's last note, how long it's been since I've felt this lovable and sexy. Lord, I feel like a teenager.

Ed drives me crazy. He tries to control everything I do and he's a fitness nut. He's in bed by 9:30 every night, eats no fat, salt or refined sugar, takes a mind-bending array of vitamins and dietary supplements, works out strenuously for an hour and a half every weekday and runs ten miles on the weekends, come Hell or high water. He has started visiting a tanning salon regularly and shaving his entire body. Recently, his favorite pastime has been looking at himself in the mirror and flexing. It's as if looking at his muscles gives him a sense of security.

He DOES have a beautiful and muscular body for a 40-year-old guy. But he's humorless when it comes to sculpting a physique and he makes it clear he thinks I'm undisciplined and somehow lacking in character because I don't choose to adopt such a rigorous regimen for the sake of

93

doing battle with the Grim Reaper. Don't get me wrong, I'm not a sedentary person. I walk briskly with two of my neighbors three days a week and I've been going to an advanced Jazzersize class with one of my friends from work every Wednesday night for seven years, except when I was pregnant this last time. Even then I went to the Pregnant and Fit class they offered at the Y. This is enough for me.

I weigh 130 pounds which is fifteen pounds more than I weighed when we got married, but I'm 5'7" and wear a size 10. Although, I still have a little "baby fat" left over from Tiffany, I don't have much and it should be gone before summer.

Ed thinks I'm too fat and flabby and he constantly makes snide and derogatory remarks about my body. He keeps saying I could have a body like Cindy Crawford if I'd just get off my "fat ass." I'm getting sick of it. Once, when he wanted to have sex, I told him to go find an aerobics instructor. He got furious and scared the shit out of me. Needless to say, he is not the world's most sensitive lover.

Griping,
Carol

---------------------------------- MAILBOX ----------------------------------

TO: CAROL BEATTY N771200C   08:50AM EST
SUBJECT: COFFEE BREAK   02-04-93

Dear Carol . . .

I have two confessions to make.

First: Buck and I have also begun to experiment with computer sex. We spent all Tuesday morning rushing our first passionate, sexually explicit messages back and forth. I was unprepared for how thrilling it can be. Incredibly, I found myself sitting naked in front of my computer, literally quivering with lust as I read how Buck was masturbating for me on his end. The sensations were primitive and powerful. Although Buck claimed he came twice during our four-hour "tryst," I wanted MORE! He promised another session that night and he electrified me again after we played on the BB at THE FOUNTAIN OF YOUTH. Who cares if my husband is never home to pleasure me if I can have regular computer sex. <laughing>

Second: Do you remember Johnny Kelly, the man who started the streaking thing in BUCK'S BASEMENT? He sent me some e-mail yesterday morning and I wrote back to him. I expect he'll write some more today . . . I hope so. He's different from Buck, not anywhere near as sweet and courtly, but he's charming, intelligent and he appeals to me on some basic gut level. I don't know why. I'm not going to tell Buck about him.

I don't know what has gotten into me! Why am I doing this? Maybe it's the excitement of having the attention of two strangers who appear ready to adore me. Up until now, my life seemed so dull and predictable. I have felt trapped lately; relegated to the role of being someone's wife and someone's mother, and that's all, for the rest of my life. On top of that, Tom has been acting strangely. I'm becoming suspicious, but I don't want to question my husband about what he does at night when he's out of town. I'm afraid of what he might say. This computer romance and sex is an effective distraction; it keeps my mind off Tom's possible extramarital activities. Not only that, but now I seem to have all this energy and a "new lease on life." Really.

You know, I read an article in a magazine recently that said men want to be loved and women want to be worshipped. Do you think there is any truth to that? All I know is this sudden feeling of control over these guys makes me feel wonderful . . . no, euphoric! It reminds me of the sexual power I wielded as a young woman. Do you think I am being wicked?

I am enjoying our chats, as well. You and I really do have something in common . . . not just our sexy computer "hobby," but also feeling slightly guilty about our physical selves. You sound like you feel okay about your body, but I hear the underlying anxiety. We women always seem preoccupied with our bodies. I was going to say men never worry about theirs, but you just proved me wrong with your description of Ed.

I have always worn a size 12 or size 14, even in high school. My weight fluctuates between 140 at its slimmest and 155 right after Christmas (I fibbed to Buck a little). At the moment, I weigh about 148. However, my body is proportional and I look better than a lot of women my age. On the other hand, I would like to look like Cindy Crawford.

My problem is I binge eat. If I am under stress of any kind, good or bad, I have a tendency to overeat. My father was also this way. I was told my eating is a part of a constellation of symptoms some addictive personalities have. I eat for the same reason alcoholics drink. I guess I should be thankful I do not weigh 250.

I was bulimic as a teenager and young woman. I even went to a psychologist for two months when I was a student at UNC in an attempt to rid myself of the terrible habit. I have a better acceptance of my body, now, but once or twice a year, when I have really done something awful (like eaten a quart of ice cream at one sitting) I will cave in to the temptation and make myself throw up.

I have become quite sluggish over the last two years. Mysteriously, a kind of ennui has set in and I just don't seem to be able to make myself get up and move. I hate aerobic exercising, it is so boring, and no sports appeal to me except snow skiing and I can't do that all year. I would like to dance, but where does someone my age go to dance? I am soft and out of shape, yet I do not feel any motivation to change my ways. I admire you since you walk regularly and have stuck with an exercise regimen for seven years. Perhaps this is why you weigh 130 and I weigh almost 150.

I keep thinking one day I will become motivated. I actually have an exercise bicycle. I asked for it one Mother's Day. Tom finally took it up into the attic because it was just taking up room in the den and collecting dust. <sigh>

Pouring another cup . . .
Katie

---------------------------------- MAILBOX ----------------------------------

FROM: CAROL BEATTY N771200C   09:30AM EST
SUBJECT: COFFEE BREAK   02-04-93

Katie,

Johnny Kelly!!!??? <LOL> Hall-lay-LOO-yuh!!! Of course, I remember the guy in Buck's Basement. I thought it was such a hoot to think of Johnny Kelly, the preacher, streaking, didn't you? I could just imagine that little moron running around naked, with Sally trotting along behind him all dolled up in her beehive hairdo.

I'm originally a country girl from Valdosta, Georgia. I remember when I was a teenager, Johnny would come to town with his Hallelujah Crusade and pitch his tent in a field about half a mile from my grandmother's house. Out front, he had this big neon cross he used to hook up to a portable gas-powered generator. You could see the cross and hear that generator from Granny's porch. I wonder how they could hear him preach over all that noise? Anyway, they caught him one year for planting fakers in the audience when he did his "healing." What a snake oil salesman! I don't have too much sympathy for the people who buy his line.

I have a cleaning lady who comes once a week. When I was still working, I suspected she was a Johnny Kelly fan because the radio in the kitchen was always set on his channel on Wednesdays. Now that I'm home, I know for sure she listens to him. I pay her a little extra so she will iron a few things for me and I notice she sets up the board in the kitchen when it's time for his broadcast. Every now and then, through the kitchen door, I'll hear her say, "Hallelujah!" It sounds like she means it.

Man, it must feel pretty weird to be writing to a guy named Johnny Kelly, though. Hey, just think of the men named Johnny Kelly who have had their names ruined from the association with that runt. I think I would have mine legally changed.

I'm glad to hear this new guy appeals to you. Why shouldn't you write to two men, or six or seven for that matter? It's a free country. I say more power to you, girl!

I've noticed a change in your writing style. You used to be so ladylike and proper all the time. Don't get me wrong, I really like that about you. You just seem to have loosened up a little. You seem more playful and happy.

I never was bulimic, but I did starve myself to a size 2 when I was a freshman at Florida State. I weighed 96 pounds. If I got up to 98, I wouldn't eat until I'd lost the two pounds. I kinda looked like a boy back then, you know, the "Twiggy" look. There was no way I'd let myself get near 100. What made me stop was I skipped a period and was scared shitless I was pregnant. The doctor told me I was malnourished, so I went up to 105 and a size 5 and stayed there for the next five or six years. Better a little "pudgy" than being continually worried I might be pregnant. You're right, we women obsess about our weight from the time we hit puberty 'til Lord knows when. Do you think we will be worrying about love handles when we are 75? Probably! <LOL>

Your chum,
Carol

---------------------------------- MAILBOX ----------------------------------

TO: CAROL BEATTY N771200C   10:13AM EST
SUBJECT: COFFEE BREAK   02-04-93

Dear Carol . . .

It's funny you should make the comment about men named Johnny
Kelly needing to change their names. As a matter of fact, I asked the
new guy if I could call him Jack and I told him why. People outside the
Bible Belt really don't know much about Johnny and the Hallelujah
Hour. Jack thought it was funny and was happy to change. He says
nobody calls him Johnny anyway. He just affected it for the BB, thinking
it made him sound cooler than just plain John. Lots of people change
their names in computerland . . . look at me.

About my writing style: I do come across as rather prissy and ladylike,
don't I? It surprised me when some man called me "stuck up" on the
board. I am really not aloof, but I guess the projection comes across
unconsciously as a result of my stint in finishing school. At Grace I was
conditioned to become a proper lady. Students were required to attend
classes where we were taught such idiotic accomplishments as serving
tea and coffee at formal receptions and calligraphing place cards. We
couldn't wear jeans or shorts (even in our own dorm rooms), had man-
datory chapel twice a week and were required to wear white gloves and
a head covering to church on Sunday.

Of course we were forbidden to wear miniskirts. It will make you
laugh when I tell you the house matrons used to stand at the foot of the
stairs with rulers and measure any suspicious skirts before we left with
our dates. If our hems were more than three inches above our knees, we
had to go up and change. Luckily, it was easy to fit a miniskirt in a
pocketbook. <laughing>

Also, my mother insisted her daughters demonstrate impeccable manners at all times. If we failed, it was a reflection upon her. Our strictest
punishments were related to some breach of etiquette.

My writing style is probably changing because I am changing. Once,
when I was in college, I experienced a metamorphosis when confronted
with the Vietnam War. Suddenly, I became a different person. I think I
may be undergoing a similar mutation as a result of my experience in
computerland. Right now I can't tell if the change is good, bad or neutral.

For the past three or four years I have felt increasingly unhappy. My
husband is never at home; my boys are slipping away from me; my
volunteer work gives me no pleasure or sense of accomplishment; and

my youth and beauty are dissolving right in front of my eyes. I have been drifting in a lonely dark place.

However, now there is a glimmer of light. Remarkably, the connections I am making over my computer modem seem to be lifting my load. I feel less alienated and hopeless, but it is troubling that I sometimes spend ten hours a day sitting at my computer. Also I frequently feel "drugged," especially since Buck has introduced me to the ecstacy of computer sex. I can't get enough of the stuff.

I am going to send Sue Veneer an e-mail note to see if she would like to be a computer friend. I confess to being nosy about her relationship with Cliff Notes. Buck told me the guy is in his thirties and married. I hate to think what he might have on his mind.

Your friend . . .
Katie

---------------------------------- MAILBOX ----------------------------------

TO: SUSAN VENEER G740094D   10:19AM EST
SUBJECT: COFFEE BREAK   02-04-93

Dear Sue . . .

Would you like to be friends and send e-mail to each other every now and then? I am a lot older than you, but here in computerland age doesn't matter, right? I am 44 years old and a homemaker. I have twin sons who are probably just about your age. I have always wanted a daughter. Perhaps we can make-believe.

Where do you go to school and what are you studying? What do you like to do for fun? Do you have any boyfriends at school?

I look forward to hearing from you soon.

Your new friend (I hope) . . .
Katie

----------------------------------- MAILBOX -----------------------------------

FROM: SUSAN VENEER G740094D   12:45PM EST
SUBJECT: COFFEE BREAK   02-04-93

Hi Katie!

Sure! I'd like to be your friend. My computer friends are the most important things in the world to me. The more the merrier and age doesn't matter.:-)

My real name is Jennifer Flinn. I'm 20 years old and a sophomore at Indiana State University in Terre Haute in the preveterinary program. Animals are my love. I don't have a boyfriend, except Cliff.

You already know about Cliff and me. Cliff's real name is Gary Sorkin. He's 32 and lives in Cincinnati. The difference in our ages doesn't matter to me at all and he says I'm very mature. He's married, but he says his wife doesn't know how to make him happy; so they're going to get a divorce in the summer probably.

I LOVE being on the computer. There are SO many nice people online. I have tons of computer friends. I usually get on for an hour before my first period classes and then for several hours in the afternoon and at night. Today, my last class was at 11:00 and my chemistry lab isn't until 2:00, so here I am. It would be good if I would cut down some and study more, though. I might lose my scholarship if I don't watch out. :-(

I always meet Cliff somewhere on the board every day and we have fun. We also send e-mail to each other every day and he has been calling me twice a week for a long time. He is going to come and visit me in two weeks. I can't wait!!! :-D I love him.

I write to about eight other people, men and women. Some of them I met on the ANIMAL RIGHTS BB. Please write soon and I promise I will write back.

> Your friend.
> @-->->----Sue Veneer----<-<--@
> or Jennifer

MASKS

------------------------------------ MAILBOX ------------------------------------

FROM: JOHN W. KELLY JR. A041178A   10:17AM EST
SUBJECT: MASKS   02-05-93

Dear Katie,

I collect African masks. Twenty-five years ago I bought my first one, a ruffed Yaka initiation mask from Zaire. In Africa, initiation masks are worn by young men when they emerge from seclusion following circumcision ceremonies. Dancing in public while wearing the symbolic disguise marks the beginning of manhood. I bought the Yaka mask to celebrate landing my first paying job as an MD. It seemed appropriate.

Over the years I've added other pieces to my collection, each one specially chosen to mark the beginning or end of an important event in my life: marriage, the birth of my daughter, sobriety, divorce, and so on. I also give them as gifts of gratitude to individuals who have made a difference in my life. Like the artists who created them, I invest the masks with symbolism and cosmic significance.

I display my six favorite pieces in my bedroom. Three are mounted on the stone wall above the fireplace and three rest on rough wooden pillars in other spots around the room. From my bed, I can see all six masks at the same time. I love to prop up on pillows and admire them at night when a fire blazes in the hearth. They have a certain beauty and a direct earthiness when the tongues of light animate them. However, a mask loses some of its power and meaning when it's brought inside and put on display. A mask needs a human wearer to achieve its full potential.

I wear a surgical mask at work almost every day to protect myself and my patients. Germs are our enemies and they are potent, dangerous and invisible. When I wear my mask in surgery, how different am I from the African healer who wears a mask to ward off harmful spirits? My disposable paper surgeon's mask has no beauty, but it's practical and suits the sterile surroundings. As a joke, I tacked one up on a wall in my den between two rare Senufo bronze masks.

Every member of AA has a sponsor who serves as an advisor and role model. My sponsor is a judge named Robert Dantzler and we have become very good friends over the past few years. One night Rob was admiring the masks in my living room. He was especially taken by a large Bantu piece on a stand. It's a helmet mask with a raffia cape attached at the bottom. The grassy cape is at least three feet long and almost brushes the floor. A person wearing the mask would become completely hidden from view.

After appraising the piece for several minutes, Rob looked at me and said something to the effect that wearing masks is what gets alcoholics into so much trouble. I understood what he meant and could agree with him on a certain level, but I contended that masks are not only used to dissemble and hide, they can also protect, transform and elevate. Masks are neither good nor bad, they're just tools. The intention of the person who wears the mask is key. We spent an interesting evening talking about masks of all kinds. On the first anniversary of my sobriety, I gave him a Yoruba mask as a gift. He keeps it on the desk in his office.

Right now, I'm thinking this computer is like a mask and can be used for good or evil. It seems to have a lot in common with the unadorned mask I wear at work. Maybe I should give some thought to decorating it. Fertility and potency masks are some of my favorites, maybe I should borrow some designs. How do you think my terminal would look with a crown of phallic symbols? <G>

A collector,
Jack

---------------------------------- MAILBOX ----------------------------------

TO: JOHN W. KELLY JR. A041178A   11:27AM EST
SUBJECT: MASKS   02-05-93

Dear Jack . . .

I enjoyed hearing about your collection of masks. Please tell me more! Before I resigned from all my nonpaying jobs, the volunteer position

I enjoyed most was my work as a docent at the local art museum. Not many people even know what a docent is . . . I didn't until I became one. The word comes from the Latin word for teacher. A docent has several teaching duties, but my favorite role was conducting tour groups (mainly schoolchildren and club members). I was a docent for almost 15 years, so after attending all the required ongoing docent classes I became quite an expert on the Mint Museum's collections.

The museum has a very small gallery of African artwork, but it is probably my favorite space. It contains masks, weapons, shields, prestige objects and religious artifacts. It's odd, but during my formal education in art history, very little time was spent studying the great artistic contributions of African cultures other than the masterpieces produced by the Egyptian and Benin empires. So I was utterly fascinated by the excellent docent classes which were taught in the African gallery.

I remember one session vividly. The lecture centered on works of a spiritual nature. The curator stood beside a small glass case which contained several boxy leather containers of varying dimensions which were studded with cowrie shells and colored glass beads. With gloved hands, she removed one piece from the case and walked around the room so we could see it better.

The curator identified the container as a "house of the head." She told us such receptacles originally held the heads of wise and respected leaders. After death, the head was separated from the body and placed in a decorated container which was then placed in a shrine where villagers could go to pray and ask for guidance. She went on to explain that the cases no longer function as small coffins for the decapitated heads of revered chieftains. Over time they have become symbolic. Some are very small (fist-size) and it would be impossible to fit a head inside; however, the containers are still placed on altars where villagers go to pay homage and seek help.

During the lesson, a woman sitting next to me tapped me on the arm and I turned toward her. She grimaced, stuck out her tongue and rolled her eyes, as if to say, "How revolting!" That bothered me.

Later that evening, I looked over my notes and thought about the reaction of the woman in the African gallery. It did not take long before it dawned upon me that the woman obviously had not given much thought to the central symbolism of Christianity which dominates our culture. A cross is a religious symbol which is also closely related to death. I wonder if a student from another planet, or from another culture in the far distant future, might be confused or disgusted by this religious symbol. The thing is, at the core of both symbols, the cross AND the house of the head, there is a message of hope. I wished the biased woman in the African gallery had been able to see this.

Like you, I respect and admire African art. It is easy to see how Picasso and the great contemporary masters were influenced by it.

> An Afrophile (is there such a
> word?) . . .
> Katie

---------------------------------- MAILBOX ----------------------------------

FROM: JOHN W. KELLY JR. A041178A   12:37PM EST
SUBJECT: MASKS   02-05-93

Dear Katie,

Your anecdote about the class in the African gallery struck a chord with me. My ex-wife, Gretchen, didn't appreciate African art in general and my mask collection in particular. Her attitude had racist overtones and we used to fight about it. She used words like "primitive," "crude" and "nasty" to describe my treasures. While we were married, she insisted I keep the masks in my den and library.

She collected Spanish Colonial works in silver. She felt they were the ultimate in refinement. In her opinion, the ornate crucifixes, chests and candelabras were much more appropriate to decorate the home of a physician than the "bestial trash" which appealed to me. She had very specific ideas about what was socially acceptable.

During our arguments, I routinely brought up the shameful cruelty of the Spanish Conquistadors and the notorious savagery of the Spanish Inquisition. However, my wife clung tenaciously to her conviction that European history, art and culture were far superior to African in every respect. There was no reasoning with the woman. Eventually I gave up even trying.

Luckily, my mask collection was one of the few possessions of value Gretchen did not demand in the divorce settlement. The day after the moving van carted away her loot, I went out and bought an Ashanti mask to mark the event. I sent one to Gretchen, too. She probably thought the gift was an attack, but I really sent it to mark the end of our relationship and as a token of gratitude for the only good thing the marriage produced, our child. Then I went about installing my masks in every room of the house. I think they helped banish the evil spirits which hovered around in the aftermath of the breakup of my marriage.

The first year after our divorce was a dark time. I missed my daughter terribly. It took every ounce of my strength to stay on the wagon.

A masked man,
Jack

----------------------------------- MAILBOX -----------------------------------

TO: JOHN W. KELLY JR. A041178A   01:16AM EST
SUBJECT: MASKS   02-05-93

Dear Jack . . .

I understand your ex-wife. My mother has always been very concerned with appearances. She is elegant and aristocratic and has iron-clad opinions about what attitudes, behaviors, dress and possessions are socially acceptable. She's a descendent of an old wealthy family and is deemed to have impeccable taste by the cream of Charlotte society. The admiration of her peers is all my mother needs or wants out of life.

Even when I was a child my mother was cold and aloof. She did not enjoy her role as a parent, so she farmed out my two sisters and me to a succession of black women who were employed as our nannies. These women gave me mothering in bits and pieces.

For a while, I tried unsuccessfully to gain my mother's love and attention, but there seemed to be some hidden secret to winning those prizes. Since I couldn't find a way to unlock my mother's heart, I finally gave up and looked to my nannies for love and security.

My sisters and I probably would have done well under the attention and kindness of our caretakers if we only had two or three. Unfortunately, my mother kept firing the women; not because they were neglectful or incompetent, but because they were not subservient enough for her tastes or for some other arbitrary reason.

My favorite nursemaid was Delores. She taught me how to dance and make biscuits and she let me sit in her warm spacious lap while she ironed. She laughed a lot. Once, when I begged relentlessly, my mother finally allowed Delores to take me home with her one afternoon. I didn't want to leave and cried when Walter, our gardener, came to pick me up before dinner.

I wanted fervently to be Delores's little girl. That night, I prayed to be turned into a black child while I slept. However, I was not blessed with a miracle.

Delores was a very large woman. She probably weighed more than 250 pounds. One day, out of the clear blue, Mother fired her. She said Delores looked like a "fat greasy slob" in the pretty pink uniform she provided for her. She wanted a servant who looked more presentable. I was devastated and cried for weeks.

My sisters and I never felt loved or secure when we were small. Both my sisters chose to remain childless. They were afraid they would be bad mothers. I took a risk and am surprised how strong my maternal instinct is. It is strangely comforting to think some women may be born without the ability to love and defend their children. This would mean my mother has a genetic deficiency, not that I was or am unlovable.

Here I go again. It never ceases to amaze me how effortless it is to blurt out painful secrets in e-mail messages. It's like free therapy.

Feeling lighter . . .
Katie

BASKETS

TO: JOHN W. KELLY JR. A041178A   09:16AM EST
SUBJECT: BASKETS   02-08-93

Dear Jack . . .

I collect handmade baskets of all kinds and have dozens on display in my house. My favorites are the sweetgrass baskets woven by women who live in the little rural communities between Myrtle Beach and Charleston on the South Carolina coast. The roping and coiling technique used by weavers in this region is an art which has been passed down from mother to daughter for 200 years. In Africa, where the style originated, I imagine the skill has been passed down for thousands of years.

Fourteen years ago, I discovered some especially well-designed and expertly crafted baskets at a roadside stand off highway 17 near Mc-Clellanville. The small operation was owned and operated by two basket-weaving sisters, Nettie and Hattie Pinckney. The women invited me to sit in an empty rocking chair and watch them work. I sat and rocked for two hours, watching their graceful and adept brown hands convert the chaotic pile of sweetgrass into watertight baskets and listened as they sang hymns or chatted in their musical Gullah dialect.

I purchased my first three baskets that day. Then it became a tradition. I visit the sisters every summer during our annual family vacation to Pawley's Island. Each year I have bought more additions to my collection.

The Pinckney talent was discovered by a Charleston specialty shop owner who successfully promoted the baskets in Charleston and Hilton Head. Now the baskets demand top dollar and sell briskly in trendy shops and galleries all over the country.

Nettie's and Hattie's daughters have not learned basket weaving. All six of them are in college, thanks to the Pinckney sisters' success. Three girls plan to be teachers, one is majoring in accounting, one is in a nursing program and the youngest is studying electrical engineering. Nettie says she will have to stop weaving next year because she is developing arthritis in both hands.

Not all my baskets were made by the famous Pinckney weavers. I also have anonymous peach and cotton baskets scattered throughout the house. And six years ago I bought a very large oval basket at the Appalachian Craft Center in the North Carolina mountains. It was made by an artist named Patty Stokes and is made of dogwood branches and muscadine vines. It has a place of honor on my kitchen table.

My boys call this particular basket "Mom's Nest." It DOES look as if some bird of prey, maybe an eagle or a condor, has set up housekeeping in my kitchen. <laughing> To maintain the image, I keep my nest filled with melons because they look so much like huge eggs. What is a nest without eggs or chicks?

There is something basic and pleasing about hand-woven baskets. I love to fill, hold and touch them. Their textures and shapes are comforting and they smell good, too. Perhaps it is a woman thing. Women have been associated with the woven containers from the beginning of civilization. I imagine the first female basket weavers invented them to simplify their work of gathering and preparing food and to cradle infants.

As I think back on it, my interest in baskets began in vacation Bible school when I was eight years old. That year the theme was "Heroes of the Bible." One week was devoted to the life of Moses. On Monday morning our teacher, Miss Margaret (who had a flair for the dramatic), told us the story of how baby Moses was found in the bulrushes by the Egyptian princess. She used a felt board for interest, moving a little cloth cut-out representing the basket bearing poor baby Moses along the imaginary Nile. It was the first time I had heard the story and the visual aid made the action seem real. I was sitting on the edge of my seat by the time the basket had lodged in the bulrushes on the felt board. I was terrified the baby might drown. When Miss Margaret put the figure of the Egyptian princess on the board, I knew Moses would be saved and heaved a great sigh of relief.

After the story, the class was divided by sex for the craft activity. The boys made Egyptian daggers out of cardboard and aluminum foil while the girls wove potholders. Weaving the potholders was supposed to give the girls an idea of what it must have felt like to be Moses' birth mother. The lesson was not lost on me. I really COULD imagine how frantic

Moses' mother must have been to save her child. She had to move fast to make sure the basket was watertight, covering it with pitch and tar so it would keep her baby safe until he was out of harm's way. That basket saved Moses' life. His basket-weaving mother was the hero of the Moses story as far as I was concerned.

A basket lover . . .
Katie

---------------------------------- MAILBOX ------------------------------------

FROM: JOHN W. KELLY JR. A041178A   10:20AM EST
SUBJECT: BASKETS   02-08-93

Dear Katie,

Two years after my divorce I traveled to Côte d'Ivoire, Ghana, Nigeria, Cameroon and Gabon. The coasts of these countries make up most of the great arc on the western coast of the African continent. The recession was formed many millions of years ago when the hump of what is now South America broke away from the mother land mass.

I went on the trip with a small group of academicians and African art collectors from the San Francisco Bay area. The three-week tour was put together by a curator/anthropologist at the California Academy of Sciences.

On the pilgrimage we visited several small hamlets situated in the fan-like Niger River delta of Nigeria. In one remote location I had the pleasure of watching an Ibo woman using a basket. She was young, tall, bare-breasted and wore a colorful length of cloth which was secured at her waist to make a long skirt. She looked about four or five months pregnant and the thin bright red material molded snugly against her body, clearly delineating the luxuriant curves of her belly, bottom, hips and legs. The woman balanced a large basket of green bananas on her head, with one arm raised and a hand clasping the basket's rim to stabilize the load.

As she walked along the path to the river landing, her plump buttocks and breasts undulated with fluid feminine grace. The many ropes of multicolored beads she wore around her neck jiggled and rolled back and forth over her swaying bosom. She was the picture of femininity. I snapped a photo just before she disappeared around a stand of tall grass.

I wanted to run after the woman, just to watch the provocative interplay of colors and movement a little longer, but resisted the impulse. I didn't want to offend our host, Edet Inwang. He was the village chieftain and although he had three other spouses, I didn't think he would take too kindly to my running lustfully after his pregnant, seventeen-year-old second wife.

The image I captured of the statuesque woman, regally bearing the basket of fruit like a crown, is my favorite photograph from the trip. The framed 11×14 print is hanging on the far wall of this room and I can see the shape of the basket and the red patch of color from here. The image is also imbedded deep in my brain, probably in the sexual center of my hypothalamus, because I can pull up a vision of the woman in motion when I want. It arouses me. I agree with you, women, baskets and fertility go together in some very basic way.

I met Janet on the trip to Africa. She was one of the tour group members. She collects shields and owns an impressive group which she displays on the walls of her office and home.

The two of us connected during the hour-long wait at the departure gate before we boarded the plane at the San Francisco Airport. Twenty minutes into the long flight, I asked the woman who was Janet's seatmate if she would mind exchanging places with me. She didn't mind, and Jan and I became a couple for the rest of the trip.

We slept together from our first night in Africa until our last. During the second week, under the mosquito net which formed a tent over our small shared bed, we made a switch from conventional lovemaking. Janet encouraged me to indulge in my secret desire. It had lain dormant for a very long time, since Gretchen found my appetite ''grotesque'' and ''unnatural.'' I experienced the best sex of my life in those compounds in the African bush.

When we returned home, Janet and I remained lovers. We eagerly experimented with a number of sexual practices which are not considered the norm, picking and choosing until we developed a repertoire which satisfied us both.

After three years together, our sex is still good. However, I've recently been craving some novelty. Unfortunately, it seems this is a weakness of mine. Perhaps I should become a polygamist like the Ibo men. That might solve the problem of my wandering eye. On second thought, I have decided not to marry again even once, so how can I possibly entertain the idea of having FOUR wives.

No candidate for polygamy,
Jack

------------------------------------ MAILBOX ------------------------------------

TO: CAROL BEATTY N771200C   11:20AM EST
SUBJECT: BASKETS   02-08-93

Dear Carol . . .

I just got the most amazing letter from Jack. He wrote about a trip he took to Africa three years ago. In a Nigerian village, he had an intriguing, sexually arousing experience watching a half-naked young pregnant woman balancing a basket of bananas on her head. I love the way he shares his experiences with me. In my mind's eye I saw the scene so clearly. I could even imagine *I* was the woman he described . . . all succulent and juicy with fertility and sexual power. Wow!

Something which also piqued my interest in this note was his reference to polygamy. Apparently the Ibo of Nigeria practice it. Of course, it is the men who have more than one wife. I'll bet the women do not have more than one husband. However, I have been thinking. Why shouldn't it be the other way around with women having multiple partners . . . like queen bees (or ants or termites)? After all, it is the egg which is precious. Sperm are a dime a dozen. <laughing>

Anyway, I wonder if I am experimenting with a little computer polygamy with Buck and Jack. Let's see what it's like to juggle sexual and emotional relationships. I wonder if I will be able to keep them straight. And just imagine the time and energy it will take to keep them both satisfied. I shudder to think. At least I won't have time to worry what Tom may be up to when he is in Charleston. Perhaps he is experimenting with juggling relationships, too. <Sardonic G>

The bad thing about this e-mail is you can not sense my underlying anxiety. Carol, I really am beginning to have strong feelings for these men . . . very strong. I actually feel as if I love Buck and I can see it won't be long before I have the same feelings for Jack. His pull is VERY strong. How will this end?

Baffled . . .
Katie

THE SEA OF LOVE

FROM: BUCK BRAZEMORE X455045A   08:01AM EST
SUBJECT: THE SEA OF LOVE   02-09-93

Happy Birthday, Sweet Thing!

I'm two days late, but I thought about you all weekend, wondering how your family celebrated your big day. I wish I could have been there with y'all. <SEG> I sent an electronic birthday card, did you get it? I've never tried that before.

I didn't have a relaxing weekend. On Friday morning, the people from Israel called to finalize the plans for my flying to Tel Aviv on the 26th of this month. This drilling project means a bundle of money for me, and a bundle and a half if we hit a respectable deposit. My lawyer, Jimbo Dukes, is going with me. He's a part-time rancher just like I am and lives on a spread about the size of mine two miles west of here.

Friday afternoon, Jimbo and I took two cars and drove down to Houston to get things lined up with the people who will be shipping my equipment. Then, I had to go to my little warehouse right outside Galveston to take stock of what I might need to add to my inventory before they crate up everything in April. Jimbo couldn't help me there, so he went on back home. It took me all of Saturday and Sunday and a good part of yesterday to get a handle on it. The drilling won't start until fall, but I need to ship the equipment way in advance. At least I don't have to worry about putting together my crew until I get back. I'll use some of Sparky's boys who have worked for me in the past. I'll hire some Israelis for the grunt work, too, but my key guys need to speak English and know what they're doing.

I'll only be in Israel about two weeks while we work out the details of the contract. Most of my time will be spent in Tel Aviv. Once the legal stuff is carved in stone and it's a done deal, I'll drive out to the site for a few days to meet the locals and do the preliminary geology stuff.

I was just thinking how grumpy it made me to be away from you for four days. Shoot, I'm gonna be one ornery cuss by the time those two weeks in Israel are over! <laughing>

It's a five-hour drive from Houston to the ranch. On the way back home last night, I was listening to some old tapes. One of the songs was "The Sea of Love." Do you remember that old tune? While I was listening to it, I started thinking about you and, before I knew it, my fly was open, "Trigger" was in my hand and that rascal had gone and made a big ol' mess. <LOL> It's a good thing there isn't much traffic between San Antonio and Kerrville late at night, that's all I can say.

It's fun drifting around on the Sea of Love with you, Katie. Why don't we have a little party on the board tonight to celebrate?

Your man,
Buck

--------------------------------- MAILBOX ---------------------------------

TO: BUCK BRAZEMORE X455045A   09:01AM EST
SUBJECT: THE SEA OF LOVE   02-09-93

Dear Cowboy . . .

On Sunday morning, when I logged on to LuxNet, I was delighted to find the electronic birthday card from you in my mailbox. It played "Happy Birthday" and it looked like the butterflies were flapping their wings. Gosh, what will they think of next? Thank you for being so thoughtful. It looks like that will be the way I will need to acknowledge your birthday, as well.

On my birthday, the men in my family surprised me with a new pair of skis, a ski outfit, and plane tickets to Denver. They have planned a week ski vacation at Winter Park. We leave this Saturday morning early and won't get back until Sunday, the 21st, in the late afternoon. The twins have this next week off from school for their winter break.

I really love to ski. We all do. This gift is not like the baseball bat the little boy gives his mother because he wants it (one year Stephen did give me an ant farm, though). They knew the vacation would be a hit. But, I had a twinge when I read your note from this morning and realized you and I will soon have to contend with two long separations.

Your weekend sounded strenuous, but exciting. Congratulations on landing the deal with the Israelis. It sounds like you have worked on it for a long time and the prospect of making "a bundle and a half" must mean a lot to you. Tom gets happy and excited when he has made a big deal. It seems it is the only time I ever see him act gleeful anymore. I really enjoy hearing about all your preparations for your work. It sounds very alien and masculine to me. I like to think of you climbing around over big complicated machinery and making deals.

Speaking of masculinity and big complicated machinery, I'm glad to hear you and your car made it home in one piece last night. <laughing> You thrill me with your description of listening to "The Sea of Love", thinking of me, driving with one hand and attending to your need with the other. It's fabulous that you are willing to surrender to abandon.

Yes! Let's celebrate on the board tonight.

The older woman . . .
Katie

************* ADULT TOPICS BULLETIN BOARD *************

TO: ALL   07:01PM EST
FROM: BUCK BRAZEMORE X455045A   02-09-93
SUBJECT: THE SEA OF LOVE

Aloha, Kanes and Wahines!

Katie and I are quite smitten with each other and have decided to take a slow cruise on The Sea of Love (or is this the Lac de Lust or the Pond o' Passion?). Anyhow, in celebration, we're hosting a beach party tonight and y'all are invited.

You can come stag or drag. However, make sure you're dressed appropriately. Katie's picked out my outfit for tonight. It looks kind of like a flowered diaper, doesn't it? Oh, well, she likes it.

The Host with the Most,
Buck

************ ADULT TOPICS BULLETIN BOARD *************

TO: ALL 07:09PM EST
FROM: KATHERINE SIMMONS S102248A 02-09-93
SUBJECT: THE SEA OF LOVE

Partygoers!

It is I, your lovely hostess. Please make yourselves at home on our blissful beach. You will notice we have a full moon tonight (Actually, we have two . . . Cliff just will not keep his pants on) and I have lined the shore with blazing Tiki torches. There is a large central bonfire and a succulent pig is roasting in the coals under the palm trees. The waves are gently lapping on the shore and, for your listening pleasure, we have hired Don Ho and his band. They are crooning in the background.

Please feel free to cast your eyes upon my person. I think you will find me especially alluring in my brightly colored sarong and orchid lei with a flame-colored hibiscus tucked behind my right ear. Allow me to put a garland around your neck and kiss you on both cheeks, as well. Welcome friends!

Now, let the games begin!

The Hostess with the Mostest . . .
Katie

************ ADULT TOPICS BULLETIN BOARD *************

TO: BUCK BRAZEMORE X455045A 07:14PM EST
FROM: CLIFF NOTES L896112C 02-09-93
SUBJECT: THE SEA OF LOVE

Salutations, Buck and Katie!

Here I am, sporting a fig leaf for tonight's festivities. I had to glue it on with Crazy Glue—I hope it'll come off.

Katie, thanks for the lei and the smooches on both cheeks. My buns look really cute with those famous lip prints, don't they?

Kindly direct me to the bar, then to Sue, then to the make-out quarters. Perhaps I'll get leied again before the night is over. <SEG>

With my butt hanging out,
Cliff

-------------------ADULT TOPICS BULLETIN BOARD --------------------

TO: CLIFF NOTES L896112C   07:22PM EST
FROM: SUSAN VENEER G740094D   02-09-93
SUBJECT: THE SEA OF LOVE

Cliffie,

Don't you think you should have chosen a larger leaf? Your butt is not the only thing that is hanging out. :-) It looks like our friend is peeking from behind a curtain. On second thought, I'll bet you wore that one on purpose. What a flasher!

How dare you let Katie lei you? That's MY job!

I'm wearing two clam shells and a grass skirt, myself. How do you like the look?

                          Doing the Hula
                          @-->->----Sue Veneer----<-<--@

************* ADULT TOPICS BULLETIN BOARD *************

TO: SUSAN VENEER G740094D   07:35PM EST
FROM: CLIFF NOTES L896112C   02-09-93
SUBJECT: THE SEA OF LOVE

Squeeze,

Will you lend me two clams?

My peek-a-boo look is for you, Sweetie! And, don't worry about Katie leiing me; you can lei me as much as you want. Go ahead, I can never have too many. <SEG>

Anyway, Katie and Buck are swimming around in the Sea of Love, the Lac de Lust and the Pond o' Passion, or haven't you noticed? They only have eyes (and everything else) for each other.

Hey! Maybe WE should take a dive into the Ocean of Orgasms, the Bathtub of Bliss and the Soup Tureen of Tenderness. Or, we can just sit here in the Puddle of Horniness, as usual. At least we don't have to worry about messing up the couch again tonight, since it would be a royal pain to drag it up from Buck's basement and out here onto the beach.

Hmmm . . . At the thought of our usual nighttime activity, I seem to be turning over a new leaf! Look, Babe, no hands!

> Peek-a-boo!
> Cliff

************ ADULT TOPICS BULLETIN BOARD ************

TO: KATHERINE SIMMONS S102248A   07:37PM EST
FROM: JOHN W. KELLY JR. A041178A   02-09-93
SUBJECT: THE SEA OF LOVE

Hi there, Katie,
I would like one of your leis and I brought one for you, too. Perhaps you would like to experiment with putting my lei on backwards, just for some variation. We wouldn't want you to be undecorated from behind.

> Coming through the back door,
> Johnny, John or Jack
> (take your pick)

************ ADULT TOPICS BULLETIN BOARD ************

TO: JOHN W. KELLY JR. A041178A   07:40PM EST
FROM: KATHERINE SIMMONS S102248A   02-09-93
SUBJECT: THE SEA OF LOVE

Aloha Jack (I like that name best) . . .
Of course I will give you a lei. Come and get it. And how can I resist your offer to adorn my backside?

> Watching you bestow your gift in
> the mirror . . .
> Katie

************* ADULT TOPICS BULLETIN BOARD *************

TO: ALL   07:43PM EST
FROM: WAYNE ROONEY F362238A   02-09-93
SUBJECT: THE SEA OF LOVE

All you sinners, hear this:
Matthew 5:27–29 says, "You have heard that it was said, 'YOU SHALL
NOT COMMIT ADULTERY'; but I say to you, that everyone who looks
on a woman to lust for her has committed adultery with her already in
his heart. And if your right eye makes you stumble, tear it out, and throw
it from you; for it is better for you that one of the parts of your body
perish, than for your whole body to be thrown into hell."

                         REPENT!!!!!!!

************* ADULT TOPICS BULLETIN BOARD *************

TO: WAYNE ROONEY F362238A   07:56PM EST
FROM: JOHN W. KELLY JR. A041178A   02-09-93
SUBJECT: THE SEA OF LOVE

Rooney:
   Will you give it a rest? If all of us amputated the offending parts of
our lustful bodies, there would be a hideous bloodbath with nothing left
but quivering featureless blobs of protoplasm. Not much to roast in Hell.

                         Just making an observation,
                         Jack Kelly

************* ADULT TOPICS BULLETIN BOARD *************

TO: KATHERINE SIMMONS S102248A   08:01PM EST
FROM: DOUG LEAVELLE P654309B   02-09-93
SUBJECT: THE SEA OF LOVE

Dear Katie,

May I come to your party? I've been sneaking around and watching you guys for days and have finally summoned the courage to jump in.

I've arrived at the party by island canoe and volunteer to be the bartender if no one has the job.

           Wearing a Speedo,
           Doug

************* ADULT TOPICS BULLETIN BOARD *************

TO: DOUG LEAVELLE P654309B   08:13PM EST
FROM: KATHERINE SIMMONS S102248A   02-09-93
SUBJECT: THE SEA OF LOVE

Dear Dougie . . .

What an impressive outrigger you have there! And, the canoe is nice, too.

Of course you may join us. And it just so happens we do need a bartender. Why don't you just go on over to the grass hut over there and set up the bar? We will be serving Pina Coladas tonight. You will find some coconut shells in the corner; you can use them for glasses. Oh yes, and don't forget to garnish them.

           Eyeing your well-packed
           Speedo . . .
           Katie

*************ADULT TOPICS BULLETIN BOARD *************

TO: KATIE SIMMONS S102248A   8:30PM EST
FROM: BUCK BRAZEMORE X455045A   02-09-93
SUBJECT: THE SEA OF LOVE

Katie!

What's the big idea!? First, you lei Cliff and Johnny right in front of everybody and now you are scoping out the bartender's "outrigger"?! You come over here, so I can keep an eye on you.

Anyway, I need to know where you want me to put this limbo pole. Carol and Ken have just arrived with their Harry Belafonte albums and have been inciting the crowd and are eager to get underway.

<Whispering> It will be fun to watch Cliff doing the limbo, won't it?

> Hugging you close,
> Buck

*************ADULT TOPICS BULLETIN BOARD *************

TO: BUCK BRAZEMORE X455045A   08:41PM EST
FROM: KATHERINE SIMMONS S102248A   02-09-93
SUBJECT: THE SEA OF LOVE

Bucky . . .

Do not fear. Since I am the hostess, I am leiing everybody tonight. It is all quite innocent, My Cowboy. And, as for the new studmuffin bartender in the tank suit . . . "Just because I am on a diet, doesn't mean I can't look at the menu," as the old saying goes. I would much rather help you position and plant your limbo pole than help Doug beach his outrigger.

Now, for the task at hand . . . let me help you with that pole, it looks heavy. I know just the spot for it.

> A Limbo Lover . . .
> Katie

---------------------------------- MAILBOX ----------------------------------

FROM: BUCK BRAZEMORE X455045A   11:51PM EST
SUBJECT: THE SEA OF LOVE   02-09-93

Lordy Katie!

I just checked to see if you'd sent any mail before I finally turned in, but I wasn't prepared for what I found! Your words have scalded me. I could see you going down on me so clear. I could almost feel the wet of your mouth and the way your lips and tongue move. My hard-on is so stiff, it hurt to have it trapped in my jeans. I had to unbuckle my belt, unzip my pants and fish it out, so I could sit comfortably enough to type this. Lucky for me Linda and the boys went to bed at 10:00. I wouldn't want them to come across me sitting here with my soldier at attention and sticking out of my britches like this. How would I explain it? <LOL>

I just wanted to write to you while I'm still hard. Maybe if you know how aroused I am this minute, it will somehow add to your pleasure of reading these words. I get so frustrated sometimes when I try to describe by e-mail what you do to me. I want to hump the keyboard and hope your monitor can translate.

That just gave me an idea. Let me try something—Here's a message from my peter—56n7mu645bttg btent5u8mj ik. I just rolled it back and forth on the keyboard. Can you read Dickese? I sure hope so. <LOL> Do you think I'm losing it? What I just did is another thing I wouldn't want anybody to catch me doing.

I'm glad we gave each other our addresses. I look at the pictures you sent me several times a day. I keep the one of you on your fortieth birthday in a can in the equipment shed and the one of you and the twins in the hammock is under the box of formatted disks I keep above the computer terminal. Linda wouldn't come near the computer with a ten-foot pole, but the boys like to play their games. I don't think they'll look under there, though.

I wish you could come and go to bed with me. I've worked hard today and I'm tuckered out, but there is nothing in the world I'd rather do than spoon your soft body with mine. Your softness would be my comfort and I could be your hard protective shell. I want to press my nose into the nape of your neck and take in the full female smell of you. In that position, you could feel the pressure of my body from the back of your neck to the backs of your knees. And my arms would hold you in, one hand holding a breast, the other spread over your sweetly rounded belly.

My cock could be hard or soft, it wouldn't really matter. We could have sex—or go to sleep. That wouldn't matter either. All that would matter is I have you.

My erection is still sitting on ready. I'm looking down and trying to decide what to do with it. Should I sit here and think about work until I can tuck it back in my jeans? Should I jack off, looking at your picture? Or, should I wake up Linda, close my eyes and imagine she is you? These have become my choices over the past week and I've tried them all. I wonder what you'd like me to do?

Would you let me call you when you get back from your ski trip and before I leave for Israel? I need to hear your voice. Please.

I love you,
Buck

GETTING 2 KNOW U

TO: JOHN W. KELLY JR. A041178A   10:27AM EST
SUBJECT: GETTING 2 KNOW U   02-10-93

Dear Jack . . .

This is exciting. Each day there is a new note in my mailbox which is like a little tile of a mosaic. With the little pieces you have offered over the period of this week, I am really coming to get a feel for who you really are. And I like the clandestine element of our secret meetings. It all seems so adventurous and naughty.

Do you remember the song, "Getting to Know You," from the *King and I*? It is permanently engraved in my brain because I played the part of Anna in the 9th grade. I must have sung that song five hundred times! I had trouble with it. As a result, sometimes fragments of the song will bubble up into my conscience. Anyway, it has been tormenting me this morning . . . you know, playing over and over again. It suddenly dawned upon me that maybe my subconscious is sending me a message. <laughing> You do seem to be "my cup of tea."

You ask me how I come to be at this particular truck stop on the information highway. Well, here's the story:

Before last month, I had only used the word processor of our computer for my volunteer activities at the art museum. Tom and the boys were the computer users in the family. Tom uses it for work-related projects (spread sheets and data bases and a bunch of other alien stuff) and the twins mainly use it for playing games of some kind or another. Every now and then I will see them using it for school work, which is the reason we justified buying it in the first place.

One of my best friends, Beverly, told me about computer bulletin boards; I had never heard of them before. She had gone on a trip to Cancun two Christmases ago and before she left she had gotten all kinds of helpful information from the frequenters of the TRAVEL BB on the LuxNet service. She pointed out to me that the information network had educational games, an encyclopedia, Consumer Reports, a cookbook and all kinds of enticements which would be of great use to my entire family. She finally convinced me the subscription price would more than pay for itself in the convenience the net offered. She sounded like one of those testimonial commercials on TV. The software had been free, so I got Tom to install it. No one ever used it to my knowledge and for six months it just lay dormant.

The week after Christmas, I got "The Mother of All Colds." By the second week, the worst part was over, but I still didn't feel much like doing anything. I got so bored I sat down at the computer and started fiddling around. A whole new world opened up.

LuxNet is very user friendly; I guess that explains part of its popularity. Anyway, that first day it didn't take me long to find the bulletin boards. The time flew by as I pored over the ADULT TOPICS BB posts and their replies. By late afternoon, my back hurt from sitting at the computer all day, but I couldn't wait until the next day, after the twins had gone, when I could sit at the computer again.

I summoned enough courage to send a post myself. From then on I was hooked. Now, it is your turn to tell me how you got to this place.

> Curious . . .
> Katie

-------------------------------- MAILBOX ----------------------------------

FROM: JOHN W. KELLY JR. A041178A   11:06AM EST
SUBJECT: GETTING 2 KNOW U   02-10-93

My Dear Katie,

I'm liking this too. It surprises me how much I've come to look forward to your mail. It's been a long time since I felt such anticipation.

My subconscious is sending me messages, as well. I feel tuned into you somehow and you seem familiar to me—like a face emerging from a crowd. You know, you rack your brain trying to figure out how you know this person—maybe it's the woman from the dry cleaners, the wife of an acquaintance, or the weather girl. Anyway, sometimes you never figure it out and it's annoying. I wonder if I'll ever figure out how I know you?

I subscribe to LuxNet because one of my partners recommended it to me. I use it to keep track of my investments and for the Internet address. Megan also uses it when she's here. Like your boys, she's into computer games and occasionally will use it for school work.

My discovery of the bulletin board was similar to yours. It happened on a cool rainy weekend in November when I was here alone. Janet was in Seattle on a business trip and it wasn't my turn to have Megan. After I checked the stock quotations, I just started poking around a little. I played that Brain Buster game for awhile and then began perusing the boards. Before I knew it, I was in the Adult Topics fantasyland.

I've corresponded with a few women on the board and by e-mail; a nurse in St. Louis, a high school teacher from Concord, Massachusetts, and even a college student at Northwestern. I had a brief hot thing with Peaches, too. Who hasn't? I think she writes one of her famous steaming scenarios and then sends it out to her long mailing list en masse. None of the relationships seemed to take, but they tantalized me enough to keep me interested. Have you had any computer flings other than the one you're having with Buck?

I enjoy sexual experimentation and I've been wondering what might be possible here. The novelty of this way of relating is stimulating and I'm hungry for something fresh and new. Are you?

Katie, I'm very interested to know what you look like in detail. Tell me more about the physical you.

Curious,
Jack

-------------------------------- MAILBOX --------------------------------

TO: JOHN W. KELLY JR. A041178A   11:30AM EST
SUBJECT: GETTING 2 KNOW U   02-10-93

Dear Jack . . .

Perhaps you and I are fraternal twins (since we are different sexes) and, by accident of birth, we were just born to different women at different times. I know about twins. Most people think it is only identical twins who have the telepathy (or whatever), but I know for a fact that fraternal twins also communicate in ways that cannot be explained. You

should see my twins when they play doubles tennis. It is like watching
a pair of dolphins swimming in tandem . . . Do you know what I mean?

I haven't had much experience with computer relationships at all. You
already know about Buck. He is my first experiment and I confess I am
enjoying his effects on me.

Self-description is such an important part of computer relationships,
isn't it? I think as one comes to care for the other person at the end of
the modem, there is a desire to give him or her more form. Then the
person becomes less wraithlike and more real. It's kind of funny when
you think about it, since vision really doesn't come into play at all.
However, I have told you as much about my face as I can think to tell.
You must want to know about my body. Wow, you move fast . . . I like
that. <laughing>

I know for a fact I look like Titian's "Venus of Urbino." I can clearly
remember actually seeing the painting at the Uffizi in Florence. It was
the summer after I had graduated from my boarding school. My parents
had given me the trip to Europe as a graduation present. It was very
fashionable among debutantes' parents to give a "European tour" to
their daughters to mark the auspicious occasion of successfully making
it through their secondary education. Several girls in my class at Grace
were on the same tour since it was sponsored by the school; one of them
was my best friend, Virginia (Ginny).

She had begun laughing hysterically when she first saw the painting
and I had looked at her blankly, wondering what in the world had gotten
into her. Then she began pointing at me, unable to speak from laughing
so hard. A few of the other girls joined in her laughter and even the tour
guide began to smile in amusement. It finally dawned on me that the
group thought I looked exactly like the young woman who was lounging
in the nude for all the world to see.

I had been chagrined and blushed mightily as the gales of adolescent
laughter surged around me. It was a rude awakening to learn I looked
enough like the model to be her twin. Her plumpness and overt sexuality
offended me. I didn't want to look like her. That night, after dinner, I
had gone back up to the hotel room, claiming to have forgotten something, and I made myself throw up before I rejoined the group for the
next outing.

Anyway, I still look like her when I'm naked. I weigh between 130
and 140. You would need to put a bag over her head and put a little
Vaseline over the lens, though (to compensate for aging, you know). I

am just a tad too voluptuous by today's standards. I have never had the "hard body" they seem to promote everywhere these days. I wouldn't want it . . . it seems to be a rather masculine look.

Now, it is your turn.

Revealed . . .
Katie

--------------------------------- MAILBOX ---------------------------------

FROM: JOHN W. KELLY JR. A041178A   12:02PM EST
SUBJECT: GETTING 2 KNOW U   02-10-93

My Dear Katie,

I've seen Titian's masterpiece and it excites me to imagine that you look like her. I especially remember her gaze, with its combination of challenge and seduction, and the luscious quality of her skin. You have the body which is my complement. I've always craved your form. Janet is big-breasted and has narrow, boyish hips. We don't fit together very well. You and I, on the other hand—

It seems my body was made from two different people. I don't match. I have broad shoulders, a big barrel chest, kind of massive, long arms, but a small butt and almost birdlike legs. I'm not hirsute, just a thatch of sandy pubic hair. Can you picture my almost hairless, gorillalike body? <LOL> When I go into surgery, I'm two-toned. I must wear a large top and a medium bottom. Since the scrubs are color-coded, I'm blue on the top and green on the bottom. It's my identifying feature. Other doctors and hospital personnel can recognize me at 100 yards.

At any rate, you and I would complement each other, since you're the wonderful pear shape I love so much and I'm lightbulb-shaped—the Yin and the Yang. If we were to couple, we would look like the symbol for Buddhism, no?

Speaking of coupling—you must be interested in my genitals. I'm certainly interested in your sexual terrain. If I show you mine, will you show me yours? Think of it as playing "doctor." <G> Here, take a peek at this first installment: My dick is chunky and ruddy and I have a large set of balls. One of them is lower than the other, due to a surgery to repair a varicocele when I was in my thirties. I like my lopsidedness, it gives my unit some personality. When my nuts tighten up, you can really see the difference, they make me look rather rakish, like arching an eyebrow, or something. I'd like to show you sometime, you might find it interesting. <G>

Would I find your sex interesting? How about giving me a tour?

Your other half,
Jack

GIRL TALK

TO: SUSAN VENEER G740094D   08:59AM EST
SUBJECT: GIRL TALK   02-11-93

Dear Jennifer . . .

In your last note to me, you said Gary is coming to visit you next week. Although I discouraged you, I hope you know I still want to be your friend. What are friends for if not to offer advice and comfort, right? I will always like you, no matter what.

It just seems to me that maybe you should wait to meet Gary until after his divorce is final, don't you? And, since he is older, you might find out you do not have as much in common as you think you do. It might spoil your fun flirting on the BB.

Well, there is my motherly advice for today. I will be leaving on Saturday to go skiing with my family for a week. I won't be here when you and Gary meet on Wednesday. However, please don't keep me in suspense. Leave me a note while I'm gone and tell me how everything goes, so I can read all about it when I get home.

Your friend . . .
Katie

---------------------------------- MAILBOX ----------------------------------

TO: CAROL BEATTY N771200C　　　　　　　　　09:15AM EST
SUBJECT: GIRL TALK　　　　　　　　　　　　　02-11-93

Dear Carol . . .

I exchanged my ski outfit yesterday. Why is it my family always gets me a size 8 whenever they buy me an article of clothing as a gift? Probably because they tell the 16-year-old-salesperson, "She's about your size." That's the only way I can figure it. Anyway, I got a really nice-looking turquoise, fuchsia and white jumpsuit. I've never had a one-piece outfit and will probably hate it when it comes time to pee. However, it looks great and that's the main thing.

I have already started packing for the trip since our flight leaves Saturday morning at 8:25. It's a big job. We will be gone for a week and winter clothes, especially ski clothes, are so bulky. In addition to packing sweaters and boots for wearing around the lodge and in town, we need to be prepared for really harsh conditions on the slopes. That means, we will all need two sets of long underwear, our polypropylene masks, glove liners and the whole nine yards. February in Colorado is cold, with a capital "C."

We are meeting Tom's brother, Ben (who lives in Richmond), and his two kids. He's divorced and has a girl in the 10th grade and a boy in 11th grade. Our kids get along fine and really enjoy each other. We will rendezvous in Denver at the car rental place. Tom has arranged for both a Suburban and a Bronco. It's a two-hour drive from Denver to Winter Park, so we will need the space with seven adult-size people and all our suitcases and ski equipment; four-wheel drive will come in handy, no doubt.

I have been writing to Sue Veneer about every other day and she has been writing back. I have discovered that Cliff is planning to come and visit her next week during a business trip. She is so excited.

The guy is surely up to no good. You know he is probably hoping to have sex with her. Sue says Cliff's wife "doesn't understand him" (or something to that effect). Can't you just hear the man, handing her that old line? It concerns me what might happen if they meet in person, but what can I do? It's really none of my business. But I did ask her if she had thought through the possible ramifications.

From what I can gather from Sue's letters, she is pretty much a loner. She wrote that she has no boyfriends at school and not many girlfriends. She apparently spends almost all her free time glued to the computer. She also mentioned something about losing some weight over the past four weeks. I wonder if she is obese.

Buck is really a nice-looking guy. Actually, it surprised me how cute he is. He sent me two pictures. I especially like this one of him sitting on the tailgate of his truck (I'm looking at it as I type this). He is leaning forward, with his weight on his arms, his hands holding onto the end of the truck and his legs dangling. He has on jeans, a plaid shirt with the sleeves rolled up, and scuffed cowboy boots. The way the light is, it makes the hair on his forearms look silvery and his ruffled hair look like a halo. How appropriate.

You know, Buck is almost too good. Although recently we have been sharing the most intimate, sexually charged e-mail you can imagine, he comes across as a "boy scout." He is sweet, courtly and very familiar to me with his Southern ways. Although I am captivated, it worries me that he is taking this courtship MUCH more seriously than I am. Maybe I should back off a little.

Jack, on the other hand, is slightly devious, unpredictable and fast. If the truth be known, I like Jack's style better. I wonder why? I have only been writing him for a week and already he has me playing "doctor" with him. You will probably die when I tell you this, but last night I found myself squatting over a hand mirror in my locked closet, looking at my bottom so I could describe it in minute detail to this guy. It was thrilling to try to put what I saw in writing and send it off to him. I wonder how he will respond?

God, I feel slightly debauched . . . and it feels so good. <laughing> I really am loving this sex play on the computer. In this day and age, when intimacy is complicated by the threat of AIDS, maybe this is the milieu where extramarital affairs should be played out. It gets rid of the middle-age doldrums and it seems harmless, since it isn't really adultery . . . or is it? I don't buy Wayne Rooney's definition, do you?

Your hussy friend . . .
Katie

---------------------------------- MAILBOX ----------------------------------

FROM: CAROL BEATTY N771200C   09:45AM EST
SUBJECT: GIRL TALK   02-11-93

Hi Girl!

The preparations for your trip sound like a handful. I've always wanted to learn how to snow ski. Probably because snowy places have such a fascination for this Southern girl. I've only actually been in snow one time in my life.

I hate to hear this stuff about Sue and Cliff. How can the man take advantage of that girl? What an asshole!

I love hearing about your sexy "triangle." I've never been lucky enough to hook into a menage a trois, myself. <LOL> How well I know what you mean about craving computer passion! Ken's letters to me drive me up the wall. It's amazing how horny e-mail can make you, isn't it? But do you know what's even better? Phone sex!

This is Ken's and my new thing. God, Katie, it is ASTOUNDING! There is something unbelievably erotic about pressing the receiver against my ear as Ken whispers and moans how he'll make love to me. Meanwhile, he's masturbating and describing that to me, too. It makes me so hot, I almost can't stand it. Before I know it, I'm there with him, grunting and gasping. It's better than real sex. Don't think I'm kidding! You haven't lived until you've tried it. I've had more mind-bending orgasms this week than in my entire marriage.

When Ken called yesterday he asked me to meet him in Jacksonville the second weekend in March. Although I'm scared to death, I'm really tempted! I think I'm going to do it, only Lord knows what I'll tell Ed. You don't feel it's a good idea to actually meet people you fall in love with on the computer, but I'm not so sure.

I'm dying to see Ken in person. He looks great in his pictures. The ones I sent him of me were taken eight years ago. I went out last night and bought a case of Slim Fast and did fifty sit-ups this morning. Next week, I'm going to make an appointment with Daniel at this really up-scale salon downtown (he charges $75 for a haircut, but he's worth it!) and then I'll go by the Estee Lauder counter and spend a fortune on makeup. I think I'll hit Victoria's Secret, too! I'm going to be gorgeous, sexy and a size 8 by the time March 5th rolls around.

Your Pal,
Carol

-------------------------------- MAILBOX ----------------------------------

TO: CAROL BEATTY N771200C   10:06AM EST
SUBJECT: GIRL TALK   02-11-93

Dear Carol . . .
 I am stunned! You sound excited about the prospect of meeting Ken in Jacksonville, but are you sure you want to risk it? He is divorced and really doesn't have much to lose. You, on the other hand, have two children and a husband. And what about disease?
 You're right, I would never want to meet a computer love. It seems there are only a few possible outcomes and they are all bad. In the first scenario, one or both of you is disappointed. In the second scenario, you are indifferent (and this spoils the on-line romance). Of course, there is always the possibility your partner is a psychopath and will spend the rest of his demented life systematically killing your family and pets. And the last scenario is the worst. In that one, you both find the answers to your prayers . . . then, what do you do? Why mess with a good thing?

     Your honest friend . . .
     Katie

-------------------------------- MAILBOX ----------------------------------

FROM: CAROL BEATTY N771200C   10:33AM EST
SUBJECT: GIRL TALK   02-11-93

Dear Katie,
 The kids and I would be much better off without Ed. I haven't told you everything. Ed isn't just emotionally abusive, he also threatens me frequently and pushes me around sometimes. Occasionally, when he's totally lost control, he's even hit me. Once, he split my lip and I had to have three stitches. I told the doctor a bottle of cleaner fell off the top shelf and hit me when I was trying to reach for something behind it.
 I've never told anybody about this, not even members of my family. I guess the only reason I can tell you is because I can't see you. It's so embarrassing. You're probably shaking your head and saying, "How can an intelligent woman put up with abuse?" I wish I could tell you.

Anyway, in addition to loving the wonderful romance and acceptance he brings to me, I guess I'm also hoping Ken might rescue me. It's a lot to hope for, but I don't feel like I can save myself and I'm so tired of being scared all the time.

Your friend,
Carol

THE CHAPLAIN'S
ROOM (II)

************* ADULT TOPICS BULLETIN BOARD *************
TO: ALL   09:08AM EST
FROM: WILLIAM RAMSEY Y082176A   02-12-93
SUBJECT: THE CHAPLAIN'S ROOM

Thought for the week:

On PBS last night, there was a taped interview with James A. Louis, the CEO of the megacorporation, Futuron. Among other things, he discussed the limitations of e-mail in business. Louis said he uses e-mail every day. However, he also reported that it's really most effective in delivering simple, positive and unambiguous messages. The example he gave was giving someone a pat on the back for a job well done. He went on to say that if the communication requires subtlety or if it contains more complicated emotions (for instance, if someone needs to be fired), then face-to-face communication is preferred and often necessary.

It struck me that this goes for human relationships, as well. E-mail is a fine venue for sharing information, telling stories and getting to know someone, but if emotions become complex (let's say, if sexual feelings begin to emerge), it's not the best manner of communication. We need our other senses to nurture and maintain intimacy.

I coined a term for the passion men and women seek on their computer screens. The new word is "<ENTER>course." In my opinion, <Enter>course is no substitute for intercourse. It's only a pale imitation.

> Offering food for thought
> Will Ramsey
> Professional Contributor,
> Adult Topics Bulletin Board

************ ADULT TOPICS BULLETIN BOARD ************

TO: WILLIAM RAMSEY Y082176A　　　　　　10:02AM EST
FROM: SANDRA WINDELL P219760B　　　　　　02-12-93
SUBJECT: THE CHAPLAIN'S ROOM

Dear Will,

How right you are! I met my second husband last year on the ROSES topic of the GARDENING BB. We're both master gardeners and members of the American Rose Society. Early last winter, we spent many afternoons e-mailing each other about our gardens, local shows and just roses in general.

We developed a wonderful friendship over our flowers and along the way we learned we're both retired Californians in our 60s. He found out I was a widow and I discovered he was a widower. Before long, we switched from writing about roses to writing about being lonely and wanting love. It was too hard to communicate by e-mail then, so he asked if he could call me on the phone. By early spring, we wanted to meet in person. We met in Pasadena in June and we were married this past December.

Our relationship outgrew e-mail in a hurry, didn't it? <G>

　　　　　　　　　　　A happy gardener,
　　　　　　　　　　　Sandy

************ ADULT TOPICS BULLETIN BOARD ************

TO: SANDRA WINDELL P219760B　　　　　　10:34AM EST
FROM: WILLIAM RAMSEY Y082176A　　　　　　02-12-93
SUBJECT: THE CHAPLAIN'S ROOM

Dear Sandy,

Thanks for sharing how your relationship outgrew e-mail. Yours is an interesting, yet typical story. It's typical in that from most of the reports I hear, when love starts to blossom it doesn't like to be confined to e-mail.

There seems to be a pattern. Sometimes a couple begins by sending overland mail and photographs. After this stage, there is a desire for voice contact and, finally, a personal meeting.

It's fortunate that you and your husband were single when you met. When one or both of the individuals involved in an e-mail relationship is married, the stories do not usually end as happily as yours.

> Regards,
> Will Ramsey

************* ADULT TOPICS BULLETIN BOARD *************

TO: WILLIAM RAMSEY Y082176A 10:42AM EST
FROM: HOUSEWIFE H797763D 02-12-93
SUBJECT: THE CHAPLAIN'S ROOM

Dear Will,

Please help me. I really don't know what to do.

I'm a 31-year-old housewife who lives in Arizona. I've been happily married for 6 years and have two small children at home. Out of boredom and as a result of my sister-in-law's advice, I found my way to the FAMILY BB on LuxNet in January.

It didn't take long before, under cover of a made-up name on the "C" ID, I began prowling around and flirting on the ADULT TOPICS BB. Within a week, I'd met "Steve" and our e-mail quickly began to include graphic sexual fantasizing.

I found myself losing control and in a weak moment, I gave this stranger my real name and telephone number; he didn't give me his. He said he wanted to pay for the long distance charges. We had phone sex twice. One day, I was overcome by guilt feelings and decided to stop this activity. "Steve" didn't want to end our relationship and he became angry. Although I'd hang up the instant I heard his voice, he continued to call my house during the day and once he called in the evening when my husband was at home. Luckily, I answered. I told my husband I'd been getting persistent obscene phone calls and finally convinced him to have our number changed.

This week, I received in the mail three Xeroxed images of an erect penis. There was no return address on the envelopes. I suspect these were sent by this man. I figure he must have gotten my address from a phone book by matching my last name to the number I'd given him. I feel I'm being stalked. What can I do? Who can I tell?

My family is very religious. They would not understand my behavior.

> Terrified,
> Housewife

************* ADULT TOPICS BULLETIN BOARD *************

TO: HOUSEWIFE H797763D   10:57AM EST
FROM: WILLIAM RAMSEY Y082176A   02-12-93
SUBJECT: THE CHAPLAIN'S ROOM

Dear Housewife,
    Please check your mailbox as soon as possible. You'll find I've sent
you a private letter about this very serious matter. I want to help you.

                              Your friend,
                              Will Ramsey

************* ADULT TOPICS BULLETIN BOARD *************

TO: WILLIAM RAMSEY Y082176A   04:13PM EST
SUBJECT: THE CHAPLAIN'S ROOM   02-12-93

Dear Will . . .
    If a computer love affair is make-believe, isn't it possible for it to
exist only in letters (e-mail and overland)? Isn't it kind of like a harmless
fantasy then? It seems it could almost be a healthy way to deal with
sexual problems in a marriage, to add excitement, experimentation and
novelty. There is no risk of disease. It isn't adultery, is it?
    I have two computer acquaintances who have spoken to their lovers
over the phone and are planning to meet these men in person. I would
never be so brave or foolish. Plus, it is really not only the sexual aspect
I find exciting about these liaisons.
    However, I am just beginning to sort this all out for myself. This way
of relating is so new and there really aren't any rules yet. You have been
around here a relatively long time and have gathered a lot of information
from the people who seek your advice. I would appreciate your input.

                              Katie

P.S. Would you tell me what you advised "Housewife"?

------------------------------------ MAILBOX -----------------------------------

FROM: WILLIAM RAMSEY Y082176A   05:07PM EST
SUBJECT: THE CHAPLAIN'S ROOM   02-12-93

Dear Katie,

I suppose it would be possible to try to keep a computer affair in letter form. From what I understand, what happens in that case is the relationship achieves a certain level of sexual intensity and then it can go no further. It stabilizes. For most people, it becomes frustrating and repetitive after a relatively short time, maybe one or two months, at most. What finally happens is one partner suddenly drops out or the letters become less and less frequent until they finally stop altogether. An exception to this rule is in the case of disabled people. These e-mail relationships can flourish for months, even years.

A major problem for many people who attempt to engage in sexual activity over their computer modems is the difficulty in resisting making the next step to telephone, and the next to actually meeting in person. This is not as much a problem for single people as it is for married folks. Singles are often disappointed when their idealized expectations are not met. Married people who indulge in this escalating behavior frequently run into any one of a number of complications. It has been known to destroy previously healthy marriages.

No, I guess it's not technically adultery, but it can be just as damaging. The computer relationships divert energy away from other relationships, especially marriage. There is also the real problem of a transfer of intimacy. It seems, because of the anonymity factor, people are willing to become very vulnerable in expressing their emotions, weaknesses and hopes to each other over the computer in addition to trading sexual fantasies. This vulnerability is usually accompanied by a sense of unconditional regard on both sides. A real-life relationship can hardly compete with this ideal one.

I'm in the process of writing a book about the new social phenomenon of computer relationships. I've been conducting research for 24 months and have interviewed hundreds. The first draft should be ready for submission by this fall.

I hope you'll understand if I don't share my advice to "Housewife" with you. I keep all my private counseling confidential.

                              Best wishes,
                              Will Ramsey

SNOWBOUND

TO: BUCK BRAZEMORE X455045A   07:50AM EST
SUBJECT: SNOWBOUND   02-22-93

Dear Buck . . .

It was a comfort to find your letters in my mailbox when I logged on just now. I have missed you. Did you get my electronic birthday card and the postcards?

I am so happy to be back here where it is warm! During my trip to Winter Park, the words "frigid," "freezing," "chilly" (and every other word that has to do with cold) were redefined for me. I even learned what a blizzard is, first hand. Brrrrr!

We have never been out West to ski during the winter months, although we have been in late November and late March. On past winter trips, we have always gone to resorts in the mountains of North Carolina, Tennessee and Virginia or to Snowshoe, West Virginia. While I have experienced single-digit temperatures before, I was not prepared for the extreme cold I was exposed to in Colorado.

The skiing was great the first three days. There was no wind and a nice 3-inch layer of packed natural powder lay on top of a deep base (my favorite conditions) and although the high was about 10 degrees, if I dressed for the conditions, I was not uncomfortable.

On Wednesday, everything changed. The blizzard moved in fast. It lasted two days, and during that period 46 inches of snow fell. It was amazing. We couldn't ski then because you couldn't see two feet and it was windy and bitter cold. With the wind chill factor, it was 30 below zero. The kids had a hard time just walking between the buildings to the swimming pool.

During the blizzard, Tom and I spent more time alone together and awake than we have in a year. It was kind of strange, almost awkward. We played some Hearts with my brother-in-law, that first morning, but Ben said he had a sore throat and felt like he might be catching a cold (which turned out to be true), so he went to his room and stayed in bed almost the whole rest of the time. Tom seemed uncomfortable being trapped in the confined space with me and, at one point, offered to do the laundry, which, amazingly enough he did. It is hard for Tom not to have a project of some kind. He is in perpetual motion. During that time we were snowbound, I was forced to see how far my husband and I have wandered away from each other.

After the blizzard we had one more good day on the slopes, although it was unbelievably cold. It was fabulous to fly through that deep powder. It was up to my knees; I couldn't even see my skis. That is an eerie sensation, not being able to tell exactly where you are going.

Well, tell me about your birthday party. I want all the details!

Thawing . . .
Katie

---------------------------------- MAILBOX ----------------------------------

FROM: BUCK BRAZEMORE X455045A   08:23AM EST
SUBJECT: SNOWBOUND   02-22-93

Dear Katie,

I'm tickled you're home safe and sound! I missed you a lot. I've never been skiing, but it sounds like it might be fun. I'd probably bust my butt, though. And, yes, I did get your electronic birthday card and one of the postcards.

For my birthday, Linda and Sparky cooked up a big surprise party on Saturday night over at his ranch, the Silver M. It's some spread, let me tell you. Most of the party was inside because it's so cold, but there was a big bonfire in the fire pit on the terrace, so you could go outside, too. They had the whole place all decorated up with Mexican stuff. Inside, there were piñatas dangling everywhere, streamers hanging down from the rafters and big branches with bright paper flowers sticking out from the walls. Outside there were luminaria lining the sidewalk and a good section of the road. It must have taken his men all day to put them out. Who knows who lit them all? It was real pretty.

Sparky has always liked to show off. He hired a mariachi band, three

bartenders and a catering company. The musicians wandered around playing, drinks flowed and the food crew set up bunches of little fancy stalls
all around the big fireplace on the terrace. They had women making
fresh tortillas on griddles and every kind of Mexican food you can imagine. Sparky had shot an axis deer, too. He had his cook, Carmelita, smoke
it and she made venison burritos for anyone who wanted something
different. Smoked venison is her specialty.

It was a fine party. After dinner they roasted me and gave me gag
gifts. In addition to a bunch of funny hats, Sparky gave me a beautiful
pair of ostrich boots. They must have cost over a thousand dollars. He
said they were to wear when it was time to "kick the bucket." I told
him they would make good butt-kicking boots and he could be first in
line.

I got so many presents it made me feel self-conscious. Sparky sent
his overseer in his truck back home with us to help tote everything. Some
fool had given me a big doghouse, and Jimbo gave me a wheelchair. It
was funny, though.

Linda was having the time of her life being hostess. There were at
least 75 people there and she just flitted around among them like a butterfly. She loves to dress up and give parties, but I'm not crazy about
them.

Sometimes I feel funny around Linda. It's just like you described
about the way it felt when you and Tom were trapped alone during the
blizzard. Sometimes it just feels awkward or something and the words
don't come.

> Your 40-year-old cowboy,
> Buck

---------------------------------- MAILBOX -----------------------------------

TO: BUCK BRAZEMORE X455045A   09:06AM EST
SUBJECT: SNOWBOUND   02-22-93

My Cowboy . . .

I wonder what has happened to our marriages? Do you think everybody our age feels this way? Is it a phase?

There is a rosewood cigar humidor with a silver lid that sits on my
dressing table. I bought it at an antique store on my honeymoon. This
morning, I went and got it and opened it. It was almost a surprise to

discover the pages I had carefully folded and placed inside so many years ago are still there.

The two cream-colored pages on top are Tom's wedding vows. Much to my mother's dismay, we had been married in a small ceremony on the lawn beside a pond behind my parents' home. I had worn a garland of flowers in my hair like the perfect 70s bride. And we had written our own vows. Reading back over them, they are so full of love.

The next six pages are the sheets of a prescription pad from a doctor's office in the little town of Marlington, West Virginia. In pencil, are the words of a passionate letter Tom had written to me while he waited in an examination room for the doctor to come and cast his sprained ankle. It had been written the week after he had proposed to me. We had gone to Snowshoe to ski with some friends as a means of celebrating.

The last two sheets are lined paper which had been torn from a spiral notebook. On them is a poem Tom wrote for me; at one time it had made me cry with joy.

These tender, hot and passionate words seem to be those of some stranger. Or this box has become a little coffin for love. Where did that love go? Did it just get worn down by the abrasion of living until it disappeared?

Perhaps it's a survival thing. I guess you couldn't carry on with the activities of daily living if you had to cope with the electricity of passion continually coursing through your veins. How would anything get done?

The passion I have discovered here entrances me. It doesn't seem to matter that the love is computer-generated. I can't tell the difference, since it has the same effect as real passion. I can't tear myself away from the source of this pleasure long enough to write checks or to feed the dog, and I'm not exaggerating. It has become like a drug for me. What would happen if everyone felt like this? I shudder to think . . . it would probably be utter chaos.

I don't know why I am telling you this. It just seems important for some reason.

Disclosing . . .
Katie

---------------------------------- MAILBOX ----------------------------------

FROM: BUCK BRAZEMORE X455045A   09:47AM EST
SUBJECT: SNOWBOUND   02-22-93

My Dear Katie,

I know exactly what you mean by the death of passion in your marriage. Since you've told your secret, I'll tell you mine.

I suspect Linda and Sparky have been having an affair for some time now, maybe even for ten years—probably longer. I'm gone so much and I've yet to see the fruits of Linda's craft classes. I think they must meet somewhere on Thursday nights. Becky has been Linda's best friend for 30 years; she'd cover for her. Sparky hasn't ever married and I know he's not gay. He's never stopped loving Linda. They're like peas in a pod. I think the problem is they love me, too.

The three of us seem to be drifting, playing parts, protecting each other. Maybe I should just put us all out of our misery and ask Linda for a divorce. But it would put everything out in the open and I don't think I have the stomach for what that would do to us.

For the last two years, I've been thinking she might finally leave me. Every time I get back from a drilling project, I halfway expect to see them standing on the patio waiting for me. They'd be happier and I would, too.

Linda and I have never really matched. But I can remember loving her body and spending many nights on a blanket on the bank of the Guadalupe just buried in the softness of her. Those intense sexual feelings I used to have for her have become blunted over the years.

You're the only person I've ever told about my suspicion. It makes me feel lighter.

                              Confessing,
                              Buck

---------------------------------- MAILBOX ----------------------------------

TO: JOHN W. KELLY JR. A041178A   10:00AM EST
SUBJECT: SNOWBOUND   02-15-93

Dear Jack . . .

It was very pleasant to be greeted by the little ember you left smoldering in my mailbox while I was gone. It has left me feeling warm and toasty (to say the least). "Tingly" is another word which pops to mind. This little game is just what the doctor ordered for my frostbitten libido. <laughing> I will have to search diligently to come up with something to match this latest explicit description of your most secret places. What did you do, use a magnifying glass? How convenient for you that the veining of your penis is an exact replica of the California interstate system. You must never get lost.

My ski trip was exhilarating, but for two days I was snowbound. I really never knew what that word meant until this trip. We were trapped in the lodge for a full 48 hours (although my kids braved the below-zero temperatures, blinding snow and howling wind to slog the twenty feet to the adjacent building where the spa facilities are). Except for the blizzard on Wednesday and Thursday, the rest of the trip was fine. I skied at least 5 hours each day.

I am an accomplished skier with good form, but as a rule, I like to "cruise" rather than test my skills. I generally start out with a few hours on the easy slopes, avoiding the congested ones at the base of the mountain. I take a lift to the ones higher up and less likely to be visited by the rank beginners who have no control. After I warm up, I progress to the intermediate trails and I am content to stay at that level for the rest of the vacation. Although, for a thrill, I might try a relatively tame black diamond (advanced) run once or twice during a week . . . just so I can say I did it. However, this year, I skied black diamond trails every day (except during the snowstorm), and I have the bruises and aching joints to prove it. <laughing>

After we arrived at the lodge, checked in, found our two suites and unloaded everything, my family members took their equipment and left me. I'm used to it. The teenagers and men took off for Mary Jane, one of the peaks in the complex with only expert terrain full of moguls, narrow trails and heart-stopping drops. They didn't even ask if I wanted to come along, since they know I am not usually up for death-defying thrills.

I went in the opposite direction from my family, toward the trails of varying difficulty on Mount Valesquez. As I ascended the mountain, instead of getting off the lift midway like I normally do, so I could take an easy trail to warm up, I took a second lift to the summit. At the top, I had a choice of easy, intermediate, or expert trails and I surprised myself by choosing the advanced one. It was like I was on automatic pilot or something.

I only fell once as I maneuvered down the steep, treacherous path between the trees. I felt young, agile and fearless. On one mogul, my weight shifted and I felt myself losing control, so I sat down and slid maybe forty or fifty (or more) feet through the roughened snow at the edge of the track. When I stopped, my skis were still on my boots and my arms and poles were over my head. I just lay there for a minute in the wonderful cold stillness and then I started laughing hysterically. It had all felt so good, even the fall. It's a good thing no one was around to hear.

With a few exceptions, I skied only expert trails for the rest of the week. Why do I have the feeling this ride we are on is over similar terrain?

> Up for a challenge . . .
> Katie

---------------------------------- MAILBOX ----------------------------------

FROM: JOHN W. KELLY JR. A041178A   10:45AM EST
SUBJECT: SNOWBOUND   02-15-93

My Dear Katie,

I'm glad you're back. And no, our path should not be attempted by the timid.

I wish I had time to send you a nice long letter right this minute. Unfortunately, I have to perform an unplanned heart catheterization at 8:30, so I need to leave in five minutes. I will be back home by noon PST (3:00pm your time), I'll write then.

> Out the door,
> Jack

---------------------------------- MAILBOX ----------------------------------

TO: CAROL BEATTY N771200C   11:04AM EST
SUBJECT: SNOWBOUND   02-15-93

Dear Carol . . .

I have had a busy morning touching base with Buck and Jack. Now, I want to write to you. Although I can tell both of the men almost anything (and do), there are still things I prefer to share with you alone.

During a snowstorm at Winter Park last week, I was trapped inside for long periods of time with Tom. The kids braved the storm to walk across the parking lot to the pool area and video game complex where all the teenagers hung out. Ben was sick in his room.

I could tell Tom was irritable because he and his brother could not engage in their accustomed combat for superiority. But, something else was going on with him, too.

I felt uncomfortable being by myself with my husband. Isn't that odd? I would catch myself looking at him out of the corner of my eye and occasionally I caught him looking at me in the same covert way.

At one point on the second day, after we had both walked over and looked out the window at the wall of flying snow for the umpteenth time, he came over and sat down beside me on the couch. He asked if I remembered the time we had gone to Snowshoe just after we had become engaged (that week seemed to have been one long string of lovemaking sessions). He put his hand under my flannel nightgown, pressed his hand between my legs and began to kiss me on the neck. Although I felt awkward (or guilty or angry) for some unknown reason, I tried to relax and get into the mood. I opened my thighs and rubbed his penis through the fabric of his long underwear.

Carol, this has never happened before, but Tom could not get an erection. I suspect his impotence had something to do with whatever has been bothering him for the past several months and was not a physical thing. Anyway, after about ten minutes of foreplay with no signs of a response from his penis, he was red-faced and gave me this strange pained expression, apologized and mumbled something about the stress of being cooped up. Then he offered to do the laundry, pulled on his jeans and left for the laundry room. He returned with the neatly folded clothes and an artificial elevated attitude. He said he had met a woman from Omaha in the laundry room and had invited her and her husband to join us by the fireplace in the main room of the lodge for some bridge.

Tom and I rarely have sex on ski trips anymore, we are usually just too tired at night and it feels so good just to sleep. And our marital relations in general have settled into a predictable twice monthly kind of rhythm. We do not set any records, that's for sure. However, I do not know what to make of this odd new development.

Thanks for listening.

Your friend . . .
Katie

CONFIDENCES

FROM: CAROL BEATTY N771200C   10:20AM EST
SUBJECT: CONFIDENCES   02-23-93

Dear Katie,

I'm so happy you're back, I'm just dying to talk to you. Sorry for not replying yesterday. I was out shopping almost all day and didn't have time to check my mailbox until this morning.

You know, they say spells of impotence begin to happen when men get over 40. Are you sure this episode with Tom isn't something pretty normal? Maybe you're feeling a tiny bit guilty about your harmless computer affairs and are letting your imagination play some dirty tricks.

In less than two weeks, I'll actually meet Ken in person! Everything is in place. I told Ed I had to go to a seminar in Jacksonville about the new governmental banking regulations in preparation for returning to work in July. He bought it.

My mother lives in Vero Beach and I'm going to swing by there and drop the kids off with her on Friday morning. I'll spend the night at Mom's on the way back Sunday night and drive home on Monday afternoon.

Ken and I have made separate reservations at the Hilton, just in case. I had to give Ed a phone number. He is VERY controlling. If I don't call him at a certain time, he will call me. Also, Mom will need a number and, who knows, Ken and I may not click. We have requested adjoining rooms, though.

I'll pick Ken up at the airport on Friday night. His connecting flight from St. Louis arrives at 8:36. The moment he steps out of the corridor from the airplane will be the first time we lay eyes on each other. It sounds like a scene from a movie, doesn't it? I wonder what it'll be like to see him for the first time? I guess it'll be a little awkward at first. Katie, I've never been this excited in all my born days. It's hard to keep it under wraps.

I've lost 11 pounds and look great even if I do say so myself. All my "baby fat" is gone. My haircut is perfect. Tiffy is content with the bottle and I'm on the pill again.

I have two Victoria's Secret numbers with the price tags still on them. They're hidden in a bag in the closet. I've never bought anything so blatantly sexual in my life, except once when I was single and I bought a vibrator from a catalogue. Actually, I'm the outdoorsy type and usually go to bed in a T-shirt and panties and sometimes socks, if it's cold.

Let me tell you about my new "unmentionables": One's a black lace Merry Widow. It has a push-up bra and satin garters. I bought some sheer black stockings with seams up the back to wear with it. When I looked at myself in the mirror, I almost keeled over. I love this new sexy me! The other thing is a gauzy, low-cut, sapphire blue, long nightgown. It's elegant and gorgeous. I leaves NOTHING to the imagination and has two slits up the sides to the waist. I can just imagine Ken pulling the hem up and pressing me against the wall with the filmy fabric bunched up between us. There I go again!

Are you ready for this? I've also shaved off all my pubic hair. Ken asked me to do it. I actually did it two weeks ago, so I could get used to it and so Ed wouldn't get suspicious. I told him my pubic hair was visible around the leg holes of my new workout outfits and I decided to just whack it all off. It looks really different, but it feels great. That is, IF I shave every other day. Otherwise it gets prickly, and drives me crazy. I guess I'll have to keep it this way unless I want to suffer through letting it grow out again.

Your bald friend, <LOL>
Carol

---------------------------------- MAILBOX ----------------------------------

TO: CAROL BEATTY N771200C   10:45AM EST
SUBJECT: CONFIDENCES   02-23-93

Dear Carol . . .

I must say I am a little jealous. I have wandered into Victoria's Secret a time or two and self-consciously looked at and fingered the pretty lingerie. I always wondered who bought the red teddies, satiny gold bras and lace thong panties. Looking around the shop, it seemed the customers were young women. They looked like they might be secretaries or college students. Some had men with them; I guess they were helping them pick things out. I felt odd and out of place in that store.

I confess I like to sleep in a big T-shirt, too, or a flannel nightgown when it is cold. I wear white or beige briefs (or what my younger sister calls "biggies") and matching, serviceable white or beige bras. When I was young, I remember feeling sexy in my two-piece bathing suit (modest by today's standards) and in my white lacy honeymoon peignoir set. I used to wear bikini panties, too. I guess I stopped wearing them after the twins were born. It just didn't seem appropriate for a mother to wear bikini panties. <laughing> I do remember feeling sexy for a few years in the 70s.

It excites me to think of walking into a store for the sole purpose of buying something to play out an erotic fantasy. A black lace Merry Widow with seamed stockings? A see-through blue nightgown which reveals nipples and a shaven mons? Electrifying!

Thank you for allowing me the vicarious thrill of being in on your adventure. Our letters remind me a little of the late-night conversations I used to have with Ginny in high school. After we returned to our dorm room, we would quiz each other about "how far" we had gone with our dates. It would make my face flame to hear Ginny tell about letting a boy "feel her up" or to confess that I had "touched it."

I feel like I am living two separate lives. This one is my secret life. My real-life friends would be scandalized to know what I do here on the computer every day. Even Ginny, who I told in detail about the first time I touched a naked erect penis and how I had let Bill Foster put his finger inside me, would be stunned beyond belief. I love this secret life and I am glad to have a friend who is sharing my experience.

I wonder where Sue Veneer is. I asked her to send me all the details of her meeting with Cliff. She wrote she would send me a note while I was on my trip. There was nothing from her in my mailbox and she has not responded to the three messages I have e-mailed to her since my return. This is not like Sue! I pulled up her number and discovered she hasn't been on the board in almost a week. I am beginning to get worried about her. I'm afraid something bad might have happened.

Fondly . . .
Katie

---------------------------------- MAILBOX ----------------------------------

TO: SUSAN VENEER G740094D   11:00AM EST
SUBJECT: CONFIDENCES   02-23-93

Dear Jennifer . . .

Where are you? Are you okay? I'm worried sick about you and I miss you. If I haven't heard from you by 5:00 this afternoon, I am going to call your school and have someone check on you. Please write.

Your friend . . .
Katie

---------------------------------- MAILBOX ----------------------------------

FROM: SUSAN VENEER G740094D   3:30PM EST
SUBJECT: CONFIDENCES   02-23-93

Dear Katie,

I'm sorry it has taken me so long to answer all your notes. It makes me feel a little better to know SOMEBODY cares about me.

I just got back to school yesterday. I had to spend last Wednesday night in the Mental Health Center in Terre Haute. My hall monitor took me there after she found me on the floor in the shower. I had my clothes on and was crying as the water poured over me. I don't really remember much of it.

My aunt had to come from Indianapolis. She's my guardian. After they decided I would be okay, she took me home with her for the rest of the week. I'm still sad. :-(

Gary called me a liar and a fat pig. I lost seventeen pounds before he got here. I thought he loved me for what I am inside, but I was wrong. He just took one look, yelled at me and drove off. :-(

You're the only person I can talk to about this. My computer friends are all I have. Will you write back?

> Love,
> Jennifer

---------------------------------- MAILBOX ----------------------------------

TO: SUSAN VENEER G740094D　　　　　　　　　　04:50PM EST
SUBJECT: CONFIDENCES　　　　　　　　　　　　02-23-93

My Dear Jennifer . . .

I am terribly sorry to hear about your sad experience with Gary. Some people are superficial and cruel. Please feel free to write me any time at all to talk about your feelings. I promise I will be your friend.

As difficult as this may seem to you now, the sad feelings will gradually fade. When you are my age, it will be hard to remember the incident at all.

I went to a girls' boarding school for high school. When I was a junior, I climbed down the fire escape one warm early fall night with two of my best friends and we sneaked into town. We ran into two older boys who were outside a bar. They'd been drinking.

The boys took us in their car out to the lake and they almost raped us. We were lucky there were three of us and the boys were too drunk to overpower us. But one of them hurt us. He broke a branch from a sapling and used it as a club. He managed to hit me three times before one of my friends threw a baseball-size rock which hit him in the face. He dropped the branch, fell to his knees and covered his eye with his hands. We escaped then, but ran a long way before we found help. Our legs were scratched and bleeding from being ripped by blackberry canes and one of my friends had a black eye. Fortunately, I was the only one who required stitches. It took seven to close the gash on my cheek.

We got into terrible trouble. All three of us were almost expelled from school (we were put on probation and confined to campus for six months). The other girls' parents were frightened, not to mention furious. My mother practically had a stroke she was so enraged by my scandalous behavior. She gave me the silent treatment when I was at home during the Thanksgiving holiday, and it took years for her to stop carrying a grudge.

The police never found the boys. The bartender said he only remembered them vaguely. There was nothing distinctive about them physically and they were not regular customers. He thought they might have been just passing through. None of us could tell the make of the car, only remembering it was blue.

I still have a faint scar on my right cheek, but aside from that, I don't have any other reminders of that terrible night. It is hard for me to remember many of the details. For example, I can't remember what the boys looked like. Really. Maybe the details of your trauma will fade away, too.

Also, have you noticed the subject on the board entitled, "THE CHAPLAIN'S ROOM"? I scan it sometimes because the man who posts there seems like a very intelligent, kind and caring guy (he is not at all like that fanatic lunatic, Rooney). He is a counselor who used to be a Methodist minister and a chaplain in the Air Force. Anyway, he seems to give comfort and good advice to the people who seek him out. Have you noticed? Why don't you E him?

E me, too, dear Jennifer. I care about you!

With love . . .
Katie

HAPPY TRAILS

FROM: BUCK BRAZEMORE X455045A   06:10PM EST
SUBJECT: HAPPY TRAILS   02-25-93

Sweetheart,

It was exciting talking to you this morning. Thanks for letting me call. Your voice sounds just like I thought it would, pretty and soft. Maybe since we've gotten over the initial awkwardness and newness of it, we might even try some of that phone sex everybody's talking about when I get back in a couple of weeks. What do you think? It sure would give me something to look forward to while I'm in the desert. <G>

Do you remember *The Roy Rogers Show* on TV? At the end, he and Dale always sang, "Happy Trails." Maybe we should sing that duet tonight.

Jimbo and I are leaving early in the morning. We'll drive to San Antonio, hop a short commuter to Houston and then take a nonstop flight to Tel Aviv from there in the early afternoon. I'll be back in Kerrville midmorning on March 15th.

I'm gonna miss you, Katie. Let's go play on the board.

> "Happy trails to yoooouuuuu,
> 'til we meet again,"
> Roy, uh—I mean, Buck

************ ADULT TOPICS BULLETIN BOARD ************

TO: KATHERINE SIMMONS S102248A   06:30PM EST
FROM: BUCK BRAZEMORE X455045A   02-25-93
SUBJECT: HAPPY TRAILS

Dear Katie,

Trigger and I would like to invite you to join us over here on this blanket by the campfire. Gabby is in the chuck wagon rustling us up some grub and we have plenty of time before the stew is ready.

Maybe you would like to pet Trigger while we wait. He really likes it when you pet him! See, he's tossing his head—a sure sign that he has found a friend.

If you want, you can even give him a little lump of sugar. That horse loves your sugar. But, watch out, cuz it might make him drool and I wouldn't want him to slobber all over your cowgirl outfit.

After we chow down, would you like to go for a little moonlight ride? Trigger can be as gentle as you please, or he can go flat out. You pick. He's a steed who's eager to please. He's at your service!

Trigger's master,
Buck

************ ADULT TOPICS BULLETIN BOARD ************

TO: BUCK BRAZEMORE X455045A   06:40PM EST
FROM: KATHERINE SIMMONS S102248A   02-25-93
SUBJECT: HAPPY TRAILS

Why Buck!

I would love to come over and snuggle up on that blanket with you and Trigger. Your steed is so beautiful, strong and proud-looking! I don't think I have ever seen such a pretty one. He looks especially fetching in the firelight with the light kinda flickering over his glossy flanks. I can't resist stroking him.

I'll bet he is responsive and well seasoned, so it will delight me to take you up on your offer of a moonlight ride after dinner. May we go bareback and ride double?

Nuzzling Trigger . . .
Katie

************* ADULT TOPICS BULLETIN BOARD *************

TO: ALL   06:48PM EST
FROM: WAYNE ROONEY F362238A   02-25-93
SUBJECT: HAPPY TRAILS

All Sinners!!!
  Exodus 20:14 "You shall not commit adultery."
  Disobey His Word and pay the price!!!!!

************* ADULT TOPICS BULLETIN BOARD *************

TO: BUCK BRAZEMORE X455045A   06:57PM EST
FROM: CLIFF NOTES L896112C   02-25-93
SUBJECT: HAPPY TRAILS

Howdy Buck!
  Mind if I stop by and roast a weenie over the campfire with you? I
like to wear these chaps without jeans. My apologies to the lady.
  By the way, did you happen to notice this impressive pearl-handled
six-shooter I'm packing? Watch me pick off that tin can on the log over
there. BING!

                          Without my pants, as usual,
                          Cliff

************* ADULT TOPICS BULLETIN BOARD *************

TO: CLIFF NOTES L896112C   07:09PM EST
FROM: BUCK BRAZEMORE X455045A   02-25-93
SUBJECT: HAPPY TRAILS

Cliff,
  I carry a pump-action, sawed-off shotgun, myself. It's a blast! Watch
this—BLAMMO! Incredible recoil, wouldn't you say? It knocked me
clear over into the chuck wagon!

                          Bragging,
                          Buck

************* ADULT TOPICS BULLETIN BOARD *************

TO: CLIFF NOTES L896112C   07:12PM EST
FROM: KENNETH LONG T017643A   02-25-93
SUBJECT: HAPPY TRAILS

Hey there Cliff,
    I'm not impressed. Check out my iron! It is a snub-nose automatic.
Throw a quarter up in the air and watch this. POW! POW! POW!

                        Just call me "Dead-Eye Dick,"
                        Ken

************* ADULT TOPICS BULLETIN BOARD *************

TO: ALL   7:29PM EST
FROM: JOHN W. KELLY JR. A041178A   02-25-93
SUBJECT: HAPPY TRAILS

Greetings,
    Hope you don't mind if I step into the circle of this cozy fire to show
off my piece. You'll notice I sport a loaded revolver. Although it is
something of an antique, it's a handsome weapon, don't you think? It's
a repeater, too.
    I've had a long career as a hunter and I find it's comforting to have
my rod on hand for getting out of sticky situations. Actually, it's pretty
handy for getting into sticky situations, too.

                        A marksman,
                        Jack

************* ADULT TOPICS BULLETIN BOARD *************

TO: KATHERINE SIMMONS S102248A   07:42PM EST
FROM: CAROL BEATTY N771200C   02-25-93
SUBJECT: HAPPY TRAILS

Girlfriend . . .
    Can you believe this!? Any time you get two or more guys together,
they always whip out their guns and start comparing them. Jeez! If they
don't watch out, there will be a shootout or a duel and somebody will
get hurt; sprain a groin muscle or something.

Maybe we should start comparing our holsters. I notice you're sporting an attractive fringed and tooled number. I like my smooth cowhide one, though. However, I'm thinking about getting mine tooled—possibly the weekend after next. <LOL>

Pistol-packing Mama,
Carol

THE CHAPLAIN'S ROOM (III)

************* ADULT TOPICS BULLETIN BOARD *************

TO: ALL   09:09AM EST
FROM: WILLIAM RAMSEY Y082176A   02-26-93
SUBJECT: THE CHAPLAIN'S ROOM

Thought for the week:

It seems many people who become involved in computer love relationships are trying to create perfection. What is the nature of perfection? Can it exist in the real world or is it an ideal? Is a perfect relationship possible? Can any one person fulfill another's every need?

It is my opinion that an individual who expects perfection in any relationship will be disappointed.

> Offering food for thought,
> Will Ramsey
> Professional Contributor,
> Adult Topics Bulletin Board

161

************** ADULT TOPICS BULLETIN BOARD *************

TO: WILLIAM RAMSEY Y082176A   09:56AM EST
FROM: NATALIE STEINER D964573B   02-26-93
SUBJECT: THE CHAPLAIN'S ROOM

Dear Will,

   I'm a 28 yo SWF from Seattle and while I agree some people are
looking for Mr. Perfect on here, I'm not. I'm just looking for a regular
guy in my area who might like to go out on a few dates and see what
happens.

   I've met two guys on the SEATTLE topic of the CONNECTIONS
BB. Although neither one of them turned out to be my type, I think this
is a better way to meet people than the singles' bar scene. You can kind
of start a conversation over the computer before you meet. It's not exactly like a blind date. If you meet in a public place, like a restaurant,
which is where I met my dates, it isn't likely to be dangerous.

                              Not perfect myself,
                              Natalie

************** ADULT TOPICS BULLETIN BOARD *************

TO: NATALIE STEINER D964573B   10:40AM EST
FROM: WILLIAM RAMSEY Y082176A   02-26-93
SUBJECT: THE CHAPLAIN'S ROOM

Dear Natalie,

   You sound like you have a realistic approach to connecting with a
man over the computer. However, from my experience, you are in the
minority. Based upon my research, people often have unrealistic expectations of a partner they meet over the computer and are often disappointed if they actually meet in real life. The disillusionment occurs
mainly in people who are already in some type of committed real-life
relationship, although it frequently happens with singles, as well.

                              Regards,
                              Will Ramsey

************* ADULT TOPICS BULLETIN BOARD ************

TO: WILLIAM RAMSEY Y082176A   10:56AM EST
FROM: JIGOKU SOSHI T936045A   02-26-93
SUBJECT: THE CHAPLAIN'S ROOM

Dear Will,

You are right. I am a graduate student at NYU and for 5 months I was writing to a woman in Maryland who I thought was my dream. It caused problems between my fiancee and me because I spent so much time on the computer and did not want to go out. She eventually broke our engagement and is now seeing another man.

I made plans with my dream to meet in Baltimore in the fall. We met at a restaurant and I was disappointed in her from the moment I first saw her. Although I had seen pictures of her before, she looked different to me. Her voice was not the same as it had seemed over the phone. She was timid rather than outgoing. The woman was not happy with me either. We did not contact one another again after that day.

Now, I'm upset because I gave up my real love for one I created in my imagination. I learned a terrible lesson from trying to bring perfection down to earth.

           Thank you,
           Jigo

************* ADULT TOPICS BULLETIN BOARD ************

TO: JIGOKU SOSHI T936045A   11:44AM EST
FROM: WILLIAM RAMSEY Y082176A   02-26-93
SUBJECT: THE CHAPLAIN'S ROOM

Dear Jigo,

I'm very sorry to hear of your bad experience. If you feel in need of some counseling to aid you in dealing with your sadness, please send me an e-mail message and I'll try to refer you. I've built a very large network of resources through my careers as a chaplain, minister, counselor and writer. Perhaps I can help.

If you do not wish to contact me personally, you may find that the university has a support system which may benefit you. Good luck.

           A friend,
           Will Ramsey

************* ADULT TOPICS BULLETIN BOARD *************

TO: WILLIAM RAMSEY Y082176A   12:26PM EST
FROM: SUSAN VENEER G740094D   02-26-93
SUBJECT: THE CHAPLAIN'S ROOM

Dear Will,

My friend Katie Simmons told me I should write to you because I'm having a hard time. I'm VERY sad because my computer boyfriend broke my heart. :-(

My boyfriend and I have known each other for a long time and he came to visit me last week. I thought he loved me and I was SO happy to finally get a chance to meet him in person. He told me he really needed to see me because he and his wife were probably going to get a divorce soon and he needed to talk to me about it because I have a mature outlook.

I waited for him at the edge of the Wal-Mart parking lot like he asked. I waited for an hour. When I saw the red Nissan driving slowly toward me, I knew it was him. My heart was beating SO fast.

But then everything went wrong. :-(He rolled down the window and said real mean, "YOU aren't Sue Veneer, are you?" When I said, "Yes I am," he cursed me. :-(He told me I was a gross fat pig and he never wanted me to contact him ever again. Before I could open my mouth, he peeled off, leaving me standing in the cold.

I don't remember how I got back to the dorm. I was crying real hard. It sounds crazy, but I walked into the first-floor bathroom, turned on one of the showers, laid down on the floor and let the water pour down on me. I had all my clothes on and I couldn't stop crying. After a while somebody found me.

They took me to the mental health center and my aunt came and took me to her house for a few days. Now I'm back at school, but I still feel SO lonely and sad. :-(Katie said you might be able to help me.

                              Love,
                              Sue Veneer

************ ADULT TOPICS BULLETIN BOARD ************

TO: SUSAN VENEER G740094D   01:04PM EST
FROM: WILLIAM RAMSEY Y082176A   02-26-93
SUBJECT: THE CHAPLAIN'S ROOM

Dear Sue,
     Look in your mailbox right now. I have written a private letter to you.
If you will e-mail the personal information I've requested, I'm pretty
sure I can help you.
     Don't delay.

Your friend,
Will Ramsey

************ ADULT TOPICS BULLETIN BOARD ************

TO: WILLIAM RAMSEY Y082176A   02:01PM EST
FROM: KATHERINE SIMMONS S102248A   02-26-93
SUBJECT: THE CHAPLAIN'S ROOM

Dear Will . . .
     What if a couple keeps a relationship confined to the computer where
it stays a wonderful fantasy? As long as the perfect relationship is seen
as an ideal rather than something which can really exist, isn't it okay?

Your admirer . . .
Katie

P.S. Thank you for helping my friend Sue! I knew you would.

************ ADULT TOPICS BULLETIN BOARD ************

TO: KATHERINE SIMMONS S102248A   03:10PM EST
FROM: WILLIAM RAMSEY Y082176A   02-26-93
SUBJECT: THE CHAPLAIN'S ROOM

Dear Katie,
     What I've seen is most of these relationships don't stay within the
confines of the computer. They branch out. And even in the few cases
where the passion remains in e-mail, the perfection that these liaisons

project often make real life relationships—marriages for example—look dull and shabby by comparison. It makes people discontented with their mates and causes discord where none existed before.

I'm happy to offer what help I can to Sue. Counseling here in computerland has become a calling. It may seem odd to you, but I think of myself as a real chaplain again. I've come out of retirement because I see a great need for ministering in this huge new domain.

Almost without exception, the troubled people who seek advice from me for problems with cyber relationships have other, more serious problems in their real lives. It's become clear to me that a continuing obsession with computer love is only a symptom of some deep and unresolved emotional pain.

Regards,
Will Ramsey

REDHEADS

FROM: JOHN W. KELLY JR. A041178A   10:15AM EST
SUBJECT: REDHEADS   03-02-93

My Sweet Katie,

Yesterday, at the hospital, I found myself looking intently at every woman who had anything resembling red hair—nurses, housekeepers, visitors, you name it. It surprises me how many redheads and how many shades of red hair there are.

During rounds, I was in a patient's room when his daughter walked in and came over and sat in the bedside chair. She might have been a few years younger than you and she wasn't particularly pretty, but she had beautiful shoulder-length auburn hair. She wore a gray sweater and a pair of black slacks. I found myself looking over the chart in my hands at the woman sitting in the chair next to the bed. She had her legs crossed and her elbows resting on the arms of the chair.

I started wondering if her body was anything like yours. Do you have the same fair skin, the freckles, the hollow at the base of your neck? Do you wiggle your foot when you have your legs crossed? How do your breasts move as you breathe?

Sometimes lately when I lie in my bed at night, I try to bring the image I have of you into clearer focus. I can see your coppery hair, olive eyes and your smile. Then I think of all the graphic images you have given me of your sex. I feel the familiar slow burn as my penis becomes rigid with trapped blood. I try to imagine your body—the Titian. I want it. Fantasizing about you gives ME a red head.

Last night, I turned over and rubbed my stiff red dick into the mattress and then into my fist, whispering and then moaning your name. It felt good to stroke my cock and come into my hand, imagining your legs wrapped tight around me.

I don't masturbate much. As a rule, I prefer womanly orifices to my fist lubricated with a little K-Y jelly. When a willing woman is available, it seems a waste to spill my seed on the sheets. Fortunately, women have not been in short supply for most of my adult life. However, beating my meat as I fantasized about you last night left me gasping. It was almost as good as some of the real live sex I've had. Hmmmmm. What would it be like to make it with you in the flesh?

I'm accustomed to being actively pursued by women. It pains me to admit it pleases me to be the quarry. During my marriage I had a few discreet liaisons with women who propositioned me, but after my divorce, it was open season. I screwed my brains out for months.

During a twelve-week spell, this one good-looking nurse regularly gave me head in a locked supply room adjacent to the cardiac catheterization lab at the hospital. Thirty minutes later she was assisting me with procedures.

About 2am one Thursday night, I screwed a young female resident while sitting on a john in a women's bathroom. We dropped our green scrub pants on the floor, but we both kept on our white lab coats. We improvised, using a fresh latex glove from her pocket for a barrier because we didn't want to waste time finding a condom. It was wild.

The two-year spree was fun, and I used rubbers, but I eventually decided the promiscuous behavior was foolishly risky. I didn't want to contract herpes or AIDS, plus, I am just plain too old for those shenanigans. I was relieved to settle down with Jan.

It dawned on me last night just after I masturbated that I've been waiting and willing for you to seduce me. My ego has been chafing because you haven't made overtures to me yet, other than giving me the tantalizing and detailed descriptions of your body I've asked for as we have played "doctor." The other women on the board immediately started wooing me with hot e-mail when they discovered I was a physician <laughing ruefully> I was expecting it from you and began wondering if I'd lost my status.

This morning, I can see my egotism for what it is and deliberately put it aside. I'm learning this skill in AA and it feels strange and good to practice it.

It would excite me if you'd share something erotic you sent to Buck.

Did you keep copies of the explicit e-mail you sent to him? I kept copies of a few of the messages I sent to other women. Perhaps we could exchange samples of our past hot e-mail as a way to begin our own adventure. It would be like starting a fire with kindling. Let's be voyeurs.

Wanting more of you,
Jack

------------------------------------ MAILBOX ------------------------------------

TO: JOHN W. KELLY JR. A041178A   10:55AM EST
SUBJECT: REDHEADS   03-02-93

My Dear Voyeur . . .
The main reason we are here in the Mexican Caribbean is because of its proximity to several Mayan ruins. Pre-Columbian art, architecture and culture have always been fascinating to me; so, you are indulging me with this trip into the interior of the Yucatan Peninsula to see the great center at Chichen Itza. It is a three-hour trip to the ruins and we are about halfway there. You are driving like a bat out of Hell down the straight road in our rented convertible.

I put some classical music in the tape player and begin telling you how much I would like to make love to you when we reach our destination. I tell you how I would love to go down on you in the Observatory, then I want to feel your tongue pressing up into me as you kneel before me on the top step of the Great Pyramid (and as I look down from that vertigo-inducing height). I want to couple face to face on the ball field and bending over the altar where the human hearts were offered to the Rain God. I want to be pressed up against the wall in the Temple, surrounded by phallic symbols and fertility signs, and be impaled by you. Let's worship sex the way the Maya did!

You reach for my hand and guide it to your lap where I can feel your erection beginning to grow. I have on a colorfully embroidered Mexican dress; I pull it up to my waist then pull down my panties, kicking them onto the floor. My knees open to you as your hand moves between my legs, your middle two fingers slide up into my lubricating vagina and your thumb finds my clitoris. My head rolls back against the seat as I luxuriate in the sensation produced by sun, wind and fingers. We speed along, surrounded by the romance of Ralph Vaughn Williams's, "Lark Ascending," and sexual electricity. I shudder and moan as you lift me up rapturously to orgasm, hearing the wet sounds of your fingers thrusting into me blending with the music.

You do not move your hand, it cups my sex gently until I look over at you with half-closed, satisfied eyes. Then, you withdraw and, with your wet fingers, lead my hand again to your erection. I unbuckle your belt and unzip your fly as you pull off onto the next dirt road into the jungle. We jolt down the lane just until the highway is no longer in view. You park under a tree which is festooned with the gorgeous magenta blooms of a bougainvillea vine.

You pull off your shorts and underwear. I hike my dress up further and giggle as I try to straddle your erection without crushing myself against the steering wheel.

Your breathing comes in gasps as you put your hands on my naked bottom and guide me down over your rigid penis. I slowly lower myself until your shaft is totally contained, as you cover my neck with hungry kisses and begin to push rhythmically up into me. Your head drops down until your damp forehead rests against the embroidered fabric over my breasts; I can hear and feel your little grunts close to my chest as you try to push deeper into my body. I love this sensation of being pinned between your relentless phallus and the steering wheel.

You cannot move as much as you would like; so, we recline your seat back as far as possible so I can move on you. I look down at your face and find it glistening with sweat. Your eyes are closed and your mouth is slack with passion. I adore the abandon reflected there. I bend down to you and we revel in an amazing face-eating kiss as I writhe over you. Your hands travel down to where we meet, the fingers of one hand exploring my distended labia with the shaft of your penis moving in and out between them as the fingers of your other hand slide down into the moist cleft of my bottom.

The pace quickens. Using my thighs, I thrust up against you mightily, gleaming with the sweat of my exertion. We are surrounded by the wonderful juicy sounds of our coupling which intensifies our passion.

Suddenly, both your hands grasp the pliant naked skin of my bottom and you pull me tight against you as your penis begins to twitch within me, filling my wet velvety interior with jets of semen. I reach down and manipulate myself for the few seconds it takes for me to come again. We gasp and moan with the joy of it.

Our breathing and heartbeats eventually return to normal, your penis gradually retracts from the folds of my sex and the warm pearly fluid we made together begins to seep from my body and onto your legs . . . a libation to the Rain God.

The Priestess . . .
Katie

---------------------------------- MAILBOX -----------------------------------

FROM: JOHN W. KELLY JR. A041178A   11:42AM EST
SUBJECT: REDHEADS   03-02-93

Katie!
You can imagine my response to your fantasy set in the sultry Mexican jungle. You turned me into a "redhead" again, and a natural one, at that. For your enjoyment, I'm sending a copy of a fantasy I wrote for the woman who lives in Massachusetts. Are you in the mood for a quickie? I'm finding it very exciting to play the voyeur, are you?

****

As I open the door, I see your reflection in the mirror. You're here, just as we've planned. We can hear the sounds of the party through the floor, but this is an out-of-the-way bathroom and we're not likely to be caught. However, I lock the door to be safe.

I stand behind you and watch in the mirror as my arms go around you and my hands knead your breasts through black velvet. I only spend a moment to savor the feel of your soft breasts through the wonderful texture of the fabric because we must hurry. I quickly tug your short, straight skirt up to your waist and liberate my cock.

You bend over the sink, bracing your hands on either side. I see that you are wearing a garter belt without panties just as I had asked. My hand opens you and I groan as I shove my insistent manhood into your wetness. My tanned fingers spread across the whiteness of your ass and we look into each other's passion-filled eyes in the mirror as I begin to move. I must look down to where we meet so I can see my dick sinking into you. My first strokes are slow, but soon I bend slightly forward, finding the ridges of your pelvis with my fingers. Then I begin rapidly lunging into you. This is what we wanted! My face registers my abandon and it makes you gasp and push back against me as you watch in the mirror.

My hand dives under you to find your clitoris. Your hand is already there, but I push it away and begin rubbing you to the rhythm of my thrusting.

Your face is close to the mirror and I watch it change as you approach orgasm. As you press your hand against your mouth to keep from crying out, I fold over you and gripping the cool porcelain I drive into you wildly. I feel my balls tighten and there is a line of fire in my cock as the semen rushes down its length and erupts into your hot cunt. I press my chest against your back and groan in oblivion as my dick spasms inside you. My heart pounds against you and I whimper with pleasure close to your ear.

We disengage and face each other for the first time. I take your cheeks in my hands and kiss you deeply—a little of your lipstick comes off on my collar and the pressure of my thumb leaves a reddened spot on your jaw.

We adjust our clothing. You reapply your lipstick and powder and pull a pair of lace panties out of your evening bag and slip them on— you don't want to leave a telltale trail on our host's carpet.

Then, I leave first and you follow in a minute or two. The only evidence of our passion is a small smudge of lipstick and a fading red spot on your chin.

Just a guest at the party,
Jack

--------------------------------- MAILBOX ---------------------------------

TO: CAROL BEATTY N771200C   10:00AM EST
SUBJECT: REDHEADS   03-04-93

Dear Carol . . .

Jack and I have made the leap to hot e-mail! For the past three days we have been sending fantasies to each other under the title, RED-HEADS (an allusion to my hair and his erection). There was an incendiary device in my box this morning involving a scene of gentle bondage! He is getting a little kinky . . . and I adore it! Exotic acts have not been in my real life sexual repertoire. Tom has always been a very conventional sex partner . . . but then, so have I. We might have missed the boat.

Did you notice there are two different kinds of hot e-mail? First, there are the florid and grandiose fantasies that have settings and are almost like screenplays. It seems the emphasis is on the scenario and the surroundings. The second kind is much more personal and seems to well up out of real feelings. It usually doesn't involve a special location or costumes. Do you know what I mean? Did you and Ken experience this or is it just me?

Anyway, Jack and I are in the flamboyant, "bodice ripper" stage now. Tuesday, we even sent copies of things we had written to other people. I sent him two things I had created for Buck and he sent me some things he had sent another woman. It didn't bother me at all that he had written the fantasies for the other woman. Actually, it was exciting . . . kind of like peeking. I have always wanted to watch another couple make love, have you?

Yesterday, Jack wrote something especially for me. He spun a fantasy about making love against the rough wall of a barn in the late afternoon sunlight. The scenario included a lengthy session of cunnilingus as foreplay. He writes artfully and precisely and REALLY gets into it! I could see the action so clearly it gave me goose bumps!

Last night was one of those rare ones when Tom was home. About ten minutes after my husband turned off his reading light and assumed his normal sleeping position, I sneaked into the loft and wrote a senario for Jack about screwing in a bathtub. Just writing it made me very warm. <laughing> And I liked the risk factor of having Tom in the next room sleeping. When I returned to our bed, I woke Tom up by coaching his penis to life. I will be perfectly content to stay in this place for a while, stewing in my sexual juices.

Buck has been my only e-mail lover and he is delightful, but there is something about Jack that makes my toes curl. He is intense and willing to totally surrender to abandon. He makes me feel a little out of control. He makes me hungry. I'm kind of glad Buck will be out of the country for awhile.

This weekend I am going down to visit my sister in Atlanta (it's a 4-hour drive). I got her to make a hairdresser's appointment for me with this man named Carmen. He is supposed to be the best. One of my friends drives down to Atlanta every three weeks to get him to cut her hair. He costs a fortune, but her hair looks great all the time. Anyway,

I have been looking through all the magazines for something new. Last month's *Vogue* said the hottest cut for this spring and summer is a "shag." If Carmen thinks it will suit me, that is what I want. I want to look hot.

> Your sexually active friend . . .
> Katie

---------------------------------- MAILBOX ----------------------------------

FROM: CAROL BEATTY N771200C   10:50AM EST
SUBJECT: REDHEADS   03-04-93

Dear Katie,

What good news to hear you and Jack are finally getting it on! I'm sure you are both relieved.

Yes, I know what you mean about hot e-mail. When Ken and I first started writing it, we'd set elaborate scenes. Sometimes we even chose different time periods and characters for our hanky-panky. For example, we had a lot of fun being Robin Hood and Maid Marian for awhile. We would screw in Sherwood Forest, in the tower and under the banquet table. <LOL>

At some point, it changed and got serious, just like you said. It was then that the horniness got out of control. It wasn't long after when we took our passion to the phone. Phone sex makes a shift, too. We felt we would die if we didn't meet. At least that is the way it worked for us.

Tomorrow, my computer affair becomes real. I wonder what's in store for me.

> Wish me luck,
> Carol

ARTISTS

FROM: JOHN W. KELLY JR. A041178A   10:10AM EST
SUBJECT: ARTISTS   02-08-93

Dear Katie,

I'm glad you find my erotica "artistic." I could use the same word to describe yours and I suspect you must have creative ability; I do.

As a matter of fact, at one time in my life I aspired to be an artist, a painter. My talent was identified when I was about ten. A well-meaning teacher at the small rural school I attended tried to encourage me. When I was 12 she gave me a volume about the life and work of Pierre Bonnard from her private collection of art books.

As I leafed through it, I came across a black and white photograph of "Nude in a Bathtub" which Bonnard painted in 1936. I was riveted to the page and developed an instant boner in reaction to the erotic image. Instinctively my hand sought my inflated dick and within seconds, I experienced my first ejaculation. I've dedicated a special place in my heart for the Frenchman's work ever since. <G>

On a trip to Paris in 1986, Gretchen and I visited the Petit Palais and I saw "Nude in a Bathtub." It's strange how age had changed my perspective. As a man in my 40s, instead of being aroused by the rendering of the naked, youthful, female figure, I was subdued by it.

Except for splashes and dots of yellow, blue is the predominant color in the work. Although there's a little pinkness in the abdominal and pubic areas, the body appears cyanotic and the face is obscured, as if covered by a shroud or veil. It seemed the young woman could be dead and lying in a coffin instead of languidly enjoying her bath. Or possibly she had just drowned.

Gretchen was 32 then and at the peak of her physical beauty. I used to love to watch her lying naked in a tub of water. I frequently asked her to take a bath before we made love, just so I could watch. The hot water made her skin bloom a deep pink. The visual stimulation was my favorite prelude to hands-on foreplay.

When we returned to the hotel room later that evening in Paris, I asked Gretchen to take a bath and pose like the woman in Bonnard's painting we had seen earlier in the day. She grudgingly complied. However, I had consumed two bottles of Merlot with dinner and was too drunk to pursue intercourse. Actually, I fell asleep, sitting naked on the bidet beside the tub with my back propped against the tile wall. When I woke up a few hours later, the tub was empty and I was freezing.

I remember standing up and looking at my reflection in the mirror. I didn't like what I saw. My hair was disheveled and my face was greenish and haggard. I looked ancient. I looked like my father the week before he died.

The Tuesday after Gretchen and I returned from France, I attended my first AA meeting. It marked the beginning of both my great struggle with my disease and the decline of my marriage.

Telling secrets,
Jack

---------------------------------- MAILBOX ----------------------------------

TO: JOHN W. KELLY JR. A041178A   11:07AM EST
SUBJECT: ARTISTS   02-08-93

Dearest . . .

Yes, I also possess artistic talent, but not enough. Fortunately, I realized this about myself early and did not pursue a degree in the applied arts only to fail. Instead I opted to study art history. I figure I saved myself a lot of pain.

Nothing is more pathetic than a determined artist who cannot quite make the grade. I have read about such people, living miserable impoverished lives and frequently committing suicide. Also, my mother made it clear a degree in art history was socially acceptable, while a degree in applied arts was unseemly for a young woman of my station in life. In her opinion, most artists are "tacky." Luckily I am perfectly content collecting other people's art instead of making it myself.

I own eight works on paper by Delphine Crabtree, a 70-year-old North

Carolina artist who has gotten a lot of international publicity lately. She has a mental condition known as bipolar disease. Since you are a doctor, you probably know all about the disorder. The afflicted used to be called manic/depressives. Since I own a collection of Delphine's work, I have read quite a bit about her mental problems.

The lithium Delphine takes allows her to lead a pretty normal life eight or nine months out of the year. However, for about two months each year she is immobilized with depression and must be hospitalized. Then, the artist must be assisted with even the basic activities of daily living. She must be diapered, fed, bathed and clothed like an infant.

The six to eight weeks a year when she is in the escalating manic phase of her illness is the period during which she creates her incredible and now famous artwork. She does not require hospitalization then and is able to work in her studio if she has an attendant present at all times.

Delphine Crabtree is known for the female figures she draws. She produces over fifty works (using colored pencils, crayons and pastels) each year when the mania drives her. Several respected galleries in the South, one in New York and one in LA represent her and she has become rich.

I met her once about ten years ago, just as she was being "discovered," at the opening of a one-woman show at the Mint Museum here in Charlotte. Luckily, I admired her work so much back then that I bought eight pieces over the next three years. These days, even her smallest drawings carry five-figure price tags. I cannot afford any more additions to my collection.

My favorite piece by Delphine Crabtree is not one I own. It was recently installed at MOMA in New York. It is a large chaotic work, but the three figures in it are clear. The small one in the left foreground is a colorful rendering of a little girl on a swing. The form in the middle is a smiling young woman. She is standing spread-eagle, with her legs braced open and with her arms flung wide. It is possible to make out the shape of a fetus superimposed over her torso. All around the woman, in red crayon, are bananalike forms (I suppose these represent erect penises). The third female in the group is far over to the right in the composition, near the edge. She is dark and skeletal with ancient breasts. She wears a capelike garment which looks from a distance to be made of some sort of print material. However, under closer scrutiny it is easy to read the word "me" written over and over again on the cape in white on the black background.

As I read over this letter it occurs to me that not only artists who fall short, but also great ones, are doomed to lives of torment. Take Van Gogh and Delphine Crabtree as examples. I am sure there are exceptions, but the odds seem pretty high that an individual who choses a life of artistic expression will suffer.

Why did you choose not to be a painter?

An art lover . . .
Katie

---------------------------------- MAILBOX ----------------------------------

FROM: JOHN W. KELLY JR. A041178A   01:15PM EST
SUBJECT: ARTISTS   02-08-93

Dear Katie,

God, our brains are in tune! It stuns me. Like you, I believe many artists, both the successful and unsuccessful ones, are condemned to lives of misery. I was a witness. My father was a musician and he wanted more than anything in the world to be a great composer.

My parents met in 1930 in a music-composition class at Trevor College, a small Lutheran institution which originally formed the hub of my little hometown in Ohio. My mother was a student and my father was the instructor. It was his first job.

I'm guessing, but I think my mother became pregnant with my brother in the spring of that year. They were married in June and my brother was born six months later. He was a big strapping boy. There was little evidence he might have been premature.

The college folded two years later in the Depression and my father was forced to look for other work to support his family. Eventually he settled for a job as a traveling salesman for the Kitchen Magician Company. Are you too young to remember the days when the "Kitchen Magician Man" sold cleaning supplies and cooking utensils door to door?

After the Depression subsided, my father didn't resume his career as a college music teacher. He had family obligations and could make more money as a salesman. However, he continued to try to compose music during his free time. When I was six, he sold a jingle to a cookie company in Cincinnati. Soon after that my father stopped sitting at the piano.

I think his growing frustration at being unable to create the music he dreamed of making is why my father surrendered to alcohol. Vodka anesthetized him so he couldn't feel the pain.

In 1952, when I was thirteen, I won the $300 grand prize for a painting my teacher entered in a competition in Chicago. However, that was also the year I decided not to be a painter.

In January, my older brother was killed in Korea and my father died of a heart attack two weeks later. Undoubtedly, my father's heart had been weakened by his years of heavy drinking. The grief was more than I could handle.

An artist's life was not for me. But it seems I followed in my father's footsteps to one destination. I became an alcoholic.

> A chip off the old block,
> Jack

I WANT DETAILS!

TO: CAROL BEATTY N771200C   10:03AM EST
SUBJECT: I WANT DETAILS!   03-09-93

Dear Carol . . .

Please, don't keep me in suspense! How did the weekend with Ken go? I am dying of curiosity!

Your Friend . . .
Katie

FROM: CAROL BEATTY N771200C   11:28PM EST
SUBJECT: I WANT DETAILS!   03-09-93

Dear Katie,

Sorry I didn't e-mail you yesterday. Please don't hate me. This is the first chance I've had to write.

When the alarm went off, I got up like a sleepwalker. Somehow I managed to get Eddie ready for the bus, changed Tiffy, gave her a bottle and put her in the playpen, but then I got right back in bed. I had to— I'm still really tired. The phone woke me up at 10:00. It was Ken and we talked for about an hour. He says he slept all the way home on the plane and he didn't go into work yesterday. Did I tell you he owns a small subcontracting and construction company? Anyway, his business is slow in winter and early spring, so it isn't the end of the world.

Last weekend contained the most valuable 48 hours of my life. It wasn't the sex orgy you're probably imagining, quite the contrary. Ken

180

and I didn't have sex or stay in the same room. Although it's true we didn't get much sleep, it wasn't for the reasons you might expect. We cried and held hands a lot and we talked until we couldn't talk anymore. We've both needed someone to listen.

I told him how terrified I've become of Ed over the past two years and Ken told me the story of how his wife left him for another woman. We've felt lonely, isolated and ashamed for so long. The release and comfort of finally finding someone to talk to without embarrassment or fear has been overwhelming.

Our meeting at the airport was like a scene out of a movie. There was no hesitation, we just moved to each other like we were magnetized. I can't really describe the first instant when our bodies touched, there are simply no words for it. We just held on to each other for the longest time. But there wasn't electricity arcing between us, just some kind of magnificent relief in finally being able to see and touch each other.

The drive to the hotel wasn't awkward, it was exhilarating. I'd already checked in, so I waited in the lounge until he checked in and took his things up to his room; then he joined me at the bar. We drank coffee and talked and talked like we'd known each other all our lives. When the bar was empty and it seemed like they were waiting to close, we moved to some chairs in the corner of the lobby. Finally, at 3:30 we went up to our adjoining rooms. You might think this sounds strange, but although we slept in separate rooms both nights, we opened the door between them and left it open.

On Saturday, we walked for miles and talked about our childhoods. Although my mother tried to hide it from me, I knew my father beat her when he'd been drinking. Once when I was very young, she bundled me up and we spent the night in the car. It was cold and I remember feeling confused about why I had to leave my warm bed. As I grew older, and her explanations of the bruises and red marks seemed contrived, I put two and two together, but we never talked about it, even after my father died.

On Sunday, I spent the night at Mom's house instead of driving straight back to Orlando. I finally got the courage to talk to her about abuse—her husband's and mine. It was an emotional night, but we're better for it, we're feeling unburdened.

In retrospect, I don't know why Ken and I didn't sleep together this past weekend. It would've been easy and we certainly had planned on it and talked about it. We've masturbated with each other over the phone and neither one of us seems inhibited. It just didn't seem appropriate, that's all I can say.

I remember being surprised when you told me it was not sex you were looking for in computerland. Maybe sex is really not what Ken and I are looking for either. We each seem to need a true friend who could understand our shame. Although we decided we would still enjoy playing our little games on the public BB because they're fun, the sexy talk is all an act now. Isn't this a strange development?

Your friend,
Carol

---------------------------------- MAILBOX -----------------------------------

TO: CAROL BEATTY N771200C   01:04PM EST
SUBJECT: I WANT DETAILS!   03-09-93

Dear Carol . . .

Lately, I have been wondering what draws us to experiment with relationships in computerland. I suspect we all (at least the people I have come to know) are looking for something other than love or sexual excitement. However, you are right, I am totally surprised by the report of your weekend. It turned out to be unlike any of the possible scenarios I had pictured. You found a compassionate and empathetic friend rather than a lover.

I would like to be a better friend to you, Carol. I am feeling the frustration with the limitations of e-mail which Will Ramsey pointed out not long ago in one of his "thoughts for the week." May I call you? Please tell me when you're available.

This whole week I will have painters underfoot; we are having the whole downstairs painted. They arrived first thing this morning in their coveralls, carrying ladders, scaffolding and drop cloths. In no time they had set up camp.

I hate to have workmen in my house! The fact that I need to be available for their questions irritates me, and it also gives me a strange feeling to hear their movements and fragments of conversation in the heart of my "territory." I always feel a little unsafe with strangers around.

Today, I started tackling some domestic chores in the bedroom and dressing area. That space is furthest from the downstairs and, if I keep the door closed, I can't really hear the painters moving around. A minute ago, one came to the stairwell and called up, "Lady?" I went into the loft to answer his question and after he left, I went over and sat down at the computer.

As the computer began to boot up with that whirring sound, I also heard a burst of muffled, raucous male laughter coming from the utility room. The laughter made me cringe with paranoia; however at the same instant I saw the NEW MAIL flashing and it occurred to me my behavior is contradictory. I hate having strange men in my house, yet here I sit at my computer, inviting a strange "new male" into my house. In different ways, the painters and Jack and Buck are providing me with a fresh new beginning. I will think about what this means later.

Your friend . . .
Katie

---------------------------------- MAILBOX ----------------------------------

TO: SUSAN VENEER G740094D   03:06PM EST
SUBJECT: I WANT DETAILS!   03-09-93

Dear Jennifer . . .

In your last e-mail, you told me you have been corresponding with "The Chaplain" and he is helping you. I haven't heard from you in more than a week. Don't keep me in the dark! What is happening?

Curious . . .
Katie

---------------------------------- MAILBOX ----------------------------------

FROM: SUSAN VENEER G740094D   05:06PM EST
SUBJECT: I WANT DETAILS!   03-09-93

Dear Katie,

Thank you SO much for telling me about Will Ramsey ("The Chaplain"). :-) He's the nicest man I ever met! He's interesting, too. He was one of the first black chaplains in the Air Force and he DID serve in Vietnam. He told me he knows how it feels to have people judge you on how you look.

Last week, he sent me the name of the Methodist church closest to campus and he sent an Internet message about me to the Youth Minister there. The minister's wife called me on Wednesday and invited me to church and to have lunch with them and some of the kids in the college youth group afterwards. The minister's name is Jeff Chapman and his wife's name is Sharon. They're young and happy about expecting their first baby in October. They're sweet and kind and I like them a lot.

Jeff says there's a woman veterinarian who is a deacon in their congregation and they asked me if I'd like to meet her. Sharon said maybe I could even work for her some. That would be so great. Anyway, they said they would introduce us next Sunday. I'm SO excited!

I don't feel as bad about Gary anymore. He really is too old for me anyway. He's bald.

> Love,
> Jennifer

PIGS

TO: JOHN W. KELLY JR. X455045A   10:45AM EST
SUBJECT: PIGS   03-10-93

Dearest . . .

I own a whimsical collection of pigs. Several years ago I bought a pig key chain to act as a reminder while I was dieting. The charm worked because I lost the 15 pounds I set out to lose. Ever since, I have taken the animal as my totem. The swine has become my protective spirit, my guardian angel, if you will. There are several around my house, in nooks and crannies. They are reminders of my nature (as if I need reminding).

"I WANT MORE!" That's my slogan; perhaps I should have it emblazoned on a sweat shirt. Or maybe it could be embroidered on a little banner underneath a little piggy face on a line of pig-logo sportswear. Who knows, it could become the rage among addicts of all kinds.

I have really become a pig where this computer-induced abandon is concerned. It has changed me. It makes me feel sexy, confident, powerful and alive! These feelings are not figments of my imagination and their effects on me are not illusions. I really do feel and look better than I have in ten years. And people are noticing the change in me.

From this vantage point, it is easy to understand why people bogged down in middle age have affairs. It is amazing how passion becomes an antidote for the creeping grayness and ennui, isn't it?

It delights me that you allow me to wallow in you morning, noon and night. I crave you constantly and want to gorge myself at the computer which has become my trough. I want more!

Oink! Oink!
Katie

---------------------------------- MAILBOX ----------------------------------
FROM: JOHN W. KELLY JR. X455045A   11:09AM EST
SUBJECT: PIGS   03-10-93

Darling Piggy,

It's funny you have chosen pigs to be your totems. They should be mine, too. In addition to being a symbol of my gluttonous nature, pigs are actually responsible for much of my practice's financial success. The sterling reputation of Marin Cardiovascular Center was founded upon our expertise in the area of porcine mitral valve replacements, that is, exchanging healthy pig heart valves for damaged human ones.

One of the by-products of harvesting pig heart valves is pig carcasses. Since the corporation owns the animals and the small slaughterhouse where the valves are removed under sterile conditions, the meat is the property of the practice. As a result, my freezer is full and I've learned to prepare an amazing array of pork dishes. I even bought a US Range, which is a restaurant-grade gigantic cooktop and oven, so I can roast a whole pig.

A porker would be a fitting emblem for my coat of arms, too. <LOL> Let's design one. How about a pair of rutting swine on a red computer screen?

I confess, I'm losing interest in Janet. For the past five weeks, I've been fantasizing about you when we have sex. At first I thought it was healthy.

Last night we went out for pizza. She had been in Portland on business for two weeks and yet I found myself feeling irritable and resentful that I had to be away from my computer and you. She even snuggled up to me and put her hand on my cock under the tablecloth, whispering she would like to spend the night. She was hurt when I gave her some lame excuse about having to go into the hospital early today. She probably suspects I'm having an affair—I am.

What's the matter with me? Here I have this lovely, flesh-and-blood woman I care about who wants to screw me, and all I want is you. Am I affecting your relationship with Tom?

It's true I can't get enough of you and always want more! In my entire life, I've never experienced such exquisite emotion. It's mindboggling, but the erotic pleasure I'm getting from our connections is better than most of the real-life sex I've ever had. But that's not all. I can tell you my secrets. And I've come to care about you. No, let's call a spade a

spade—I've come to love you. The rational part of me can take a hike.
I'll take whatever this is, Katie, and be grateful!

> Just call me "Porky,"
> Jack

---------------------------------- MAILBOX ----------------------------------

TO: CAROL BEATTY N771200C   11:29AM EST
SUBJECT: PIGS   03-10-93

Dear Carol . . .

Buck will be home in less than a week. I have been trying to decide
how I will manage both my computer lovers when he gets back. It seems
impossible.

Jack and I write to each other at least four times a day and usually
more often. Writing letters to him takes hours of my time, he wants so
much of me. I can't get enough of him either. Some of our notes are
full of the mundane details of our lives, others hold secrets and still
others are dripping with passion and descriptions of kinky sex.

We both seem hungry for the same things. We long for the purification
of confession and we are both gluttons where the sex is concerned. I
enjoy Jack's demands . . . he pushes me hard to consider new ideas about
love-making and I admit to craving the freshness of his approach more
than Buck's rather romantic and conventional one.

Buck has said he wants to try phone sex when he gets back. I confess,
I would like to try it, but with Jack instead. However, if I try phone sex,
will I be on the slippery slope like you and Will Ramsey say? And, if I
add the dimension of phone sex, where will I get the energy to satisfy
both my lovers?

Maybe my only recourse is to give one of them up . . . but I don't
want to do that. I love them both. I really do . . . I'm such a pig. So
THIS is what it feels like to be a polygamist.

A few weeks ago, on a rainy Sunday afternoon, I watched an old Cecil
B. DeMille movie, *Samson and Delilah*, on TV. Do you remember this
spectacular old flick? It stars a handsome, virile Victor Mature and a
young, ravishing Hedy Lamarr.

DeMille movies are such fun. They are extravagant and gorgeous and
totally unbelievable. *Samson and Delilah* would have one believe the
Gaza of Biblical times was like some sparkling clean circus. Philistines
clank around in gleaming golden suits of armor, complete with giant

sunflowerlike helmets; townspeople parade about in splendid, jewel-encrusted garments; and Hedy slinks around in one fabulous, glittering, midriff-bearing ensemble after another. I love it! I wonder what it was really like in that sun-baked and dusty corner of the world a few thousand years ago.

During the movie and after, I pondered the Delilah character. This woman uses her sexual confidence to control men . . . she makes them her slaves. Delilah is much more powerful than the subservient, guilt-wielding Danite woman whom she sees as her rival for Samson's love. All the Philistines, men and women, are vocal in their praise of her. Really, if you think about it, even without the awesome added ingredient of God's favor, she is at least as powerful as Samson.

I can confess this to you . . . playing at being the temptress and the power it gives me over men is the real appeal computer relationships have for me (although, don't get me wrong, I enjoy the sexual titillation as well). I have been at the mercy of men all my life and have served them. I love turning the tables. It makes me feel invincible and young. In real life, I can't wield this power anymore.

Recently, Jack asked whether our computer affair was having an effect on my marriage (apparently it is making him unsatisfied with his real-life lover, Janet). I am avoiding the question. The truth of the matter is our computer passion is having an effect on my marriage, but it is a good one.

As a result of our hot e-mail, I find myself in a state of almost constant (yet, in varying degrees) arousal. I have developed new confidence in my allure and have become aggressive in bed with Tom. Since we got back from Colorado, there has been no evidence of impotence. We have had intercourse several times. I have had no qualms about waking him up in the middle of the night or before dawn to initiate sex. I have become uninhibited, experimental and vocal. Tom is responding. He asked me the other day whether I had decided to take the hormone therapy for menopause after all. <laughing>

Tom is becoming a different man. His eyes have begun to sparkle again when he looks at me and his physical displays of affection have become more frequent. He has been coming home earlier. He even asked me if I wanted to go out to dinner and a movie on Friday night . . . by ourselves. We haven't had a ''date'' in ages.

Just call me ''Delilah'' . . .
Katie

---------------------------------- MAILBOX ----------------------------------

TO: CAROL BEATTY N771200C   11:50AM EST
SUBJECT: PIGS   03-10-93

Dear Katie,

I don't share your hunger for power over men. I really love the support and kindness I get from Ken. He's such a pleasure after what I get from Ed. All Ed cares about is himself. He is hard and cruel and over the years he has become meaner and meaner.

Hey, you haven't told me about your new hair style. Are you totally gorgeous?

> Your friend,
> Carol

---------------------------------- MAILBOX ----------------------------------

TO: CAROL BEATTY N771200C   02:17PM EST
SUBJECT: PIGS   03-10-93

Dear Carol . . .

My hair looks great! Carmen gave me a short "shag" cut and I am just crazy about it. It is a youthful hairstyle. My sister, Marilyn, went nuts when I walked out. Right then and there, she made an appointment for herself for next Tuesday.

After my trip to the hairdresser's, we went to Morrowfield, a nearby upscale shopping mall. At the Lancôme counter in one of the stores, a makeup artist was doing makeovers and I had one. Usually, I wear only a little light coral lipstick and some blush, but I told him I wanted "the whole nine yards." Marilyn told me I looked gorgeous and that was all the impetus I need to buy $287.00 worth of creams and cosmetics.

The lipstick shade I bought is called "Fauve." The French word means "wild beast" or "savage." I love the idea of having a savage, vermilion mouth! <laughing>

My marriage seems to be improving as a result of my experiments with computer love. Something nice and unexpected happened when I returned home a little after noon on Sunday. Tom was bending over his laptop computer at the dining room table when I came in and asked where the twins were. Without looking up, he told me they had gone to friends' houses and wouldn't be home until after dinner. Then he looked up and his mouth dropped open. He liked my new look and he told me so.

Anyway, I went into the kitchen and started making some sandwiches for lunch. I was standing in front of the sink washing a tomato when he walked up behind me, pressed himself against me and whispered it would be fun to take advantage of the boys' absence by going up to our bedroom. I was stunned! We made love in broad daylight at 1:00 in the afternoon. It has been a long time since we did anything so spontaneous.

> Just call me . . .
> Fauve

---------------------------------- MAILBOX ----------------------------------

FROM: CAROL BEATTY N771200C   02:36PM EST
SUBJECT: PIGS   03-10-93

Dear Katie,
 You're lucky! It looks like some of your computer-induced sexiness is slopping over into your real life. Tom sounds like a much nicer guy than Ed.
 In an earlier note, you asked if you could call me. I'd love to talk to you on the phone sometime. Could you call this afternoon? My number is, (407)555-1212.

> Yours,
> Carol

---------------------------------- MAILBOX ----------------------------------

TO: CAROL BEATTY N771200C   03:00PM EST
SUBJECT: PIGS   03-10-93

Dear Carol . . .
 Sure, I'd love to talk to you in person. How about if I call at 4:00?
 In my last note, I forgot to mention I heard from Sue Veneer yesterday. She seems to be doing very well. The minister at the church is going to introduce her to a veterinarian in the congregation and the girl is hoping to get a part-time job.
 In an afternoon note, she told me she has lost 30 pounds since November (apparently she weighed about 190 then, because she says she weighs 159 now). Since her clothes were hanging on her, the minister's wife went with her to Lane Bryant and helped her pick out a few new things. Sue was ecstatic to report she wears a size 16 instead of a size 24. Wow, success in weight loss is relative, no?

It strikes me as odd that all three of us (you, Sue and I) have changed our appearances over the past few months. We are actually becoming different people. Once, I wrote jokingly to Buck that the computer is a lot like Aladdin's Lamp. Then, I was referring to the fact that one can create a character behind which to hide. Now, I am wondering if the computer actually does possess some magical properties. <laughing> It would seem so.

                              Your friend . . .
                              Katie

THE ROCK HARD CAFE

TO: ALL   08:00PM EST
FROM: KENNETH LONG T017643A   03-11-93
SUBJECT: THE ROCK HARD CAFE

Hi Folks!

Welcome to my Rock Hard Cafe! It's THE place in computerland to meet your friends. I also have the best menu in town. You can tell I'm a good short order cook by my white apron, paper hat and the pencil stub behind my ear.

There's plenty of seating available tonight. Slide into one of the red leather-upholstered benches at the booths along the wall, stake a claim on one of the chrome chairs around the Formica tables in the middle of the room, or sit on one of the stools here at the counter and talk to me while I do my thing. There's a dimly lit back room if you'd like a little privacy.

I offer take-out service for the ladies. My motto is: "When I take it out, I deliver! Satisfaction guaranteed!" If you want it to go, I recommend the "Chef's Special."

Elvis is singing "Jailhouse Rock" on the jukebox and pretty, sassy waitresses are on hand to take your orders. Come on in, we're always open!

> Handing you a menu,
> Ken

************* ADULT TOPICS BULLETIN BOARD *************

TO: ALL   08:09PM EST
FROM: CAROL BEATTY N771200C   03-11-93
SUBJECT: THE ROCK HARD CAFE

Hi!

I'm Carol and I'll be your pretty sassy waitress this evening. You'll notice our menu is packed full of tantalizing delights! We have delicacies to whet your appetite, we have things to fill you up and we have a wide selection of goodies for your sweet tooth. We've got hot and spicy, we've got cool and creamy, we've got sweet and tangy and everything in between. If you don't see what you want on the menu, just ask.

Now, what can I bring you?

Pencil and pad in hand,
Your waitress

************* ADULT TOPICS BULLETIN BOARD *************

TO: ALL   08:17PM EST
FROM: CLIFF NOTES L896112C   03-11-93
SUBJECT: THE ROCK HARD CAFE

Hi Cats!

It is I, the Cliffster, wearing a black leather jacket, motorcycle boots and a sneer. You will notice, I own a powerful-looking chopped hog, and my motorcycle looks tough, too.

Carol, since I don't see furburgers on the menu, I'll have a cheeseburger—all the way, fries and a chocolate shake. And, if you have any chicks around here who go "all the way," I'll take one of them for dessert.

Swaggering over to my usual
booth,
Cliff

************* ADULT TOPICS BULLETIN BOARD *************

TO: CLIFF NOTES L896112C   08:28PM EST
FROM: CAROL BEATTY N771200C   03-11-93
SUBJECT: THE ROCK HARD CAFE

Hi Cliff!

I see you are naked from the waist down as usual. Hey, that reminds
me, we have a bratwurst and sauerkraut special tonight. Would you care
to change your order?

> Admiring your tattoos,
> Carol

************* ADULT TOPICS BULLETIN BOARD *************

TO: CAROL BEATTY N771200C   08:37PM EST
FROM: CLIFF NOTES L896112C   03-11-93
SUBJECT: THE ROCK HARD CAFE

Carol,

Nah. I think I'll stick with the cheeseburger. But, on second thought,
you better leave off the onions. I'm a free agent now and am on the
lookout for a new Motorcycle Mamma.

> Combing my hair and eyeing the
> babes over by the jukebox,
> Cliff

************* ADULT TOPICS BULLETIN BOARD *************

TO: KENNETH LONG T017643A   08:40PM EST
FROM: WILLIAM RAMSEY Y082176A   03-11-93
SUBJECT: THE ROCK HARD CAFE

How's it going, Ken?

I think I'll just sit here at the counter. Have you got any more of that
coconut cream pie left? If you do, give me a piece with a cup of black
coffee.

This is a nice place. You don't see many real diners these days. The fast food joints have taken over. Used to be, you could go into a place like this and have a conversation with a stranger. I guess the computer is becoming the place where people can do that again.

> Nostalgic,
> Will

************** ADULT TOPICS BULLETIN BOARD **************

TO: WILLIAM RAMSEY Y082176A   08:56PM EST
FROM: KENNETH LONG T017643A   03-11-93
SUBJECT: THE ROCK HARD CAFE

Hello Padre,
   Yep, I like my little place. Since Buck's basement is being overhauled while he's out of the country, I've been doing a brisk business here. I'm even thinking of expanding. I may open another diner over on the CON-NECTIONS BB. How does that grab you?

> Pouring your Java,
> Ken

************** ADULT TOPICS BULLETIN BOARD **************

TO: CAROL BEATTY N771200C   09:04PM EST
FROM: KATHERINE SIMMONS S102248A   03-11-93
SUBJECT: THE ROCK HARD CAFE

Hi Girl!
   Here I am, fresh as a daisy and dressed in a pink fuzzy sweater and matching poodle skirt. Please make sure to admire my strand of pearls, saddle shoes and ponytail, too.
   I am meeting Jackie here for burgers and later we are going to the drive-in. Would you and Ken like to come along?

> Smacking my gum and putting a
> nickel in the jukebox . . .
> Katie

************** ADULT TOPICS BULLETIN BOARD **************

TO: KATHERINE SIMMONS S102248A   09:12PM EST
FROM: CAROL BEATTY N771200C   03-11-93
SUBJECT: THE ROCK HARD CAFE

Hi Katie!
   Ken and I would love to double date with you and Jackie to the drive-in. As a matter of fact, we'll take Ken's DeSoto. But, you'll have to wait until we get off work and Jackie will have to drive, 'cuz we have dibs on the back seat!

                         Wearing Ken's ring on a chain
                         around her neck,
                         Carol

************** ADULT TOPICS BULLETIN BOARD **************

TO: KATHERINE SIMMONS S102248A   09:24PM EST
FROM: JOHN W. KELLY JR. A041178A   03-11-93
SUBJECT: THE ROCK HARD CAFE

Hi Kid,
   You look good enough to eat in that sweater.
   Could we go in the back room? It's nice and dark back there and I could pet your poodle under the table while we wait for our burgers.

                         Your date,
                         Jackie

************** ADULT TOPICS BULLETIN BOARD **************

TO: JOHN W. KELLY JR. A041178A   09:33PM EST
FROM: KATHERINE SIMMONS S102248A   03-11-93
SUBJECT: THE ROCK HARD CAFE

Jackie . . .
   You look keen in your letter jacket and chinos . . . what a hunk! Do I smell Old Spice? My favorite! Come on over here and snuggle up with me in this booth and you can pet my poodle all you want.
   Ken and Carol are going with us to see *The Creature Who Ate Cleveland.* We'll have a tough time deciding whether to watch the action on

the screen or the action in the back seat. They really know how to steam up the windows.

Here comes Carol with our cheeseburgers and a vanilla shake (with two straws). Let's dig in.

Fluttering my eyelashes at you over
our milk shake . . .
Katie

************* ADULT TOPICS BULLETIN BOARD *************

TO: ALL   09:40PM EST
FROM: WAYNE ROONEY F362238A   03-11-93
SUBJECT: THE ROCK HARD CAFE

Beware Sinners!!!!

It says in the Book:

Proverbs 6:26–29 "For on account of a harlot one is reduced to a loaf of bread, and an adulteress hunts for the precious life. Can a man take fire in his bosom, and his clothes not be burned? Or can man walk on hot coals, and his feet not be scorched? So is the one who goes in to his neighbor's wife; whoever touches her will not go unpunished."

************* ADULT TOPICS BULLETIN BOARD *************

TO: WAYNE ROONEY F362238A   9:52PM EST
FROM: JOHN W. KELLY JR. A041178A   03-11-93
SUBJECT: THE ROCK HARD CAFE

Well Wayne,

You sure know how to brighten a place up, don't you? At least you had a loaf of bread in that one. That phrase makes your post remotely related to the topic at hand, since there is some food involved.

You're getting a little more lucid. The medication must be working.

Jack

BLACK VELVET DRESS

TO: BUCK BRAZEMORE X455045A   09:30AM EST

SUBJECT: BLACK VELVET DRESS   03-16-93

My Dear Buck . . .

The September I was 12 years old, my mother took me to Atlanta to shop and to visit her sister. While we were shopping, we came across a store called, La Belle Jeune Fille. In the window was the most beautiful vision my young eyes had ever seen. On a mannequin, displayed in a blizzard of gilt leaves, was an exquisite black velvet dress. It had a white lace collar, a pink satin sash and a bodice which was intricately embroidered and studded with seed pearls. The dress stopped me in my tracks and I begged my mother to take me into the shop.

In the fitting room, as I looked at my reflection, I was transfixed. Something miraculous happened after I put on the dress. My mother and aunt were strangely quiet and their expressions changed subtly as they appraised me in the long mirror. I think it was then that I knew I would be beautiful.

The tag on the dress was handwritten and read $250.00 (isn't it odd I can still remember that?). Even by today's standards it is an extravagant price to pay for a child's dress . . . back then it was exorbitant. And even though I was a spoiled child and I begged and cried until my eyes were red and I breathed in little jerky gasps, my mother would not buy the dress for me.

However, at some point the grownups must have conferred because after lunch, my Aunt Chris took me to Pet World to see the schnauzer puppies and my mother went to La Belle Jeune Fille and bought the dress. It stayed in its lovely pink box on the top shelf in her closet until two weeks before Christmas.

Although that dress was the most magnificent gift I ever received, sometimes I wish I had never been given it. Perfection simply cannot hold up to the abrasion of real life.

You see, before I got the dress, I thought about it frequently and dreamed about it at night. I saw myself resplendently arrayed in it, standing amid a sea of admiring faces. I always envisioned it in its pristine state, in a flurry of golden leaves or as it looked the first time I had seen it on my just-budding woman's body. It gained magical properties in my imagination.

I wore the gift at every opportunity . . . to Sunday school, all the holiday festivities and my birthday party. Frequently, I put it on and just wore it in my room. Over the late winter and early spring it began to show the wear of my adoration. By April, the collar had become limp, the sash slightly frayed, the fabric over my bottom became shiny and a few of the pearls had been lost. The next year, it looked rather bedraggled when I took it out of my closet. When I put it on, the bodice pulled across my newly plump breasts and it had become too short. Eventually it went into my younger sister's dress-up box and finally became our maid's favorite furniture-polishing rags.

I hope you are beginning to understand why I am telling you the story about the black velvet dress. You see, in so many ways, our carefully built computer relationship is like my dress. It is perfect.

I have been thinking a lot lately about what Will Ramsey has written about the nature of perfection in some of his CHAPLAIN'S ROOM posts. It strikes me that we might be trying to create something perfect and imaginary to take our minds off the troubles in our real-life marriages. Is this possible?

If our computer relationship becomes any more real, it will be subject to the same wear and tear our marriages are. It wouldn't be long before we would be left with the furniture-polishing rags. That is just the way it is. I don't want it to happen, Buck. That's why I called you yesterday, asking if we could scale down our involvement.

I don't blame you for hanging up on me or for calling me in the wee hours this morning. It was a shock. This just seems like the best time to start disengaging.

As I said on the phone, I feel TERRIBLE about this. My tears were real. I honestly still care deeply for you and I feel almost sick with remorse. I know I have hurt you. Please find it in your heart to forgive me and tell me we can be friends. Carol and Ken have managed to convert their passion into a special type of friendship. Maybe we can do that too.

Love . . .
Katie

---------------------------------- MAILBOX ----------------------------------

FROM: BUCK BRAZEMORE X455045A   12:23PM EST
SUBJECT: BLACK VELVET DRESS   03-16-93

My Dear Katie,

Can you find it in your heart to forgive me for last night? I'm thankful Tom was out of town, so you didn't have to explain why someone would call you at 3:00 in the morning. I'm embarrassed that I cried, you know I was drunk. Damn, I hate a crying drunk!

I don't know what has gotten into me. I can't ever remember feeling this low, even when I think about Linda and Sparky. You must think I'm loco for taking it so hard. It's just that I was lonely for you while I was in Negba. I found myself dreaming that somehow we could be together, run away or something. How could we do that—where would we go?

I don't want this to end, but I reckon there's not much I can do about it. I'll respect your wishes, although I don't see how we can "be friends." I wouldn't know how to do that.

This afternoon, I rode out to the place on my property which has always given me comfort. There is a little escarpment between my land and the adjoining property on the backside. It's loaded with fossils and I've spent lots of hours gouging out thousands of bivalves, sea urchins and other sea creatures which have turned into rocks, with my pick. Today, I found a rare, absolutely perfect, fist-sized shell. It looks a little like a pair of child's hands in prayer.

Fossils have always mesmerized me. They prove anything is possible. How can it be that Texas was at the bottom of the ocean? How is it conceivable giant creatures lived here in forests of fantastic plants? But I held in my hand the proof of it. Pressure and heat had preserved it in rock.

How is it possible I love you? It seems inconceivable, yet, as a result of heat and compression, I hold the evidence. My love isn't any more fantastic than an ammonite or a triceratops, is it?

Why can't we go on? It still doesn't quite make sense to me. Before I left for Tel Aviv we were thick as thieves. Now, suddenly, you don't want anything to do with me. I smell a rat. Is there something you're not telling me? Please be honest with me.

I love you,

Buck

------------------------------------- MAILBOX -------------------------------------

TO: BUCK BRAZEMORE X455045A   01:45PM EST

SUBJECT: BLACK VELVET DRESS   03-16-93

My Dear Cowboy . . .

It used to amaze me how my sisters could get away with sneaky stuff all the time; I have never been very good at hiding things or keeping secrets. My sisters were good liars, but I never quite got the hang of it. Dishonesty makes me uncomfortable. My mother always caught me. Probably, I wanted to be caught.

I am feeling guilty now. The truth is, there IS another reason I want to end our connection. While you have been gone I have developed very strong feelings for another computer lover. Actually, he has been in the picture for several weeks, even before you left on your trip to Israel.

This man is not as sweet and good as you are, but he answers some need I have. Don't ask me what the need is because I haven't been able to figure it out myself.

While you were in Tel Aviv, my feelings for this man escalated to the point that it has become clear I do not have enough energy for you both. I had to make a choice.

I hope this confession will make you hate me so you will not feel so bad.

Unfaithful . . .

Katie

---------------------------------- MAILBOX ----------------------------------

TO: CAROL BEATTY N771200C   03:13PM EST
SUBJECT: BLACK VELVET DRESS   03-16-93

Dear Carol . . .

During the past 48 hours I have been riding a roller coaster of emotions. I can't resume my affair with Buck, it will be impossible if I want to keep my connection to Jack. I don't have enough energy for both of them. I made a choice . . . there was no contest.

While I love the sweet courtliness of Buck, Jack pulls me in with his demanding, hungry abandon. The Californian is out of control and he creates a kind of vortex which draws me with incredible force. We act like addicts when we connect . . . we can't seem (and don't want) to help ourselves.

Anyway, there was a note in my mailbox from Buck on Monday night, asking me to call him in the morning. He must have written the note the moment he got home. I did call him yesterday, but we only talked for about 20 minutes. He hung up after he heard I wanted to end our computer affair.

Buck sounded incredulous and bewildered after I confessed I no longer wanted to be his lover. At first, I tried to convince him my decision was based on the fact that our relationship was perfect and I didn't want it to change, but he suspected something else and asked me point blank. I am not a convincing liar, so I avoided his questions.

Buck called me at 3am, crying and begging me to meet him somewhere . . . anywhere. He said his life would be miserable without me. He'd been drinking.

Luckily, Tom was in New Orleans. How could I explain Buck's call to my husband? I can hear it now, "That was one of the two guys I secretly write every day on my computer. We reveal our innermost thoughts and secrets and get off on some fantastic imitation screwing while you are at work. I have never met him in person, but the man loves me passionately and wants me to run off with him."

However, as shocking and potentially disastrous as the call was, it thrilled me. It made my heart beat wildly to hear the passion, romance and grief in his voice as he begged me to come to him. I became weak in the knees (and sexually aroused) to be adored so. I confess, I love this adoration from strange men. It makes me feel powerful and sexy again. After he hung up, I felt almost sick with desire. Do you think I'm terrible to admit this?

This morning, I e-mailed Buck a lame and sentimental "Dear John" letter entitled, "BLACK VELVET DRESS." It was pathetic . . . Buck deserves better. He responded by apologizing for his behavior and asking again if I am hiding something. I never could lie, so I just told him about Jack. I figured it might make him mad and then he wouldn't feel so miserable about my infidelity. Maybe I will never hear from him again.

I AM sad, but it is a strange sad. If I had the energy, I would gladly keep both my computer lovers. I would become bloated on their craving for me. I love the effect their ardent emotion has on me . . . it fills me up and energizes me. This must be what it's like to be a vampire. Poor Jack! Now, he must fill all my needs.

The way I am feeling about getting high on computer passion is the way I used to feel in college about getting stoned on pot. I would get wasted and later not be able to remember what I did or how it felt, but I knew I wanted to do it again.

You know what is really surprising? I don't feel much anguish or guilt any more. Last night I had terrible pangs of remorse for breaking Buck's heart, but this afternoon all I feel is a little twinge. Mainly I feel this big flood of relief as if a burden has been lifted from my shoulders. How do emotions develop and recede so fast around here? I don't get it.

Carol, thank you for listening to me. Who else could understand or listen to something that sounds so incredibly crazy?

May I call you again tomorrow morning?

Your Insane Vampire Friend . . .
Katie

SPRING BREAK

MAILBOX

TO: JOHN W. KELLY JR. A041178A   01:22PM EST
SUBJECT: SPRING BREAK   03-17-93

Dearest . . .

Next week is Spring Break for the twins. One of Tom's business connections owns a vacation place in Providenciales, a small island in the Turks and Caicos chain, below the Bahamas in the Caribbean Sea. For years the man has offered us the use of the house and we are finally taking him up on it. We leave on Saturday morning for Miami and will return to Charlotte on the following Saturday night.

I want to pack a few final memories into this last year Greg and Stephen will be home. Trips seem to be the best providers of good ones. In late May, after graduation, we will have one more family vacation to Pawley's Island, South Carolina. My sons will leave directly from the beach house for their summer jobs as counselors at a large boys' camp on the North Carolina coast. Then, in mid-August, I will have them for one more week before they leave for college.

My friend, Ginny, is childless so she really cannot empathize with what I am feeling about losing my boys. Beverly was delighted when her youngest daughter left for Vanderbilt last year. She said she loves her empty nest. I dread mine. It is difficult to imagine a life without my children at the center of it. It makes me panicky to think about it.

I have told you a little about Carol Beatty, my computer buddy from Orlando. She has become a friend in a very short time. I tell her things I don't tell Beverly and Ginny and she confides in me, as well. Last week and this past Tuesday, I called her on the telephone and we had two long conversations. Carol is a much different person than the character she projects on the BB and in my mailbox. It surprises me that she is not the fearless brassy woman I have imagined. I don't know why it surprises me. In computerland, it is possible to play a completely different role than the one we have in real life. She does . . . I don't. Do you?

Carol has some very big personal problems. Her husband physically and emotionally abuses her. I don't understand how abusive relationships work and I don't know what I can do for her or even how to advise her. All I can do is listen. It is frustrating to feel helpless.

Buck has returned from Israel. I've ended my computer affair with him and he is unhappy about it. However, I simply could not maintain my high voltage connections to both of you. I don't make a very good polygamist . . . how do they do it? Anyway, I was forced to choose, otherwise I would have been bled dry of every drop of energy. It is hard enough to fill your ravenous needs.

It will be difficult being away from the computer while I am in the Caribbean. What will I do without my daily fix of ferocious passion? In our recent exchanges, I am learning the joys of bondage . . . and not just the sexual kind.

Bound . . .
Katie

---------------------------------- MAILBOX ----------------------------------

FROM: JOHN W. KELLY JR. A041178A   03:51PM EST
SUBJECT: SPRING BREAK   03-17-93

Darling,

Jan and I are leaving for Santa Fe on March 26th to visit some friends. I won't be back until Sunday, April 4th. Two weeks is a long time to be without you.

This morning there were two notes from you in my mailbox. I wish you could have seen my reaction to your daydream. It generated the most massive, throbbing and incredibly stiff hard-on in recorded history. What a monster! <he says with typical manly pride> I could have driven nails with it.

I even made a copy of the fantasy and took it into work with me. After reading it again, I was trapped in my office for almost twenty minutes with my second erection of the morning. I had to resort to examining old x-rays as a means of distracting myself because my patient was already on the table in the lab. My pecker was still at half-mast when my nurse knocked on the door. I walked kind of hunched over down the hall. Maybe the staff thought I was examining my shoes. <LOL> A little later, as I was washing my hands, I looked down and noticed a dark golf ball-size wet spot on my scrubs. I quickly pulled out my shirttail to cover the evidence. How undignified! How fun! I feel like I'm fifteen years old again.

The reason I didn't write to you first thing this morning is because Megan spent the night last night. We always have breakfast together before I drop her off at school. It's hard to watch her walking away from me and up to the building. We're very close and the separation is hard for both of us.

My daughter may come to live with me after this school year. My ex-wife remarried last May. Megan was recently stunned and embarrassed to learn her mother is three months pregnant, at 40. Also, she isn't too fond of her new 30-year-old stepfather. I'm sorry about all that, but I'm also ecstatic because it may mean we'll live together again. I really miss her.

My daughter is the light of my life. At almost sixteen, she's lovely and athletic. She's a swimmer and on both her school and Marin County Aquatic Club teams. Her best events are the 100-meter butterfly, the 200-meter Individual Medley and the butterfly leg of the Medley Relay. I love to watch Megan swim—she's a marvel—like a seal or a mermaid. Her movements are powerful, yet fluid and graceful. She has a county meet next Wednesday night and I've volunteered to be a timer.

In the late spring, she plays softball on a recreation league team. She usually plays third base and she's always one of the big hitters. I love to watch her come to bat. As she assumes the batting position, she extends her right hand out into space, just briefly (looking a little like a tightrope walker), before she grips the bat with both hands. I'm a photographer of sorts and I took the most wonderful picture of her in that instant when she looks like she's balancing on a wire. I had it blown up to an 8×10 and have it on my bedside table.

I'm telling you about Megan because I want you to know I understand the apprehension you are feeling about being separated from your boys. I empathize.

I'm sorry to hear about Carol's problems. I know a little about "abusive teams." Since alcoholics are often involved in them, it's a topic at some AA meetings. She probably knows there's a battered woman shelter in her community. However, from what I understand, abused partners frequently must fear for their lives before they have enough energy to break free. It must be frustrating to feel limited in what you can do to help her. This is one of the drawbacks of long-distance friendships.

Speaking of the drawbacks of long-distance relationships, I'm feeling some of the frustration, myself. Katie, I need to see your face. Will you send me some pictures? You can send them to either one of my addresses. They are:

Dr. John William Kelly Jr.
c/o Marin Cardiovascular Center
6100 Arroyo Blvd.
Suite A
Mill Valley, California 94941

and

Jack Kelly
50 El Oceano Rd.
Mill Valley, California 94941

Please send them today or tomorrow, so I will get them on Monday. If I have your face, then maybe I won't miss you so much while you're in the West Indies and I'm in New Mexico.

Finally, I'm not sorry to hear that you've decided to end your computer affair with Buck. If the truth be known, it's the best news I've gotten in a long time. I've wanted you all to myself from day one.

Your lover,
Jack

---------------------------------- MAILBOX ----------------------------------

TO: JOHN W. KELLY JR. A041178A   04:44PM EST
SUBJECT: SPRING BREAK   03-17-93

Dearest . . .

Your note from last night made me laugh! It is hilarious to imagine you trapped in your office with a "stiffy" and crabbing down the hall trying to hide it. It thrills me to hear the extent to which I have invaded your life.

Thank you for empathizing with my empty nest apprehensions. Maybe what I need is a new job to keep my mind off of being "laid off." I have been a volunteer at the art museum for years and Beverly told me last week that the board has allocated funds to hire an Assistant Curator of Education. It is only a part-time position which would begin in September. It doesn't pay much. The duties will include scheduling tours (mainly school field trips), interfacing with the volunteer docent corps and helping the curator with special events. The job appeals to me and I know I could do it. Beverly is prodding me to apply. She says I would be great. What do you think?

Carol seems frightened of her husband. She tells me Ed has always been very controlling. He must know where she is at all times and he interrogates her about the most mundane things . . . like the grocery receipts. She says the threats and physical abuse are sporadic. Mainly he threatens her, but he also pushes her around and slaps her. Once she had to get stitches when he punched her in the face. I did ask her if there were some services in Orlando where she might get some help and she says there are, but she is too ashamed to contact them. Recently, Carol told her mother about the situation. However, my friend is terrified of what her husband might do if she takes the children and leaves to go live with her mother in Vero Beach. I feel totally useless. I guess most people feel powerless where domestic violence is concerned and that's why it is always with us.

In the guest room closet is a giant box of photos which haven't been put in albums yet. This morning, I have been rummaging through it, looking for a few snapshots to send to you. Perhaps you will enjoy an assortment of pictures from different times in my life. Look for my envelope on Monday.

Now, you must look through your photos because I want some pictures of you, too. They will help me through our separation and it would be rather nice to finally see the face of the man with whom I have lately been sampling the most exotic and erotic of practices. <laughing>

> Getting out the handcuffs . . .
> Katie

P.S. My address:
    Katherine Simmons
    4761 Old Church Road
    Charlotte, NC 28207

THE MIDLIFE BOAT

TO: ALL   07:30PM EST
FROM: KATHERINE SIMMONS S102248A   03-18-93
SUBJECT: THE MIDLIFE BOAT

Ahoy Passengers!

The big ship is going down, but I managed to commandeer one of the midlife boats. It is a commodious craft, well stocked with provisions and life preservers (including a wide array of cosmetics and hair products and an impressive stack of diet and self-help books).

Actually, it is a beautiful day to be adrift. The sun is brilliant in a cloudless sky and the Caribbean Sea is calm, clear as glass and the impossible turquoise blue you see on postcards.

I am dressed in a spiffy crisp white captain's uniform and am looking for a crew. Would anyone care to join me?

> A Castaway . . .
> Katie

TO: KATHERINE SIMMONS S102248A   07:50PM EST
FROM: WILLIAM RAMSEY Y082176A   03-18-93
SUBJECT: THE MIDLIFE BOAT

Dear Katie,

Let me compliment you on your choice of subject title; it made me smile. The computer really does become a refuge for people in distress. Most of my mail comes from middle-aged people with real-life relationship problems. I like your analogy.

I'll be happy to float with you for a spell. Where are you headed?

Regards,
Will Ramsey

************** ADULT TOPICS BULLETIN BOARD **************

TO: WILLIAM RAMSEY Y082176A   08:01PM EST
FROM: KATHERINE SIMMONS S102248A   03-18-93
SUBJECT: THE MIDLIFE BOAT

Dear Will . . .
    I appreciate the companionship. The shoals of midlife are treacherous,
since they are full of dangers and have not been mapped. It is reassuring
to have a little company during the passage . . . especially your company.
    Actually, I am headed to the desert isle of Providenciales. It is in the
Turks and Caicos chain and is the last of the British-owned West Indies.
The island is supposed to be very scenic . . . full of wild orchids and
white sugary beaches. I am looking forward to being marooned for a
week.

Scanning the horizon . . .
Katie

************** ADULT TOPICS BULLETIN BOARD **************

TO: KATHERINE SIMMONS S102248A   08:01PM EST
FROM: JOHN W. KELLY JR. A041178A   03-18-93
SUBJECT: THE MIDLIFE BOAT

Ahoy there, Mate!
    Allow me to enlist in your motley crew. I'm in the mood for a little
swashbuckling. We can take turns swashing and buckling, okay?
    Want me to raise the Skull and Crossbones? It'll be an appropriate
banner for a midlife boat. <sardonic G>

The Ancient Mariner,
Jack

************* ADULT TOPICS BULLETIN BOARD ************
TO: JOHN W. KELLY JR. A041178A   08:13PM EST
FROM: KATHERINE SIMMONS S102248A   03-18-93
SUBJECT: THE MIDLIFE BOAT

Dear Jack . . .

As skipper, I reserve the right to hoist the flag. However, since I don't have one and you are never without your Jolly Roger, maybe we can make the flag-raising ceremony a joint effort.

Run over there and fetch that length of sturdy rope and stand by to elevate your pennant. It will be quite inspiring to see your standard straining in the breeze.

A stickler for protocol . . .
Katie

************* ADULT TOPICS BULLETIN BOARD ************
TO: KATHERINE SIMMONS S102248A   08:29PM EST
FROM: CLIFF NOTES L896112C   03-18-93
SUBJECT: THE MIDLIFE BOAT

Shiver me timbers!

It is I, Peg-leg Cliff, without my pants and waving my cutlass in your general direction. I'm quite a swordsman. You ought to try fencing with me sometime.

Pretty Polly is sitting on my shoulder. When I'm finished with her, perhaps you would like to walk my plank. My wooden leg is not the only piece of lumber I carry around with me.

A Buccaneer,
Cliff

************* ADULT TOPICS BULLETIN BOARD *************

TO: KATHERINE SIMMONS S102248A	08:43PM EST
FROM: CAROL BEATTY N771200C	03-18-93
SUBJECT: THE MIDLIFE BOAT	

Dear Cap,
  Scoot over! It's not fair for you to get all the seamen. Save some for me!

          Hopping on board,
          Carol

************* ADULT TOPICS BULLETIN BOARD *************

TO: CAROL BEATTY N771200C	08:50PM EST
FROM: KENNETH LONG T017643A	03-18-93
SUBJECT: THE MIDLIFE BOAT	

      Seaman 1st Class, reporting for duty!

************* ADULT TOPICS BULLETIN BOARD *************

TO: ALL	09:00PM EST
FROM: WAYNE ROONEY F362238A	03-18-93
SUBJECT: THE MIDLIFE BOAT	

SINNERS BEWARE!!!!!
FORNICATORS AND ADULTERERS ARE BOUND FOR THE
LAKES OF FIRE IN THE PIT OF HELL!!!! REPENT BEFORE IT IS
TOO LATE!!!!!

************ ADULT TOPICS BULLETIN BOARD *************

TO: KATHERINE SIMMONS S102248A   09:15PM EST
FROM: BUCK BRAZEMORE X455045A   03-18-93
SUBJECT: THE MIDLIFE BOAT

Man Overboard!

---------------------------------- MAILBOX ----------------------------------

FROM: BUCK BRAZEMORE X455045A   09:20PM EST
SUBJECT: THE MIDLIFE BOAT   03-18-93

Katie,

I'm miserable without you. Watching you playing around on the board today is about to drive me crazy. Please don't leave me! I wouldn't mind sharing you. I share Linda.

Is one of the guys who wrote today on the board your new lover? Is he Will or Jack or Cliff? I thought these men were my friends. I can't believe one of my buddies would steal my treasure.

                              The victim of a pirate,
                              Buck

PROVIDENCIALES

TO: SUSAN VENEER G740094D   10:02AM EST
SUBJECT: PROVIDENCIALES   03-30-93

Dear Jennifer . . .

Last week, my family and I had a wonderful vacation on the little Caribbean island of Providenciales. I think the Spanish name means "providence" in English. I looked the word up in the dictionary and discovered it means God's or nature's benevolent guidance. It can also simply mean, God.

It has kind of stumped me why the Spanish would name a desert island, "Providenciales." There is no water at all. Every house has a cistern and residents must collect rainwater for bathing and for flushing toilets. Most of the native people even drink the rainwater. The small colony of European and American expatriates have their drinking water shipped in and the Club Med, at the southern tip of the island, has its own desalinization plant which converts sea water into potable water.

Maybe the Spanish named the island "Providence" because they were just happy to have made it across the Atlantic Ocean intact. Or perhaps it is simply because the place is so incredibly beautiful, but then, there are many stunningly beautiful Caribbean islands. It's a mystery.

My boys had a ball (and you probably would have, as well). Although we stayed in a private house on an inlet called Thompson's Cove, we had guest passes for use of the Club Med facilities. Greg and Stephen practically lived there. The Club Med has windsurfers, jet skis, sailboats, swimming pools and all kinds of planned activities. However, I think the biggest draw was the beach, since European women frequently enjoy the sun without their bathing suit tops. <laughing>

I haven't heard from you in a long time and I was wondering how you are doing. Please write.

                    Your friend . . .
                    Katie

---------------------------------- MAILBOX ----------------------------------

FROM: SUSAN VENEER G740094D   12:06PM EST
SUBJECT: PROVIDENCIALES   03-30-93

Dear Katie,

Wow! That island sounds great. I've never seen the Caribbean Sea except in magazines. It looks like Heaven. :-)

I LOVE my new job! I work on Monday and Wednesdays after classes and all day on Saturdays. I just got back to the dorm about an hour ago.

The vet's name is Marianne Sanders. She has been a vet in this area for twenty-two years. She has a partner named Beth. They take care of the big farm animals around here, mainly cattle and horses.

Last Saturday, I went with them in the van to make rounds. At one farm they palpated the cows. That means they put on these big, rubber, combination sleeve and glove things and stuck their entire arms into the rectums of the cows to do internal exams. It's very dangerous to palpate cows since they can kick. While the vets did the exams, I checked the ear tags and then wrote down the findings as they called them out. At the next farm, I learned how to do the documentation for giving equine encephalitis vaccinations and Coggins tests on horses. I also did the paperwork when they filed the horses' teeth. This is called "floating teeth," don't ask me why.

Marianne is going to show me how to sterilize, sort and store the instruments this coming Saturday. This is SO interesting! I just love it AND I get paid five dollars an hour. :-D Maybe if I get very good, she will let me be a partner when I get out of vet school, too. She says there is more than enough work for ten vets around here.

Marianne is nice, too. She told me to call her Marianne even though she is 50. She isn't married and doesn't have any children, but she and Beth have eight dogs. I had dinner with them last night at their house. It's a big farmhouse. In back is where the office, dispensary and surgery are.

A lady at church sells Enchante cosmetics. Last week, Sharon (the minister's wife), two of the girls from the youth group and I went over to her house and she gave us some make-up tips and a BUNCH of free samples. One of the girls taught me how to French braid my hair, too. Everybody has been telling me how good I look since I started wearing lipstick and fixing my hair. I feel great. :-D

My mother died of cancer when I was 6 and my dad never remarried. When he died two years ago, I went to live with my aunt for a year until I started college. Nobody ever showed me how to make myself look better. I really like the way I look now. I wear a size 14 and I don't have to go to "fat lady" stores anymore. I bought a pair of jeans at The Gap yesterday with my first paycheck.

Well, I need to go eat dinner. E-me soon.

> Your happy friend, :-D
> Jenny (that's what everybody calls
> me at church)

---------------------------------- MAILBOX ----------------------------------

TO: CAROL BEATTY N771200C   01:30PM EST
SUBJECT: PROVIDENCIALES   03-30-93

Dear Carol . . .

Where are you, girl? I wrote you yesterday and you didn't answer. A few minutes ago, I called your house, but no answer. Jack is in Santa Fe. I feel kind of lonely without my computer buddies. I did get a nice letter from Sue Veneer, though. You will be happy to learn she is doing well.

While I was gone, Jack sent me a note. He got my pictures last Monday and he is delighted with them. What a relief! I got his, too, and I am pleased with the way he looks. His face and build remind me of Spencer Tracy. He has a rugged-looking face with intense eyes, energetic-looking gray hair and a compact, almost stocky, body. He looks like he could be a wrestler or a fighter instead of a doctor.

It makes me blush to tell you this, but in addition to the "G-rated" photos, he also included two Polaroids . . . before and after shots of his erection. I was not expecting them and they made me absolutely weak in the knees. I hid them in a box of pantyliners under my sink. <laughing> Did you and Ken send each other pornographic pictures?

Jack asked me if he could call me on the phone after he gets back.

We set a date for next Monday morning. I sent him my number. Now what's in store for me?

Today I am doing laundry. We came back with four suitcases full of dirty clothes. Water is at a premium in Providenciales, so I only did a little hand washing during our vacation.

Tom's friend had left four guest passes for the Club Med on the table for us to use while we were in Provo. The twins spent almost the whole vacation there. They met two cute French girls on the beach and the four of them paired off into couples in no time. They had a wonderful time on the beach, swimming, playing volleyball and dancing. The boys came home after midnight and left every morning as soon as they rolled out of bed. Although one day, at my insistence, they brought the girls to the house for lunch and afterwards they went snorkeling in the cove.

It was a little disconcerting at first to watch from the deck as my sons cavorted in the inlet with the pretty, topless young women. However, I got used to it eventually. I even took pictures of them with their arms around each other, standing knee-deep in the clear water . . . four beautiful smiling young people, nude except for skimpy strips of cloth around their hips which did not leave much to the imagination. I wonder what they did when they were out of my sight.

I asked Tom to make sure my sons had condoms. Although I have talked about sex with Greg and Stephen since they were little boys, I think this vacation marks the first time I really have thought of them as being full-grown men with adult sexual appetites.

One afternoon, Tom and I took an outboard boat to a little cay on the eastern side of the island. It is still populated with iguanas. The animals have been exterminated from the inhabited islands by human predators and their attendant cats. We had fun watching the big lizards eat the peanut butter sandwiches we had brought along as bait.

Later, we took off our swim suits and made love on a towel spread out on the sand. Afterward, we talked. I hardly ever accompany Tom when he travels, but my husband surprised me by asking me to come with him to Yokohama in September when he goes to negotiate the Ishii fax machine contract. He said we could make stops in the Pacific and Hawaiian islands on the way back and suggested it might be a good way to become reacquainted after the twins have gone off to college.

The sun was setting when we headed back. It was glorious.

Isn't it strange that although my relationship with Tom is improving by leaps and bounds, I still want to escalate to phone sex with Jack? Perhaps it is because I know this triangle is responsible for the change in my marriage. If Jack and I reach new highs, then Tom and I will, too. My computer affair is saving my marriage.

Your friend . . .
Katie

---------------------------------- MAILBOX ----------------------------------
FROM: CAROL BEATTY N771200C   04:25PM EST
SUBJECT: PROVIDENCIALES   03-30-93

Dear Katie,

Ed found out the bank didn't have a seminar in Jacksonville. He came home early last Tuesday afternoon. He slapped me hard, grabbed me by the hair, pushed me to my knees and threatened to kill me if I didn't tell him everything. I told him I had met a computer friend, but that nothing had happened. He threw me against the wall, screaming he didn't believe me.

At one point, I was able to get away from him. I got the baby and Eddie and managed to lock ourselves in my car on the street. Ed ran out of the house and started pounding on the windows and yelling, but when some of the neighbors began to walk out on their porches and lawns, watching him, he got in his own car and screeched off.

One of my neighbors stayed with the kids while I ran inside and got a few things, including my laptop, and I drove to Vero Beach. The children and I are now living in the other bedroom of my mother's condominium.

My husband has called two times. Once he threatened me again and the other time he apologized and begged me to come back. I almost caved in because I'm feeling so guilty and scared, but he has apologized before. Yesterday, he came here and tried to get to the elevator, but the guard wouldn't let him through.

I've finally called a hotline for battered women and I'm learning what I can do about Ed. A woman named Karen has become my contact person. She is very kind and knowledgeable. Also, Mom is helping and Ken is driving down here Friday night after work. I still don't know what I'm going to do. I need to talk to you. May I call?

Your friend,
Carol

---------------------------------- MAILBOX ----------------------------------

TO: CAROL BEATTY N771200C   04:56PM EST
SUBJECT: PROVIDENCIALES   03-30-93

Carol!

Of course you may call! I will stay glued to this spot until I hear from you.

Yours . . .
Katie

LONG DISTANCE

TO: JOHN W. KELLY JR. X455045A   08:44AM EST
SUBJECT: LONG DISTANCE   04-08-93

Dearest . . .

You have the most magnificent, rich and resonant voice . . . I could listen to it for hours (and have)! I am feeling a little weary and wrung-out from our four-day phone sex extravaganza. It is hard to believe, we have talked every day since Monday for at least two hours, and usually more. Carol was not kidding about phone sex . . . it is better than real sex!

God, I have had to resort to taking afternoon naps. <laughing> It feels a lot like we're on a honeymoon. If an actual penis were involved, I would have certainly developed honeymoon cystitis or a limp or something.

As exciting as this new discovery is, I must confess my ear hurts and my batteries seem in need of recharging (and not just the ones in my vibrator). <laughing> Would it be okay with you if we spend a few days away from the phone? Why don't we try a break from Friday through Monday?

It still makes me chuckle that you insisted on giving me your beeper number. I realize you are just demonstrating your trust in me, but it makes me laugh to think of actually beeping you. What in the world could be so important I would need to contact you in that way . . . a horniness emergency? <laughing> That having been said, I confess, I would enjoy beeping you sometime when I know you are at home, just for the fun and novelty of it. May I beep you on Tuesday after lunch (that sounds so naughty)? We should be well rested by then and probably in need of some critical care.

What a coincidence! The FedEx man just left. The package surprised me. When I saw the return address was San Francisco, I knew it was from you and tore it open like an eight-year-old with a Christmas present. The bronze pig is fantastic! I adored him the moment I laid eyes on the little beast. The idol is already ensconced on the counter in the kitchen where he glowers balefully.

I feel perfectly safe displaying my little boar in plain sight, since Tom will just think I picked it up while shopping with Ginny or Beverly. He does not understand my pig collection and is not remotely interested in it. Thank you, my dearest, for such an appropriate and lovely gift. I will make a little altar for him and worship at it regularly. <laughing>

I love to get things from you in the mail. Do you realize that during the past three weeks, you have sent me over a dozen cards and letters? I have bundled them up into a little parcel, tied it with a red ribbon and stashed it, along with your hottest e-mail and the vibrator you sent, in an accordion file on the bottom shelf behind the door of my closet. My sacred treasures won't be discovered there; the men in my family have no interest in that space. I wish I had a safe like you have, though.

I have stored most of your photographs in the file, too. However, I keep the picture of you holding the chain saw and the one of you wearing your mismatched scrubs in a book beside my bed. I think of these special photographs as my icons. Lately, Tom has not been traveling as much, but on nights he is out of town, I sleep with the pictures in my bed. Do you think I am losing it? <laughing>

Worshipful . . .
Katie

-------------------------------- MAILBOX ----------------------------------

FROM: JOHN W. KELLY JR. X455045A   10:13AM EST
SUBJECT: LONG DISTANCE   04-08-93

Darling,

I'll reluctantly go along with your request for a long weekend separation, but it'll be tough. By next Tuesday, I'll be ready for another 6-hour enduro like we had on Monday. By all means, beep me after lunch. <LOL>

It pleases me that you like the gift. I like surprising you.

The wife of one of my partners is an interior designer. Christine owns a popular shop in Mill Valley which carries some pretty pricey inventory. I like to go there when I'm looking for a special gift because she has exquisite taste and a wonderful selection of unique things from all over the world. I went there to find a special gift for you.

The Japanese pigs (a pair—a sow and a boar) stopped me in my tracks and I had to buy them. I kept the female and have her on top of the bookcase in my bedroom. Maybe I should build an altar for her, too.

The Pagan,
Jack

----------------------------------- MAILBOX -----------------------------------

TO: CAROL BEATTY N771200C   10:35AM EST
SUBJECT: LONG DISTANCE   04-08-93

Dear Carol . . .

I just called your mom's place and she said you had gone to Orlando and probably wouldn't be back until late tonight. She said she would tell you to check your computer for my message. I have gotten so used to talking to you daily on the phone it feels a little odd to revert back to this form of communication. Despite its limitations, e-mail does come in handy.

Your mom told me the restraining order seems to be working and Ed has backed off. She also said after you meet with your lawyer today about the divorce, the deputies will escort you to your house to get your things. If you can, please call me in the morning and let me know how everything went.

You know Jack and I have made the leap to the phone. Today, I asked him if we could take a break until Tuesday. I have been on the phone for hours every day this week with you and Jack and my ear actually hurts. Also, the intensity of the emotions simply exhausts me. This coming weekend is special, so I need to conserve my energy.

Easter Sunday is the twins' birthday. It is hard to believe they will be eighteen. As gifts, we are giving each of them a computer system to take to college. Their girlfriends are staging a party for them on Saturday night. It makes me sad to relinquish that pleasant job. Although, the boys did accept our invitation to a celebration brunch at the club on Sunday . . . if their girlfriends are invited, that is.

Those girls are moving in on my territory. However, I am still going to play Easter Bunny this year and I'd like to see Allison and Jill try to wrestle that pleasure away from me! <laughing> There will be baskets on the porch on Sunday morning, as always. I just can't give up my last opportunity to play the role. I know I do it for myself rather than the kids, though.

I got a message from Sue Veneer last night. She told me she is letting her LuxNet membership expire this month. She says she doesn't have time for it anymore and will just use her computer for school work from now on. She asked for my address, so she can send an occasional note by snail mail. I gave it to her because I really care for Sue. She is my friend and I need to stay connected to her.

Sue seems to be headed down a much better path than the one she was on earlier. It strikes me the computer has actually been the instrument which enabled a positive change in her life. If she had not plugged into Will Ramsey, who knows what would have happened to her?

It has surprised me you and Ken have become such good friends and have both felt comfortable giving up the erotic aspect of your relationship. This is a development I did not expect. However, it supports my theory that we middle-agers are drawn to computer involvements for reasons other than lust. Although you have suffered, it seems ultimately your computer experience has been rewarding for you. It has provided you with the catalyst you have needed to break away from your abusive marriage.

I am still wondering if the computer is a boon or a bane for me.

Your Friend . . .
Katie

LOVESICK

TO: JOHN KELLY A041178A   09:59AM EST
SUBJECT: LOVESICK   04-14-93

Dearest . . .

Is there a doctor in the house . . . a heart doctor?! I think I have taken an overdose and I wonder if my cardiac muscle can take the jolt.

Actually, I know quite a few other doctors. Several of our friends practice some form of medicine. My father-in-law, Jim, and Tom's older brother, Ben, are both successful orthopedic surgeons. They were partners in the same practice until Jim retired. My father-in-law wanted both of his boys to follow in his footsteps. However, Tom has always been the rebel in his family.

I think my husband's competitive relationship with his brother and his desire to prove himself to his father are mainly responsible for his relentless preoccupation with work. It does not seem enough for him to enjoy the same financial success as the other men in his family. He is determined to eclipse them. Now that Tom has gotten his wish (when he gets the Ishii fax machine account, it will certainly catapult him to victory in this race for the bucks against his father and brother), I wonder if he will be content? I doubt it.

Let's spend a few days writing about something other than sex, okay? Tell me some of your deep dark secrets.

                    Your favorite patient . . .
                    Katie

---------------------------------- MAILBOX ----------------------------------

FROM: JOHN KELLY A041178A   10:20AM EST
SUBJECT: LOVESICK   04-14-93

Darling,

It's true. We've both been taking some great big doses of strong medicine this past week or so. However, I'm building up a tolerance. I doubt
if I could ever get too much of you. It's fun to try, though. Actually, I
enjoy this new habit immensely and am content to allow this particular
monkey to sit on my back indefinitely. It doesn't hurt to take little breaks,
though. I will tell you some of my "dark secrets" as you have requested.

I really love my work, but will be content to pack it in and rest on
my laurels next year. There's only one blot on my otherwise unblemished
career. The cloud, which still lingers on my professional horizon, is an
unresolved malpractice suit.

I'm what is known as an interventional cardiologist, which simply
means I do some invasive procedures in addition to assessments and
noninvasive testing. About three years ago, I arrogantly performed a
balloon angioplasty on a tricky patient who, in retrospect, I probably
should have referred to a vascular surgeon. It might have been an error
in judgment, but the incident was neither malpractice nor negligence on
my part. I am fully qualified to perform angioplasties and have done
hundreds over the span of my career.

An angioplasty is a relatively simple procedure performed to reduce
the risk of a heart attack. A catheter with a little ballooning device is
inserted into a narrowed artery. As the balloon is inflated, the channel is
widened so blood can course through more easily to the heart. Unfortunately, in maybe 2% of cases, the artery does not respond as expected.
It is like trying to widen the mouth of a crystal goblet. The vessel reacts
like it's brittle rather than pliant and it shatters. Which is what happened
in my case, resulting in a minor heart attack for my patient and a rush
to the operating room for emergency surgery.

Unfortunately, my patient is an attorney. Many doctors cringe at the
prospect of treating a lawyer, and with good reason. Although it was a
risk which was stated on his consent form, the patient thought it was
solely my fault that he had to submit to "unnecessary surgery." Granted,
the man had come in for what he thought was a routine procedure and
ended up suffering a mild heart attack, spending three weeks in the hospital and running up a $50,000 bill, but it was really not my fault.

Although the case has been brewing for almost two years, it will not go to court until this August. It's been hanging over my head like an anvil.

Isn't it ironic? One of the main reasons I decided to finally seek help for my alcoholism six years ago was because I didn't want it to affect my ability to be a good physician. My sobriety had a stiff price. My beautiful young wife could not accept the changes it wrought in me and asked for a divorce within a year. And now, here I am, at the end of my illustrious career, facing a malpractice suit. It doesn't seem fair.

Now it is your turn. What black secrets do you have for me?

On call,

Jack

---------------------------------- MAILBOX ----------------------------------

TO: JOHN KELLY A041178A   11:40AM EST
SUBJECT: LOVESICK   04-14-93

Dearest . . .

Here is my dark secret. As a result of my dysfunctional family (and who has a functional one?), I must have the approval, no, the adoration, of others. I think it is an overblown reaction to my need to feel loved and secure. I am a slave to this neurosis, but it gives me tremendous energy. It is my "driver" and it allows me to do wonderful things.

Although I have never worked for money, I have worked like a Trojan for glory. You see women like this all the time in the world of "professional volunteering." We are the wives of successful men; the ones who run the Junior League, the Arts Council, the Symphony Auxiliary, the Girl Scouts, the PTA, ad infinitum. We supply the vision, oversee boards, develop projects and build consensus, just like the high-powered executives in our men's dominion. We surround ourselves with lieutenants, yes-men and groupies.

At first doing good deeds was its own reward. The work was gratifying. However, it was no substitute for a career. After years and years of giving my time and energy to others, I seemed to reach the bottom of the well. There wasn't anything else to give. It hit me one afternoon about four years ago as I did my usual Tuesday job of managing the volunteers sorting and folding used clothes at the Crisis Center.

I suddenly felt totally exhausted, sucked dry, dizzy. I blacked out and collapsed on the floor. They sent for an ambulance and my husband. At the hospital, the doctor could find nothing physically wrong with me. After that day, over a period of 12 months, I gradually pulled back from all my volunteer roles . . . first from the leadership and, finally, from even membership in the myriad activities I had plunged into.

Last year, I began to pull back from acquaintances. Now I have reached the point where I will only go out with Beverly and Ginny, who offer me the refuge of unconditional affection and regard. My friends are worried about me. I know I am depressed.

My husband is bewildered by my behavior. He really cannot handle it and, as a result, he has flung himself even deeper into his work. This is the way he has learned to handle stress. Up until recently, he had been spending at least three nights a week in Charleston. I guess he is having an affair, and somehow I don't blame him.

Until a few months ago, my energy seemed to be bleeding out of me. Some days I felt like I was beginning to disappear. However, the computer has connected me to a new power source. I can feel it recharging my dead battery.

> On life support . . .
> Katie

--------------------------------- MAILBOX ---------------------------------

FROM: JOHN KELLY A041178A   01:00PM EST
SUBJECT: LOVESICK   04-14-93

Darling,

Do you want my blackest secret? Down deep in my soul somewhere, I hold this terrible fear of being abandoned. I can trace it back to a particularly traumatic experience I had when I was seven years old because even now, at fifty-four, I can clearly remember the incident.

I grew up in the small town of Matthews in rural Ohio. One day, my father took me on an outing to Cincinnati which is a thirty-minute drive away. It was a mild early summer day and I remember walking along the river docks, looking at the big working boats and barges.

At some point, my father took me to a park and told me to wait for him there, saying he'd be back soon. He went looking for a bar. As you know, my father was an alcoholic. I sat on that park bench for hours. By late afternoon, I was sobbing and had wet my pants. Finally, a woman came up to me and soon a policeman arrived. He took me down to the station and it was just like a scene out of one of those old movies. They gave me a lollipop and entertained me.

Luckily, I had recently memorized my address. When they could not locate my father, they called Matthews and located my mother. She and my uncle came and picked me up.

My father called that night and I could hear my mother screaming at him. He didn't actually show up for several days. After he walked in the house pale, filthy and shaking, he had hugged me to him and cried with remorse. He smelled foully of vomit and a dirty unwashed body, yet I submitted stiffly to his embrace. I loved him.

From that time forward, I have harbored the fear I will be abandoned. Sometimes it almost seems like I plan for and work toward it.

My marriage was a terrible, wounded, halting thing. My wife was 14 years younger than I. She was beautiful and I loved her, but I always knew she'd eventually leave me. Our codependency was hideous to see. When I finally joined AA in desperation, she couldn't handle it. Divorce is a common outcome when one partner seeks help for alcoholism. You would think it would improve a marriage, but often the pathological behavior is so ingrained in the relationship that when the addiction element is torn out by the roots, the marriage can't survive the trauma. Sad.

I'm learning to love my solitude and self-defensive privacy. I don't want to remarry. This is a big problem for Janet and we are beginning to have vitriolic arguments around my "lack of commitment." The other night she complained harshly about the distance I've been putting between us lately. The pressure is becoming intolerable. Perhaps I'm drawn to you because I know the emotional energy I'm investing will ultimately mean the end for Jan and me. Permanence in any relationship is an alien concept to me.

Enough of these bitter dregs! Let's wallow around in passion and drown our sorrows. Take off your clothes, pull out the new toy I sent you and call me, now.

> In need of a transfusion,
> Jack

THE CHAPLAIN'S ROOM (IV)

ADULT TOPICS BULLETIN BOARD

TO: ALL   09:13AM EST
FROM: WILLIAM RAMSEY Y082176A   04-16-93
SUBJECT: THE CHAPLAIN'S ROOM

Thought for the week:

There are two types of addiction; substance addiction and process addiction. Substances which may be abused, include: drugs, alcohol, tobacco and food. Processes which may become compulsive include gambling, work, shopping, exercise and sex.

It strikes me that some computer relationships may cross the line and become addictive. Comments?

Offering food for thought,
Will Ramsey
Professional Contributor,
Adult Topics Bulletin Board

ADULT TOPICS BULLETIN BOARD

TO: WILLIAM RAMSEY Y082176A   11:54AM EST
FROM: AMANDA LEE C567210B   04-16-93
SUBJECT: THE CHAPLAIN'S ROOM

Dear Will,

I must be addicted. I don't seem to be able to stop what I'm doing and it's affecting my real life.

I'm married, have three school-age children and work part time for
an attorney. As irrational as it seems, I'm also in love with a man whom
I've never met and who lives 900 miles away.

At first, it all seemed manageable. It was fun and exciting to have a
fantasy lover. Now, I'm losing sleep, am late for work and am guilty of
neglecting my family so I can spend more time with this man in my
computer. It's also beginning to be quite expensive, since we communicate several times each day and the LuxNet rates for e-mail have gone
up so much. And we've begun talking on the telephone, so I dread to
see the bill this month.

I feel guilty and remorseful, yet don't seem able to let go of the
passion and joy I receive from my affair. What can I do?

> Agonizing,
> Amanda

************* ADULT TOPICS BULLETIN BOARD *************

TO: AMANDA LEE C567210B   02:17PM EST
FROM: WILLIAM RAMSEY Y082176A   04-16-93
SUBJECT: THE CHAPLAIN'S ROOM

Dear Amanda,

In your note, you mention the cardinal symptom of a process addiction: a feeling of powerlessness in the face of a compulsive behavior
even though the behavior has a negative impact on the quality of life.
You sound like you want help in regaining control.

I will be glad to offer some suggestions for your individual situation.
Please check your mailbox.

> Sincerely,
> Will Ramsey

************* ADULT TOPICS BULLETIN BOARD *************

TO: WILLIAM RAMSEY Y082176A   02:54PM EST
FROM: BRAD FLETCHER K967210C   04-16-93
SUBJECT: THE CHAPLAIN'S ROOM

Will,
   Hey man, give me a break! I've had lots of computer flings. When I
get tired of one, or it gets too heavy, I just quit. This is all fantasy.
What's the big deal?

                              A cyber Romeo,
                              Brad

************* ADULT TOPICS BULLETIN BOARD *************

TO: BRAD FLETCHER K967210C   03:17PM EST
FROM: WILLIAM RAMSEY Y082176A   04-16-93
SUBJECT: THE CHAPLAIN'S ROOM

Dear Brad,
   When I was a chaplain in Vietnam, I talked to lots of pilots who were
involved in bombing raids. Many of them had delayed feelings of remorse about bombing civilian targets. At first, the target was an abstract
for them. However, later it hit some of them that people lived in those
spots on the map—mothers, fathers, children, grandparents.
   I'm not equating hit-and-run computer relationships with killing people in bombing raids. But, it might be interesting for you to think about
this: There is a person, not a fantasy, on the other end of the modem.

                              Just trying to be helpful,
                              Will Ramsey

************** ADULT TOPICS BULLETIN BOARD **************

TO: WILLIAM RAMSEY Y082176A   04:14PM EST
FROM: MERRY MICHAELSON U453744C   04-16-93
SUBJECT: THE CHAPLAIN'S ROOM

Dear Will,

I was an addict and let my computer affair rule my life for four months. I have to repeat German III this summer because I missed so many classes and labs. My parents are pissed. They think I overslept every morning.

My lover's wife found out about us one day last week and gave him an ultimatum. He chose her and dumped me. He even stopped his subscription to LuxNet so I can't ever e-mail him again.

The end was sudden and it was a major shock. I had to go "cold turkey." It really sucked that first night. The next night, I went out and got drunk with some of my friends. And within two days I was totally okay. I bounced back in no time. It's not at all like when you break up with a guy in real life. I wonder why.

Now I feel kind of embarrassed and real stupid. I can't believe I have to go to summer school because I was strung out on this older guy. I'm glad it stopped before we got into the phone sex thing. That was going to be next. Now, the whole thing seems dumb. Know what I mean?

Merry

************** ADULT TOPICS BULLETIN BOARD **************

TO: MERRY MICHAELSON U453744C   05:27PM EST
FROM: WILLIAM RAMSEY Y082176A   04-16-93
SUBJECT: THE CHAPLAIN'S ROOM

Dear Merry,

Yes, I DO know what you mean. You mention a common characteristic of the new social phenomenon of computer affairs. They often end suddenly and without warning. One day a relationship will be on an even keel and the next day a lover simply drops out of sight.

However, you also point out another common thread in cyber romance break-ups. Frequently the grieving period is short. Speed is a hallmark in both the flaring up of passion and in the grieving once it's snuffed out. Your recovery period of two days is one of the shortest ones I have heard reported to date. A week or ten days is the norm.

I don't know why it is easier to recuperate after a computer affair dies. I guess it has something to do with the fact that the intimacy does not actually exist in the first place. It's rather like waking up from a dream. The situations and characters which are believable during sleep do not seem rational in the light of day. When one looks back at a computer love after it has disappeared and its intoxicating effects have worn off, it is revealed for what it is, an illusion.

Sincerely,
Will Ramsey

*********************** MAILBOX ***********************

TO: WILLIAM RAMSEY Y082176A   08:00PM EST
SUBJECT: THE CHAPLAIN'S ROOM   04-16-93

Dear Will . . .

Your post on addiction has struck a chord with me. I am trying to figure out if I have a process addiction. Can you help me?

I am married, but over the past few months have become rather deeply involved with two separate men over my computer modem. Each relationship began with a simple exchange of information and gradually escalated to include sexual passion and deep emotional investment. I really don't understand how it happened. It seems my love affairs began with conversations which took the form of a flow of consciousness. Eventually the notes became strings of stories and secrets. All of a sudden, love and passion seemed to be there, too.

At 45, I have enjoyed this rebirth of passion . . . I have missed it so much. It adds excitement to my life, makes me feel desirable again and floods me with a sense of power. At first, this outlet for my sexuality seemed harmless and the perfect antidote to my midlife angst and ennui. It did not seem like real adultery and there is no worry about disease. It seemed to be the ultimate in discreet "safe sex."

When handling two computer affairs simultaneously became unwieldly, I was able to disengage from my first lover without much problem. But, it is beginning to worry me because I am becoming very dependent upon the second relationship and my lover seems to be similarly attached. Now, I seem to be at the mercy of both my libido and my craving for adoration. I cannot tell whether this is safe or not. It is impossible for me to be objective.

Although I have never lied to my husband, I have kept my computer activities secret, and I feel some guilt for this "sin of omission." However, the effects the computer affairs have had upon me seem to actually have helped my marriage. By that, I mean my new elevated self-esteem, confidence and sexual energy have sparked my husband's interest and we are reconnecting with each other after a long time of being apart. We seem to be falling in love again.

On the other hand, I have very strong, indisputable feelings for my computer partner. I have grown to love him. You say this is an illusion, but I do not know what else to call this easily recognizable constellation of emotions if it is not love. It seems real to me.

This man is like me in many ways. He seems to understand me and our sexual inclinations are compatible . . . we both want to be totally out of control with passion. We want to experiment. I confess we both tend to "overdo" and have histories of addiction; him to alcohol and me to food.

Our passion has grown out of the confines of the computer to include the overland mail and, recently, the telephone. We have sent many letters, postcards and photos and several gifts. The past ten days have been a phone sex orgy. My lover has requested nude photographs of me and has suggested we begin videotaping ourselves and our surroundings and the details of our lives and send these cassettes to each other. Inexorably, we seem to be coming closer and closer and becoming more and more tangible. The natural next step is to meet. Although neither one of us has mentioned it (actually, we avoid the subject), the pull toward physically meeting might become irresistible.

Two women friends I met here on LuxNet staged meetings with their computer lovers. One is Jennifer Flinn. She was devastated by the experience, you advised her and, as a result of your connecting her with a caring supportive community, her life has headed in a healthy positive direction. The other woman, whom you don't know, has dropped the sexual component and become a very close friend of her computer lover as a result of their meeting. And, of course, the bulletin board is full of both ecstatic and tragic reports of what happens when a computer affair becomes real. Your mailbox must fill up with reports, too. I have always thought it would not be a good idea to meet a computer love, but now . . . I don't know.

This is a strange place to be and I do not know of anyone in the real world who could understand my quandary. I have seen the nonjudgmental advice you give others and I have seen firsthand its wonderful effect on my friend, Jenny. Will you advise me, as well?

> Asking for help . . .
> Katie

---------------------------------- MAILBOX ----------------------------------

FROM: WILLIAM RAMSEY Y082176A   04:59PM EST
SUBJECT: THE CHAPLAIN'S ROOM   04-16-93

My Dear Katie,

Let's say, for the sake of argument, that both your loves ARE real. They are still very different. By way of explaining the difference, please take the following trip with me:

In early summer, it is wonderful to camp on the wild, rugged Canadian coast of Lake Superior. It's fabulously beautiful, with its spruce-fringed, sunset-colored cliffs towering over dazzling water. Can you imagine pitching a tent on a spectacular, stony beach somewhere? The air is clean and fresh and everywhere you look there is something new and marvelous to capture your imagination and delight you. It is spellbinding if you have never seen it before.

Wouldn't it be terrific to spend a week or two, or even a month, in your tent on the shore? You could invite a stranger to join you and experience the newness of him, as well. Sex would be especially exciting in such surroundings with a new partner.

However, what if you were forced to spend a year in the tent on the shore? How would your ideal vacation spot hold up in the dead of winter or during a storm? Would the temporariness of the accommodations seem as romantic when you are craving a nice long bath or inside plumbing? Maybe you would miss your home.

Can you get in touch with the way it feels sometimes to return home after a long time away? What is it about "home" that we love so much? There are other places which are more beautiful and exotic, for sure. Perhaps, it is because it is "ours." It was tailor-made to suit us. It feels comfortable and safe. It has permanence to it—indoor plumbing, doors with keys, food. Oh sure, it is not perfect by a long shot. Sometimes it becomes dusty, it needs redecorating from time to time and occasionally it may require repairs (even big ones). But, we usually have a large investment in our homes and, as a result, it provides us with a haven upon which we can depend.

This analogy seems to fit the two loves you are experiencing, doesn't it? Can you see the difference between narrow love, or infatuation, with its transitory nature and its domination by self-gratification, and wide love, which is long-term, based on commitment and centered in compassion and nurture? To take this analogy a step further, can you see not only your marriage, but yourself, as "home"?

You must be the one to determine whether you are addicted or not. Almost always, people engage in addictions as a way of distracting themselves from something painful and unresolved. Can you answer honestly if your computer liaison is helping you avoid dealing with something? This is the test of all addictions.

I am interested in your responses. Please keep in touch.

Sincerely,
Will Ramsey

--------------------------------- MAILBOX ---------------------------------

TO: WILLIAM RAMSEY Y082176A   05:27PM EST
SUBJECT: THE CHAPLAIN'S ROOM   04-16-93

Dear Will . . .

It is so helpful for me to have "pictures." Your analogies are perfect and have given me food for thought. Let me think for a week or two and I will get back to you about what I discover.

Thank you for caring about me. I appreciate your advice more than I can say!

Gratefully . . .
Katie

CAUGHT IN THE ACT

TO: CAROL BEATTY N771200C   03:27PM EST
SUBJECT: CAUGHT IN THE ACT   04-27-93

Dear Carol . . .

I am sorry I did not write or call you this morning at our usual time. Something horrible and traumatic has happened. Jack, Tom and I are reeling from it.

My husband has read some of Jack's and my hottest e-mail. The notes are full of descriptions of gentle bondage and oral and anal penetration. They also contain words of love and tenderness and refer to phone sex. Surely you can imagine how incriminating the letters are. The whole experience has been what I imagine it is like to be caught by a spouse in bed with a lover.

I made copies of our most passionate and uninhibited e-mail because I love to reread it. I usually keep the notes in a manila envelope in a hiding place behind the door in my closet. Unfortunately, yesterday morning I took four copies with me into the downstairs bathroom, left them on the shelf next to the sink and forgot about them (They say there are no accidents).

Last night, Tom came home with a headache and went into the bathroom to get some Tylenol. He came back out into the kitchen with a stunned look on his face and the pages of e-mail in his hand. I was horrified.

We are having a terrible time. Of course, Tom cannot comprehend how Jack can possibly love me. At first, he was incredulous and full of rage and righteous indignation. He said I was out of my mind.

He wanted to know everything, so I was honest and told him in detail about my experiences in computerland. In addition to Jack, I told him about Buck and you and the other people I have come to know over the net, too. I have never lied to my husband. He was alternately furious and bewildered to learn I had fallen in love and engaged in the most explicit sexual play over the computer with not one, but two, strangers. When I had finished, he sat looking miserable, speechless, shaking his head in disbelief.

After what seemed like a very long silence, I saw a change come over his features. Finally, he looked at me sadly and confessed to his affair. For six months he had been embroiled in a relationship, which included sex, with a 30-year-old woman from Charleston. She lives in the complex where he keeps his condominium. They met in the parking lot.

I already knew deep down that Tom was having an affair. I was not amazed to learn the details. My husband said he was not in love with the woman, he had just felt lonely and despairing when he met her. Apparently, middle age is proving to be a difficult time for him, as well. The week after we got back from Colorado, he ended the involvement with the woman. My husband said he saw a change in me and it had given him hope we might recapture the passion we once had and learn to truly care for each other again.

We spent almost all night, into the wee hours, talking. It became clear we'll be needing some professional help if our marriage is to come through this intact. It surprises me Tom seems willing to consider counseling. He must really love me, even after all of this.

Jack and I talked for a long time this morning. We decided the best thing to do is to stop our communication until I can get a handle on my real relationship. I promised my husband, after I talked to Jack on the phone and reached an understanding, I would not connect with my lover again until Tom and I have had a chance to reach some state of equilibrium. It is only fair; my mate deserves this consideration. Jack and I have agreed to reconnect on May 11th, two weeks from now.

I would be glad not to have to deal with this turmoil in my life. Carol, I feel tired and drained. Finally reality begins to take its toll. Among my friends, only you and the Chaplain could possibly understand.

Weary . . .
Katie

----------------------------------- MAILBOX -----------------------------------

TO: WILLIAM RAMSEY Y082176A
SUBJECT: CAUGHT IN THE ACT

Dear Will . . .

I need your advice. Everything has come crashing down around me. My spouse has found out about my computer lover and I have finally learned the details of my husband's real-life affair.

The funny thing is, as disruptive and awful as the revelations have been, there is a kind of peace and hopefulness in their wake. Now that our secrets are out, we feel clean and open. There may be a chance for a new beginning. Where can we go for help?

Will you call me? My number is (704) 375-6711.

> In trouble . . .
> Katie

PAWLEY'S ISLAND

TO: WILLIAM RAMSEY Y082176A   09:00AM EST
SUBJECT: PAWLEY'S ISLAND   06-01-93

Dear Will . . .

Yesterday, my family and I returned from the beach. It was a perfect trip and I have returned feeling refreshed and renewed.

I will be forever in your debt for recommending Sofia to me. I have a standing appointment with her every Tuesday morning now. Tom has been seeing her associate, Peter Mahan, on Mondays after work. On Friday evenings, the four of us meet together for couples' therapy. My husband and I are gratified at what is beginning to happen to us as we begin to set goals. I think we will acheive them.

The vacation to Pawley's Island marks a special point in my marriage. Tom and I spent hours together, walking on the beach or sitting on the porch, talking and reconnecting. We are so different from the young people we were. It has been quite a revelation, the discovery of this new person to whom I have been married for 20 years.

Thank you from the bottom of my heart.

> Your Friend . . .
> Katherine

----------------------------------- MAILBOX -----------------------------------

TO: CAROL BEATTY N771200C   10:08AM EST
SUBJECT: PAWLEY'S ISLAND   06-01-93

Dear Carol . . .

Perhaps you will notice a different tone to this letter. I have been on a journey and returned a different woman.

Pawley's Island is an unpretentious spot when compared to the newer upscale seaside resorts which encrust the curve of South Carolina's Grand Strand. Driving over the bridge from the mainland is like stepping back in time. Due to restrictions, there are no commercial ventures on Pawley's (unless you count the two 100-year-old inns, the one Coke machine and the newspaper rack). There are no high-rises, no signs, no neon. What a relief.

Although Hurricane Hugo did a tremendous amount of damage, the dunes have been restored. The cottages nestle into lush vegetation: the stunted live oaks, youpon hollies and myrtle bushes that form the cool, green, sheltering "caves" and "tunnels" for which the island is known.

Twelve cottages date back to antebellum times and the others are required to conform to the same architectural conventions, so the island has a special appeal and a kind of roofiness to it. There is a rustic, weathered grace about the island which brings to mind other seaside communities steeped in history, most notably in New England.

Sixteen years ago my mother inherited one of the historic houses along the beach. Inheritance is almost the only way one may acquire property on the island, especially one of the buildings with historic significance. Mother's house is called "Seaside Home" and it was originally the summer retreat of a rice planter named Mason Childs. Tom, the twins and I have spent our end-of-school vacations here ever since Mother came to own it. "Seaside" (as we call it) has been the setting of many of our sweetest family memories.

During this particular trip, I let go of the twins. Like so many summers before, I watched them from the rocking chair on the screened porch as they cavorted on the beach with their cousins; as they pushed the cata-maran out into the surf; as they rode the waves. Only this summer, it struck me that my time with them is over and they must leave me and begin their own stories. I wallowed in self-pity for a day or two as the realization sank in.

I played back the tapes stored in my memory . . . remembering the weight of them in my lap and the puppy smell they had as children, the suppleness of their bodies under my hands as I protected them with Coppertone . . . that intimacy would become the territory of their girl-friends and wives.

Without warning, it dawned upon me that, in the future, it would be rare for them to even sleep under the same roof with me. Soon after they return from their summer jobs as camp counselors, they will leave for college; Greg to Duke and Stephen to UVA.

At a certain point, near the end of the week, I found a kind of peace. It settled down over me as I watched a mother osprey fishing. It was a spiritual moment for me when I suddenly gained insight. It was kind of an epiphany. Anyway, after that morning on the beach, I let the boys go in my heart and understood I had done a good job in preparing them for life. And what more important job is there than raising healthy, well-adjusted human beings?

On the same "magical" morning, I really understood the treasure I have in my marriage. Although both Tom and I have been guilty of neglect, it has a stronger foundation than I realized. We have recommitted ourselves to making it better and our counseling is helping us plot a course.

Everything is different.

Transformed . . .

Katherine

-------------------------------- MAILBOX --------------------------------

FROM: CAROL BEATTY N771200C   11:00AM EST
SUBJECT: PAWLEY'S ISLAND   06-01-93

Dear Katherine (a new name for a new woman?),

I'm so happy for you! It seems you have finally reached a resolution for much of the conflict in your life. I'm beginning to finally feel comfort and peace in my life, too. Every journey is different, no?

Yesterday during my support group session, I was searching for something in nature with which to compare the violence in my marriage. Suddenly, I had a vision from my childhood in Georgia. When I got home, I wrote it all down because it marked a breakthrough for me. I want to share my insight with you because I know you'll understand what I mean when I use the image of kudzu, that tenacious, suffocating Southern weed.

Here is what I wrote:

"When I was little, my family lived right outside Valdosta. At the end of our road there was a small lake which was surrounded by dense green foliage. On two sides, it had a backdrop of kudzu. The leafy vines blanketed and weighted down the trees and brush, making them appear lumpy and ghostly, like shaggy green spirits rising from the ground or the living dead. It cascaded down from the tall limbs like curtains or waterfalls.

"Kudzu takes over. It grows like wildfire and the roots go deep, making the weed almost impossible to eradicate. It'll grow over anything, grasping, clutching, crawling and ultimately choking to death every growing thing in its path. It can even kill giant oak trees by blocking the sunlight. The tangled thatches it creates are also havens for snakes, insects and rodents.

"The vines form tendrils which curve out into space like feelers, searching for new surfaces. If nothing is available the tentacles will coil around themselves, making strong braided cords.

"The weed is deciduous, so in winter the leaves turn brown and begin to fall off after the first freeze. Then, the ropy, tattered, dormant vines hang from bare trees, or telephone poles, or whatever else might get in its way. Kudzu is very ugly in the cold months. It is then, especially, that it's possible to see how kudzu binds and tethers down its victims.

"The only way to get rid of kudzu, is to dig it up."

The other native Southern women in my group understood exactly what I was trying to say about abuse. I know you will, too.

Yesterday, I heard from the bank. They have agreed to my transfer to Jacksonville. I am planning to move this summer, after the divorce is final.

Now, tell me what will become of you and Jack.

Your friend,
Carol

--------------------------------- MAILBOX -----------------------------------

TO: CAROL BEATTY N771200C   12:45PM EST
SUBJECT: PAWLEY'S ISLAND   06-01-93

Dear Carol . . .

Katherine is my real name. I am just taking it back. It is more comfortable to me; it is "home," if you know what I mean.

I am pleased to hear you are healing. And, yes, I can see exactly what you mean when you compare domestic violence to kudzu. I understand the abuse must have overpowered, stunted and strangled anything good in your marriage. Your decision to "dig it up" is all you can do.

Jack and I have agreed to wait until Thursday to communicate with each other again. Then, I will tell him of my resolve to recommit to my marriage. It will mean giving him up completely. I am sure my decision will not come as a surprise.

This is something we both need. Jack and I are addicts, Carol . . . pure and simple. I accept this and have surrendered the idea I have any control. If something didn't happen to prevent it, we would have planned to meet in person, then what would have happened? Fortunately, we will never find out.

Yesterday morning, when I walked over to our neighbor's house to retrieve the mail, I found a package from Jack. I opened it first thing when I got back home. It contained a gift, a small African mask. You will not understand the significance of the mask and it would take a very long time to explain. So, I will just tell you it is a signal that he understands this is the end of our relationship.

On a different tack, I have decided to let my subscription to LuxNet expire next month. I do not need it anymore. However, I want to stay connected to you. Make sure I get your address when you are established in Jacksonville!

As always, thank you for being my friend.

Fondly,
Katherine

------------------------------- MAILBOX -----------------------------------

TO: JOHN W. KELLY JR. A041178A   08:01AM EST
SUBJECT: PAWLEY'S ISLAND   06-03-93

My Dearest John (I want to use your real name, this time) . . .

Pawley's Island, South Carolina, owes its existence to malaria. Although the wealthy 19th-century rice planters did not know the cause of the mosquito-borne disease, they did know if they moved their households across the salt marshes to the coast during the hot season, fewer members of their families would fall ill.

I have come to feel I can escape, not malaria, but the miasma of depression which has afflicted me over the past three or four years when we travel to the island. My hopelessness always goes into remission after a week spent on the spit of land. However, this year, I think it has completely healed me with a miracle.

Early one day, as I walked along the beach, I saw an osprey, or fish hawk, hovering high over the breakers. I stopped and sat down on the sand, feeling privileged to be an audience for the mother bird. For the fifteen years I have been vacationing on Pawley's Island, I have enjoyed watching these predators fish. They are beautiful to watch . . . graceful and swift.

Their nests are in the tops of the tall trees on the landside of the salt marsh. Every morning, they make the short trip across the creek and over the cottages to the beach. Fishing is a solitary pursuit and the hawks come singly. They glide over the dunes, catching the air currents which push them aloft and enable them to survey the water for signs of schooling fish.

I admired the smooth, fluid, rhythmic beating of wings as the hawk patrolled the swells for prey. Suddenly, she pirouetted in midair and came hurtling down toward the scintillating surface of the ocean with her talons outstretched. The hooks struck the water, sending a shower of glittering drops in every direction. The osprey wobbled violently for a moment, struggling to keep her quarry and stay aloft. Finally, with great effort, flapping her wings mightily, the bird rose slowly from the surf, clutching a thrashing, dripping mullet in her claws. She labored upward until she caught another air current to help her stay airborne with the good-sized fish in tow.

It is rare to see an osprey returning to her nest heavily laden with a catch. A lone fisher must plummet down, strike the water and struggle back upward empty-taloned many times for every dive that is successful.

So, I watched with a feeling of satisfaction, until the bird, with her booty flapping and glinting in the sunlight, disappeared behind the dune.

As I stood there, the miracle happened and I became the bird. I mean, I suddenly understood why I had been a witness and a partner in this scene of rewarded persistence (in the natural world where truth is easy to see, as allegory).

Like the osprey, I have been scanning and searching for the thing that will feed me. I have plummeted down, hit the water and come up empty-handed so many times I have become weary. However, at last, I have caught the elusive prey and I am returning home with it.

The fish I have been searching for this long, lonely time is the acceptance of myself for what I am . . . not perfect, but unique. I am an osprey; no better or worse than any other living thing on the planet, but valuable just the same. I do not need others to define or adore me. The insight was like an air current, lifting me way up over the water with the treasure still secure in my grasp. In that blinding instant, I understood I can nourish myself.

I have used my sexuality and I have used you, John, to try to fill the gaping hole inflicted by my self-loathing. It is not your passion I need, it is only a compelling distraction. My addiction relieved me from the misery of my depression. What I really needed was to simply let go of the idea I am not lovable, and it was much easier than I thought to do that.

I have made the decision to recommit myself to my marriage. I can't do this and love you, too. So, I feel it is time for us to let go. Since you are my "twin" and we have been in sync since the beginning, it gives me hope that you have come to the same conclusion. I know you have because I have opened your gift . . . the mask. I will treasure it as the emblem of a beginning and an ending. Thank you.

Let's help each other. Call me when you get this and let's say, "Good-bye."

Waiting . . .
Katherine